I0739496

The al-Andalus trilogy

Book Two

THE EYE OF THE

FALCON

The Scottish novelist Joan Fallon, currently lives and works in the south of Spain. She writes both contemporary and historical fiction, and almost all her books have a strong female protagonist. She is the author of:

Daughters of Spain
Spanish Lavender
The House on the Beach
Loving Harry
Santiago Tales
The Only Blue Door
The Shining City (Book 1 in the al-Andalus trilogy)
Palette of Secrets

(all are available in paperback and as ebooks)

www.joanfallon.co.uk

JOAN FALLON

THE EYE OF THE FALCON

Scott Publishing

ISBN 978 0 9931797 3 0
First published in 2015
Scott Publishing
Windsor, England

ACKNOWLEDGMENTS

My sincere thanks to my editor Sara Starbuck whose advice and support have been invaluable, as always.

PART 1
976 AD

CHAPTER 1

It was barely light when she came to his room. The night sky was turning to milky white on the horizon but the songbirds were still asleep; even the cock had not yet begun to crow. She stood by his bed, looking down at him. Her nightdress shone and glittered in the flickering light of the night lamps; it reminded him of the kingfishers that stole in to the palace gardens to steal fish from the lakes. Gently her hand stroked his hair.

'Hisham, my son, are you awake?' she asked.

'Yes mother. What's happened? Is something the matter?'

He was well aware of the commotion in the women's quarters; the wailing and crying, the sound of heavy footsteps as the guards marched through the palace, the slamming of doors and loud voices all spoke of some catastrophe. It had broken into his sleep and woken him before his mother arrived at his bedside. Now she knelt by his side and said, 'You must get up, Hisham. The Khalifa is dead.'

Dead? Baba was dead? He felt a chill pass over him and hot tears sprang into his eyes. He looked at his mother; her face was impassive, not a tear marred her beautiful face. She pulled the covers off him and took his hand in hers.

'Do not cry, Hisham; there is no need for tears. You are the Khalifa now, my son. You will be a great and glorious ruler,' she continued, her eyes gleaming, 'like the Omeyyads before you. Al-Andalus will thrive and prosper with you as Khalifa and with me by your side.'

She bowed low so that her face touched the carpet next to his bed, her long blonde hair cascading over the elaborately woven silks, and would have kissed his hand but he snatched it away. Baba was dead. Who was this woman who did not weep for her dead husband? He had seen her shed more tears when her pet peacock died.

He turned his face away from her. Was she telling him the truth? Was Baba really dead? His father had been unwell for some time, confined to his rooms, only able to walk a few steps at a time, but Hisham had never really expected him to die. He was sure he would get better. He believed the doctors who came each day and gave him potions made from *habba souda* and warm milk - said by the Prophet to cure everything but death - who made him infusions of anise and applied myrrh to his lips to sweeten his breath, who massaged his legs and prescribed salt water baths. He believed them when they said that with time he would recover, that he would return to his books and be as he was before. But they had been wrong. Baba had not recovered from the affliction that had twisted his face and stolen the strength from his limbs. He had lain in his room surrounded by his ministers, listening silently while they told him what was happening in his kingdom. Then, tired from his inability to do anything, he had sent for Hisham and asked him to read to him.

What would Hisham do now? He had loved his father. Al-Hakim had been more than a father; he had been Hisham's friend and his teacher. Each day, when his father had finished with the business of the court, he went into the harem to look for his son and together they walked in the palace gardens while he recited the great Persian poetry of times past. He recounted the exploits of his father, Hisham's grandfather, the mighty al-Rahman III, who had died before the boy was born, of how he had subdued all the rebellious tribes and united al-Andalus into the most powerful kingdom in Europe, of how he had defeated the Christian princes yet allowed Christians, Jews and Moslems to live in peace, side by side. Hisham had listened to his stories and was proud to be part of such a powerful family. On other occasions he accompanied his father to the great library, al-Hakim's pride and joy, and there he learnt the secrets that were held within his countless books, sharing his father's excitement when a new manuscript arrived from some distant land or a copyist presented him with something fresh to read and explore. Hisham loved to trace his finger over the beautiful illuminated characters and follow the words across the page or watch as books in Latin or

Greek were carefully translated into Arabic. His father had taught him many things it was true, but Hisham was not sure that he had taught him how to be Khalifa of Muslim Spain.

'Hisham, you must get up, the ministers are waiting to see their new Khalifa. Come child, I know you are upset at the news but you have responsibilities now,' his mother whispered so that his attendants could not hear her.

He looked at her and wished he could just pull the covers over his head and stay there until she went away but he knew he could not. *Al-Sayyida al Malika*, the Queen Mother, was not someone to be easily ignored; she was as fearsome as she was beautiful.

His mother stood up and clapped her hands. She looked annoyed with him. At that signal Hisham's personal slaves hurried across to him and, reluctantly, he rolled out of bed so that they could begin to prepare him for the day. Khalifa? How could he be Khalifa? It was only a few months since he had celebrated his eleventh birthday.

***

Subh looked at her son, standing there in his undergarments, meekly submitting to the hands of his manservant. He was the new Khalifa, ruler of all al-Andalus, Hisham II, the most powerful person in the civilised world and there he was, a weak, timid boy, his face stained with tears. This was what she had worked for all her life, to have one of her sons made Khalifa but now she was not sure that Hisham was up to it. If only al-

Hakim could have hung on a few years longer until Hisham was older, but that too would have had its risks. For how long would the vultures have waited while their ruler slobbered and drooled like a child? No, she was amazed at the respect al-Hakim had commanded from his people but she knew it would not have continued indefinitely. Al-Andalus was a rich land with a strong economy and al-Hakim had accumulated a lot of money - despite spending a fortune on his useless books - and she knew he had left his son some forty million dinars in the treasury. There were many people would have their eyes on the throne; already there were rumours about al-Hakim's younger brother planning a coup.

True Hisham was still a child but then she had been younger than him when she had been sold into slavery and look how she had won through. With her help he could do likewise. She watched as the slave stripped him of his clothes and led him through to his bath. How puny he was, a skinny little lad with long blond hair and a soft girlish face. Well he would change as he grew older; once he reached puberty he would fill out and his chest would thicken. In a few years he would be a man. She prayed that God would be on his side and he would not be like his father, more interested in young boys than women.

'*Sayyida*, would you like me to send for some tea while you are waiting?' one of al-Hisham's servants asked.

'Yes, that is a good idea. Bring it to me in the garden. I will wait for my son there.'

She pulled her robe around her shoulders to ward off the chill of the morning air. The grass was covered with dew and she walked carefully so that her slippers would not spoil. One of the palace cats slunk away into the undergrowth, nervous at her approach. Already the sun was climbing steadily through the sky and it would soon be time for the morning prayers . She sat down by the edge of the pool and gazed at the surface of the water, a liquid mirror reflecting pink tinged clouds and a brightening sky. As she leant forward her own reflection stared back at her. Here she was at last, mother of the Khalifa, *al-Sayyida al-Malika*. She smiled at the memory of how far she had travelled since the day she first arrived in Córdoba, so long ago.

***

At last the caravan halted, the camel driver screeching his commands at the tired animals. Clara fell to her knees, exhausted. Please God that they were almost there. She had lost count of the days and nights she had been walking, chained in a line of other exhausted children, all as dirty, ragged and hungry as she was. She had never had to go without food before; her mother had fed them all, her and her brothers, with bread she baked herself and vegetables from the garden, with big bowls of steaming broth and chicken stews. Clara's stomach rumbled as she remembered the delicious things her mother made: little honey cakes, biscuits topped with seeds and berries from the hedgerows, baked apples and syllabub, creamy milk from the cow. Where was her mother now? Where were her father, her uncles, her brothers? Her father was an important man, a merchant, so why hadn't he sent anyone to find her? Her uncles worked for the bishop, so surely they could have done something to help her. She was frightened and confused. Why had nobody come to save her? How had this happened to her? So many questions were crowding her brain.

All she could remember was that she had been walking towards the miller's house with her friend Ana, ducking in and out doorways, trying to avoid the river of mud that the main road turned into every spring. It was her birthday and her mother had promised to make her some raspberry buns if she went and bought some flour. Then suddenly people started screaming and running. At first the two girls just stood still and stared around them in astonishment. Everyone had gone crazy. It took them but a minute to realise that the townspeople were running from their attackers. Men on horseback, with long cloaks and their heads swathed in turbans swooped down upon them, slashing to the left and the right with long, curved swords. People fell to the ground, blood pouring from their wounds as the men ploughed on, killing everyone who got in their way. Some carried firebrands which they threw into the doorways of the houses, setting them alight; others rode straight to the market place and started to round up the women and children. Smoke was pouring from the houses, making it hard to see but Clara knew they had to move from the doorway. She pulled

Ana by the arm and tried to run but before they had gone more than a couple of yards a man stepped in front of the girls and grabbed them, tucking them under his arms as though they weighed no more than a couple of sacks of flour. Clara screamed and kicked, but his grip was like iron so she began to shout for her father but, even as she did so, she knew it was useless. Nobody would hear her small voice in all that chaos. She could hear people screaming that the Moors were here, that the Infidel was upon them, that they would all die. The women had begun to wail and cry in terror. She didn't understand any of it. Who were these Moors? Why did they want to kill them? And where was her family?

She still did not know who these men were or what they wanted but she knew that many people had died that day. Not her nor her friend Ana, they were still alive, just. As for her family, she had no idea whether they were with the living or the dead.

She pulled her dress straight. It was torn and stained as though she had worn it for weeks. Her hands were blackened and her fingernails broken where she had clawed at the rope, trying to undo the knots. The rope was tied around her waist and attached her to another child of about fourteen, who in turn was tied to another and so on. There must have been about twenty of them, all children and all girls, shackled together like animals. The boys, kept separate, were manacled round the wrists and the ankles and stumbled along in single file ahead of them, looking for all the world like a drunken centipede.

Clara's feet hurt. She twisted them round to see what was causing so much pain. Both her feet were bleeding from cuts and blisters and there, in the sole of her left foot, was a long splinter of wood. She pulled at it until she thought she would faint but it wouldn't budge.

'Can you help me?' she asked the older girl roped next to her. 'Can you see that splinter?'

The girl picked up Clara's foot and looked at it. 'Yes, I think I can get it. Hold on.' She pinched her nails around the splinter and pulled hard until it came out.

Clara wanted to scream with pain but she didn't make a sound. She just rubbed her foot with the hem of her dress and said, 'Thank you.'

'You're a brave little thing,' the girl said. 'How old are you?'

'I'm seven. It was my birthday, the day when …' Clara started to say and stopped, tears welling in her eyes at the memory of that day when her life had changed forever.

'Well happy birthday then,' said the girl.

'Here. Drink,' one of the men said, shoving a gourd of water into Clara's face.

She drank greedily, but before she was satisfied, it was pulled away and offered to the next girl and then passed along the line. The man was dressed like all the others, with a scarf wound around his head into a turban and wearing a hooded cloak over his grubby brown tunic. His skin was dark and swarthy, burnt by wind and sun, and his eyes glowed like coals. His beard was black and matted from a lack of combing and he wore a gold earring in one ear. Maybe he was a pirate, Clara thought. She had heard of pirates who raided the towns along the coast from the travellers, who told tales of their cruelty to anyone who had the time to listen and that was usually the children. Or maybe he was a bandit from high in the Pyrenees. They too were bad men who came over the mountains from Gascony to raid the towns of anything of value. But what would bandits or pirates want with children? Surely they wanted to steal gold and jewels or take the horses and round up the livestock, not children. What good were children to them? Unless, maybe they were taking them to work for them on a pirate ship or up to their hideouts in the mountains. Neither prospect sounded good and both filled her with fear.

She looked behind her at the exhausted file of girls, some squatting on the ground, some clinging to each other and crying, others slumped over in the resignation that no-one was coming to help them, some even stretched out as though dead. She looked past the kneeling camels, along the dusty track into the distant haze, hoping to see where Ana was but it was hard to know which of those dirty, dishevelled girls was her friend.

'Up. We are moving now,' one of the men called.

He spoke a language similar to her own but with a strange accent, and he seemed to be the interpreter for the group. The children had come to learn that when the men said 'up' that was what they meant and they meant 'at once'. Clara pulled herself upright, wincing as her feet touched the ground again; her legs were like jelly, the muscles tight and sore from walking. She felt that she could not take another step but she had no choice. She walked or she fell. It had happened to one of the girls behind her. She had tripped and fallen and then could not get up again. It made no difference to the men. The one who had given them the water hit her with a stick until she managed to drag herself to her feet.

How many more days would they have to keep walking? How much further was it to wherever they were going? All Clara had worked out was that they were heading south, because she watched the sun rise each day on her left and sink below the crimson horizon on her right. All she knew was that with every step she was moving further away from her family and her home. She would have cried but there were no tears left to cry. All she could do was stumble forward, murmuring her prayers to herself and hoping that God would save her.

***

It was three days later that she saw a large city on the distant horizon and she could tell from the reaction of her captors that this was the place they had been heading for. The men relaxed and chatted amongst themselves, cracking jokes and talking of what they would do when they reached the city. For them too it had been a long journey and they were as grateful as the children to have their destination in sight, at last. The caravan, prisoners and captors both, walked on with renewed spirits, across a fertile plain, with stalks of green corn as high as a man's waist, where partridges and corncrakes flew up startled by their heavy-footed approach, where the hum of buzzing insects and the vibration of cicadas were the only sounds to be heard. Their route travelled alongside an old stone aqueduct that brought water to the crops, their only reference point in this sea of waving green. Hot and tired, the children followed the camels that plodded steadily forward, leading the way, their necks stretched, their heads forward, the tents and baggage that they carried on their broad backs swaying gently back and forth in time to their slow, ponderous steps. Before them stretched a wide, but shallow river, and on its far bank was the city. Such a city she had never seen before. The buildings were built of stone and, as it was now evening, they glowed a rich warm sandy colour in the rays of the setting sun. The man with the gold earring was pleased with himself.

'Córdoba,' he said, beaming at them and pointing to the city. 'Córdoba.'

So this city was to be their destination; that much was clear but what was still not clear was their fate.

The caravan eventually stopped by the edge of the meandering river and the men led the camels down to drink. Once they had had their fill, it was the turn of the children.

'Wash,' one of the men said and mimed washing himself in the water.

The children did not need to be told twice. They clambered down the bank, hamstrung as they were with the heavy rope, stumbling and pulling at each other until they were in the river. Suddenly they were children again, jumping about in the cold water, squealing with pleasure as they kicked their tired legs and splashed each other. It was wonderful. Clara had never thought she could enjoy anything so much. She ducked under the water and shook her head about, letting her hair float around her like seaweed until it was thoroughly wet then she sat down in the shallows and rubbed at her feet and legs, next she washed her face and then her arms and hands. Gradually the dirt and grime of the journey, which had lain like a hard crust on her body, began to soften and soak away, the caked blood, the faeces from sleeping next to the camels, the mud, all washed downstream leaving her feeling cleaner and fresher than she had for many days. She twisted her long hair into a rope and squeezed out as much of the water as she could then shook her head and let it hang down her back to dry, a gleaming cloak of dark gold. She straightened her wet dress, which seemed so much more dirty now that her skin was clean, and stood up with the others. As soon as everyone had finished washing, the men shouted for them to get back in line and the caravan began to move along the riverbank, on towards the Roman bridge that led into the city.

They camped on the banks of the river. The men set up their make-shift tents, tethered and fed the camels and saw to their prisoners. Whatever they had planned for the children it was not going to happen that night; she would have to wait one more day to know her future.

***

A slight movement made Subh look behind her; it was Gassan, Hisham's personal slave, an old man whose father had served al-Hisham's grandfather.

'The Khalifa is waiting for you, *Sayyida*,' he said, giving her a slight bow.

'Very well.'

She stood and stretched, feeling the cool breeze on her cheeks. It did no harm to remind herself from time to time about her past but she had no intention of telling anyone else. As far as everyone else was concerned, life for their queen began when al-Hakim had made her his favourite concubine.

CHAPTER 2

Makoud ibn Qasim, better known to his friends and family as al-Jundi, the soldier, was distraught at the news of his master's death. He had served al-Hakim for many years, ever since he had been promoted to the Khalifa's personal bodyguard after saving his life in a battle against the Christian princes. Al-Hakim had been a good Khalifa, wise and just, a learned man whose wisdom was respected throughout the civilised world and he had kept their country at peace. If anything he was too virtuous to be a ruler; al-Jundi knew how the ministers took advantage of him, how they were happy to take over the duties that he, the Khalifa, found onerous until, little by little, they amassed more power than was right for their station. He had seen it happen over the years since al-Rahman's death - it would never have happened in his lifetime. The old Khalifa was as sharp as a razor, trusted nobody except his son and he kept the reins of power firmly in his hand, but al-Hakim was different. He was a shrewd, wise man but he was not given to political intrigue nor was he a warrior. He defended his country when necessary but at heart he was a scholar. His love lay in his library and the books that he collected. Nobody could say he was a bad ruler or that he did not do his duty, but he had allowed too many power hungry men to worm their way into positions of influence and, worse than that, he had allowed the women in his harem to meddle in affairs of the state. This was something al-Jundi could never understand. Al-Rahman had had his favourites in the harem. He had lavished them with jewels and money and given them their hearts' desires, but never would he have stood for their interference in the government of the land. Now al-Hakim's favourite concubine, the ex-slave, Subh, mother of the prince al-Hisham, was determined that her young son would take over the reins of power. Al-Jundi had met the boy prince on many occasions and liked the young man but even he had to admit that he was not ready to rule a kingdom as rich and diverse as al-Andalus.

'Must you leave now?' his wife Amina asked, bustling about the kitchen, preparing his morning tea. 'You have had nothing to eat or drink since last night.'

'Don't fret, woman. Of course I must go. The young prince needs me. This is a time of danger for all of us. Al-Hakim may not have been the strongest ruler we have seen but he was well respected and obeyed. Now he is dead who knows who will come crawling out of the woodwork seeking their chance at power. I must be there to protect his son. I swore an oath of allegiance to al-Hakim and all his family.'

Al-Jundi's youngest son came toddling into the room, rubbing the sleep from his eyes. 'Baba,' he said, holding out his arms to his father.

'Come here, little one and give your Baba a kiss.' He lifted the toddler up and kissed him. 'Baba must go now. He has important business to see to. Run along to your Mama and I will see you tonight. Don't worry, wife,' al-Jundi added gently, and strapped his sword to his side.

He must be prepared for anything to happen today. Everyone already knew that al-Hakim's brother, the prince al-Mughira was planning to take the throne. Rumours had been flying around the court ever since al-Hakim had had that first stroke which left him partially disabled. Now was the time to see if the traitor planned to take action or not.

A movement in his sons' room told him that they too were awake. He put his head through the doorway just in time to see a tousled head emerge from beneath the blankets. It was Ahmad. The others were sleeping soundly.

'Good morning Ahmad, isn't it time you were out with the birds? Up with the lark and all that?' he teased.

Ahmad worked with al-Jundi's father-in-law, the Grand Falconer and was learning to become a falconer too, so he was used to his father's jokes about birds.

'Yes Baba. You realise that you say that every morning,' the boy said with an exasperated smile as he rolled off his mat and stood up.

He was a skinny lad for his age with a face that reminded al-Jundi a lot of his own brother, an artistic face, finely featured with dark soulful eyes.

'The early bird catches the worm,' he said, unable to resist one last joke at his son's expense.

'Here,' his wife said, handing him his soldier's red cloak. 'Don't tease the boy.'

The uniform of the Palace Guard was green and gold but he always wore the red cloak to signify that he was ready to shed his blood for his master. It was a concession that al-Hakim had awarded him when he had appointed him his royal bodyguard.

'You will need it. The air is cold,' she added.

He touched her cheek lightly, tenderly and stepped out into the chilly morning air, closing the door behind him. This had been his parents' house, and when al-Jundi had married, he and Amina had moved in to live with them. His father was dead now, a heart attack had taken him from them, or so said the doctor, but al-Jundi knew differently; his father had died of grief and shame. He had never been the same man after the trouble with al-Jundi's brother Omar. It had broken his father's heart to have to send away his youngest son, but there had been no alternative. Omar, with all the recklessness of youth, had fallen in love with one of the Khalifa's concubines, and in so doing had set off a chain of events that had led to his exile.

Al-Jundi headed towards the North Gate of the palace; it was a short walk. The streets were quiet save for a few early risers setting out their market stalls and a man shovelling up manure left by some passing camels; curls of smoke from household fires rose lazily into the misty air and the smell of baking bread awoke in him pangs of hunger. How well he remembered when the city was being built. That was what had brought him and his family to Madinat al-Zahra all those years ago, when his father had hoped to make his fortune selling his pottery to the rich and powerful members of the new court. It had been a time of prosperity and hope. Al-Rahman III had made al-Andalus the most powerful and richest country in the civilised world. Everyone had shared in the wealth that a strong economy and years of peace had brought with it. Nowadays the future looked uncertain and al-Hakim's death would have made people nervous.

'*As-salama alaykum, Quaid,*' the sentry by the gate greeted him.

'*Wa alaykum e-salam,*' he replied.

'You have heard the news?' the sentry asked.

'Yes soldier, I have heard the sad news about our Khalifa.'

Al-Jundi walked through the arched entrance and headed straight for the Khalifa's private quarters. Even before he reached there, he could make out the sound of wailing coming from the harem as the women ululated in their grief. Their heartfelt cries tore through him. How easy it was for women to grieve. They did not have to hide their sorrow behind a stoic facade and carry on as if this were just another day. He felt an intense sadness at the passing of his lord and master, a man he had grown to love and respect over the years, but nobody would know how he felt, not even Amina. It was not a man's way.

As he approached the Khalifa's private quarters he was stopped by two Palace Guards.

'What is your business here, soldier?' one of them asked in heavily accented Arabic. He was one of those arrogant Slavs, a mercenary willing to serve whoever would pay him the most money. Al-Jundi could never leave al-Hisham's safety in such hands.

'What do you mean? Don't you recognise me? I am Makoud ibn Qasim, al-Hakim's personal bodyguard,' he replied indignantly.

'Al-Hakim is dead.'

Al-Jundi felt the blood rush to his head in anger and his hand went automatically to his short sword. This impudent Slav. He could cut him down in an instant.

'Al-Jundi, how nice to see you. Have you come to pay your respects to the new Khalifa?' al-Hakim's widow asked, appearing before him with a radiant smile.

Instantly he dropped his hand from his sword and bowed towards her. *As-salama alaykum*, Your Highness. Did you say the new Khalifa?'

'Yes, you do know al-Hakim is dead?'

He nodded.

'Well you, above all people, must agree that al-Hisham is the only legitimate heir to al-Hakim and so he has been appointed Khalifa. The coronation will be in a couple of weeks.'

'So soon?'

'Is there any reason to wait? Quite the opposite I would have thought. These things need to be settled quickly before there is any unrest.'

He bowed once more. It made him uncomfortable to hear a woman, especially a woman who used to be a slave and a concubine, talk so freely about matters of state but there was little he could do about it. She was the young Khalifa's mother and that gave her immense power. She was a queen now, the Queen-Mother, *al-Sayyida al-Malika*.

'My son is in the throne room. You may go in. He is waiting for you,' she said.

'Thank you, Your Highness.' Al-Jundi bowed once more and made his way along the passage to the throne room, a place he knew as well as his own home, because every day for the past thirty years he had stood guard there, protecting his sovereign.

'Al-Jundi, how pleased I am to see you,' a childish voice called out before he had barely entered the room.

'As-salama alaykum, Your Highness,' he said, bowing so low his head touched the marble floor.

'Wa alaykum e-salam,' the boy replied politely. 'Thank goodness you have come. My father is dead.'

'Yes, I know, Your Highness. I am overwhelmed with grief. He was a good man.'

'They have made me Khalifa, al-Jundi. What am I to do? I don't know what to do. Baba often spoke of me being Khalifa when he died but I thought that would be in the future when I was much older. Not now. I am so scared. Mama says I must be very careful because there are many bad people who would want to kill me.'

He looked at al-Jundi with his big, blue eyes, as dark as the night sky, his face pinched and white from crying.

'Don't worry about that, Your Highness. I will be by your side always. I promised your father I would look after you and my word is my bond. Nobody will hurt you while I am here.'

He patted his sword to emphasise his words and smiled encouragingly at the frightened child, sitting there on the magnificent throne where his father and his grandfather had sat before him. The boy had been dressed that morning in a *djubba* of fine white cotton and its wide sleeves were embroidered in gold thread. His head was swathed in a white turban that seemed too big for him and on his feet were sandals of the finest leather. Someone - his mother no doubt - had placed the huge ruby ring that his father always wore on the child's middle finger and garlanded him with chains of gold. He looked to al-Jundi like a child caught dressing up in his mother's clothes, and he felt pity for him.

'Your Majesty,' a voice called as a figure approached the throne.

Unlike al-Jundi, who had strode directly to the young Khalifa's side, this man advanced part way and stopped and bowed to the ground, then repeated the process twice more until he stood in front of al-Hisham. It was Yafar al-Mushafi, a childhood friend of the boy's father. Al-Jundi knew him well. He was of Berber descent like al-

Jundi himself, and although few Berbers were appointed to the government, this man had risen to power through his loyalty and hard work. Now he was a respected elder statesman, Grand Vizier to the Khalifa. He had been well liked by al-Hakim although al-Jundi was aware that there was no love lost between him and some of the others in the government.

'Your Majesty, let me express my immense sorrow at the death of your father. He was a good man and to me personally, a beloved friend. I am here to pledge my allegiance to you as I did to your father,' Al-Mushafi said, bowing low and kissing the ground in front of the boy's feet.

'Thank you, *ammu*. You have always been a good friend to my family and you have been like an uncle to me. I will not forget that.'

The Grand Vizier beamed at these words and began to mumble about the importance of having the coronation quickly and forming a new government.

Al-Jundi moved away from the throne and took up his place at a discreet distance. This was just the first of the men who would be prostrating themselves before the new Khalifa in order to gain some advantage for themselves. Al-Jundi was a simple man. Some would say he was a brave soldier, some a loyal friend. He would say he just did his duty. It was his duty to serve the Khalifa and for him that came before everything else, fame, wealth, even family. But simple man though he was, the years he had spent in the court had taught him many things; it had taught him how to identify a self-seeking man from a generous one, how to spot the sly and greedy, the traitors in waiting. It would have been impossible to stand within earshot of al-Hakim, as he had done for many years and not have learnt these things. How often he had wished he had the freedom to warn the Khalifa of his suspicions but it was not his place to do so. All he could do was watch and wait, always ready to ward off any attack on his sovereign. The only time he was not needed was when al-Hakim withdrew into his harem. Al-Jundi had heard the rumours. Everyone in the court knew of the former Khalifa's partiality to young men but no-one spoke of it. It was not his place to judge. As far as Al-Jundi was concerned, what his master did behind closed doors was between him and Allah.

His gaze took in the whole scene. The throne room was unchanged save for the child sitting in the place of a man. It was an imposing room, designed to impress foreign dignitaries with the Khalifa's wealth and power. The Palace Guards, in immaculate green and gold uniforms, stood in an unbroken line with their backs to the walls, their lances by their side, their scimitars tucked into their belts, as still as statues. The room had been built with the most precious materials that the architects could find, pure gold for the ceiling, marble from Valencia for the columns that supported the beautifully painted arches, brightly coloured stucco, carved and painted with blue lapis lazuli, green malachite and scarlet made from cinnabar. It was furnished with equal luxury, with fountains from which flowed crystal clear water, and gold statues studded with precious gems. But the feature which never ceased to amaze visitors and courtiers alike was the suspended tank of mercury positioned so that the rays of the sun made it gleam and shimmer like something from another world. His eyes drifted back to the boy-khalifa who was dwarfed by the luxurious throne and overwhelmed by what was happening to him. Strands of his golden hair had escaped from his turban which now listed slightly to one side. His bewildered face reminded al-Jundhi of the last days of the boy's father when he had sat propped on his throne, neither in this world nor the next. He swore to himself then and there that he would stand by this child no matter what happened, no matter where he had to go.

CHAPTER 3

Abu Amir Muhammed ibn Abi Amir al-Mafari strode into the palace, his black *djubba* flapping behind him like the wings of an injured crow but Abu Amir was not injured, he was buoyant. He had just received news from his mistress that the Khalifa was dead. The news was like fire to his blood. Now was his time. This was his opportunity to make his name.

'Dearest, you managed to come,' Subh whispered as she slid into his open arms. 'I knew you would not desert us.'

'I came immediately I heard the news. Where is al-Hisham now?'

'I sent him back to his room. He is still upset about his father.'

'Good. We need to talk. Who else have you sent for?'

'Only the Grand Vizier, al-Mushafi, and General Ghálib.'

'Why did you send for al-Mushafi? He is no friend of ours.'

'I know, my dearest one, but he is liked and respected by the people and after all, he is the Grand Vizier. I had no choice. He has already been to pay his respects to the Khalifa.'

'And General Ghálib?'

'He is on his way. Abu, I am worried. I have heard that the Khalifa's brother is going to claim the throne. What can we do to stop him?'

'Don't worry, my precious. I too have heard this news. His advisers have filled his fool's head with the idea that Hisham is too young and that he should reign in his place and name the boy as his heir. Well if they think that they can get away with that they are very mistaken. Hisham is al-Hakim's legitimate heir and no-one is going to take his throne away from him.'

'*As-salama alaykum*, my Queen, and you too, Abu Amir,' the General said, striding into the room and bowing before Subh.

'*Wa alaykum e-salam*, General Ghálib. I am glad you could come so quickly.'

Abu Amir had barely had time to return the greeting to the veteran general when the Grand Vizier made his entrance.

'Welcome my dear Grand Vizier,' Subh said, as Yafar al-Mushafi bowed in greeting. She looked around at the assembled group and added, 'Good. We are all here. Come and sit down. I will send for some refreshments.' She clapped her hands and instantly an ebony skinned slave was at her side. 'Bring us some mint tea and sweet cakes,' she told the slave, 'and don't be all day about it.'

'It's a bad business,' al-Mushafi said, pulling over a cushion and sitting down beside Abu Amir. 'The boy's too young to rule. There can be no dispute about that.'

'So what do you suggest we do, let that fool Mughira rule in his place? The people would not stand for it,' said Abu Amir.

'No, of course not. But the boy will not be able to manage on his own,' continued al-Mushafi. 'The country will fall apart. Once our enemies see a sign of weakness they will break through our defences and attack.'

'Yes, that is true. I do not often agree with you, I admit, but on this occasion you are right. We must keep al-Andalus strong and, above all, united. It is not just the Christian princes who will smell blood and try to destroy us, there are plenty of Muslims who have their eyes on the throne. It would not take much for some upstart prince to think that he had the right to usurp al-Hisham and take the throne for himself,' said the General.

'Yes and then there are the Fatimites in North Africa. They have had their eyes on al-Andalus for some time. Don't forget they have a formidable army,' added al-Mushafi.

'My son is the legitimate heir to the kingdom. Surely that is all that matters,' Subh interrupted.

'Of course, *Sayyida* but it is not so simple. He is still a child,' Abu Amir said before addressing the two men. 'I agree with both of you. The country needs a strong ruler, someone to hold the country together, to send a signal to our enemies that nothing has changed, that we are as strong and powerful as we ever were. This is why we are here this morning. The Khalifa's mother, our new *Sayyida*, has asked for our help to protect her son and his throne.

She proposes that we form a regency to rule in place of al-Hisham until he is old enough to govern on his own. Ghálib, as a loyal and experienced general in the Khalifa's army, you, al-Mushafi, as a friend of the royal family as well as being the Khalifa's Grand Vizier and I, as chief administrator of the Khalifa's property, will form a triumvirate and govern in the name of al-Hisham until he is of age.'

The men nodded in agreement. There seemed to be no better answer to the predicament. Although it was two years since al-Hakim had had his first stroke and the topic of the succession had been in everybody's mind, no-one had dared to voice their thoughts aloud. Now at last they could do something to try to maintain the peace. He turned to the new *Sayyida al Malaka*, to make sure she was still in agreement.

'It is an excellent idea, Abu Amir,' she said. 'What about al-Mughira?'

'Ah, yes, al-Hakim's cousin. Do we really consider him a threat to the throne or do you think this is just posturing on his part?' asked al-Mushafi.

'I think he believes he has a legitimate claim to the throne,' the General said. 'We cannot ignore him. I know he is a fool but he is, after all, the Khalifa's uncle. If we stop him claiming the throne, what is to prevent him from setting himself up as sole regent and taking control?'

'My son's life could be in danger,' Subh said, accepting a glass of mint tea from the Nubian slave. 'Al-Mughira may be a fool, as you say, but he is a dangerous fool. If anything were to happen to Hisham then the throne would go directly to him.'

'The *Sayyida* is right. We cannot ignore this threat. It must be dealt with swiftly. I will go and speak to him in person,' said Abu Amir. 'Maybe we can come to a compromise with him that will not threaten the Khalifa's position.'

The slave girl placed the pot of tea and a plate of tiny sweetmeats, made from honey and almonds, on the low table in front of them and walked away as silently as she had come, her gossamer dress swaying back and forth with the rhythm of her hips. Abu Amir watched her for a moment and then said, 'So, are we in agreement?'

'Of course. I will arrange for the regency to be ratified by the Council of Viziers, immediately. Then we must arrange the coronation,' the Grand Vizier said.

'Good.'

'And now my friends, , I must leave. There is important work to be done and no time to lose,' the Grand Vizier said, rising from his seat and bowing low to the Khalifa's mother.

'I too must leave you. Do not worry, *Sayyida*, your son's future will be safe in our hands,' said the General. *'Ma'a salama.'*

'Ma'a salama, dear friends,' repeated al-Mushafi, pulling his cloak around his shoulders. 'We will be in touch before the sun sets.'

Abu Amir, lay back on the couch and smiled at the Grand Vizier and the General as they bowed and left. He knew the General would go straight to the throne room to prostrate himself before the new Khalifa. He too would have to pay his respects to the child but not right away, later. Now he had much to think about. He helped himself to a second cup of mint tea and mused over the morning's meeting. It had gone as he hoped. The first step had been taken. The Triumvirate would rule the country and he would rule the Triumvirate. He had little love for the Grand Vizier, even though he had been the one who had helped Abu Amir to move from his humble letter writing post to more important positions within the government. Al-Mushafi was a man too steeped in the traditions of the past, unable to move with the times. It was true that he was an experienced statesman but he was cautious and wary of any change. It would be hard to work with him because he would always regard Abu Amir as a youngster, who should bow to his long years of experience. General Ghálib on the other hand could be very useful to him, especially as he had the army on his side. He too was an experienced man who had served al-Hakim throughout his reign and he saw himself as the protector of the young Khalifa. Fortunately the General was not overly fond of the Grand Vizier either, even though the two families were in the midst of negotiations over marrying Ghálib's daughter to Mushafi's son. Abu Amir had seen the girl. She was young and comely, not beautiful and exciting in the way that Subh was, but she would make a suitable wife for any man. Maybe this was a way to insert a wedge between the two men and remove al-Mushafi from power, while binding the General closer to him.

'What are you thinking of, my lover?' asked Subh, sliding onto the couch beside him. 'Your brow is furrowed and your eyes are dark. Are you not pleased with the way that the meeting went?'

He put his arm around her and pulled her closer to his chest. She smelled of lilies and lavender water and her skin was as soft as rose petals. Around her neck hung a gold chain encrusted with sapphires which matched the colour of her eyes perfectly. She was a beautiful creature there was no doubt about that, but she was ambitious; ambition gleamed in her eyes in the same way it did his. They were two of a kind. What a shame he could not take her for his wife, but that would never do. People might see him as power-hungry, someone with his eyes set on the throne. They would not be incorrect in these assumptions, but he did not want to gain his supremacy in that manner. He wanted the people to support him; he wanted to be remembered as a good, wise ruler and for that to happen he had to manage things carefully. He was a man who had always been very conscious of how others saw him. His image was important to him and he knew that it could ruin his popularity if he married the widow of the old Khalifa. Besides which, he thought unkindly, Subh was too old to be his wife. He needed someone young and nubile, someone who could give him many sons. But she was useful, for now, and she adored him. He bent over and kissed her on the lips.

'I was thinking of you, my love.'

***

That evening he sent for his most trusted slave, a man called Abbas - the Lion - and in appearance, he was indeed a lion of a man. Originally from the Nile Valley, where he had been captured as a young boy, Abbas had come into Abu Amir's household ten years previously. He was now head and shoulders taller than Abu Amir and as wide as a barn door. His skin shone like burnished copper and he wore both his beard and his hair, in a long tawny tangle. Abu Amir sometimes thought that the slave would have been better named Haytham, the hawk, for he had the eye of a hawk, cold, deadly and all-seeing, but maybe his parents had had another life mapped out for him, before his capture, a warrior's life rather than a life of secrets and lies.

As a servant, he was invaluable to Abu Amir. Nothing missed his notice and he knew everything that was happening in the palace and outside it. He was ruthless to the point of having no emotions for anyone, pitiless, cold and unrelenting. On top of that he was fiercely loyal to his master, who had promised him wealth and power that would have been outside his grasp otherwise. All these were qualities that Abu Amir admired and used to his advantage. He knew that he could always rely on the Lion to execute his plans without question.

'*As-salama alaykum,* my Lord,' Abbas, said. 'How may I be of service?'

'*Wa alaykum e-salam*, Abbas. I need your assistance to get rid of a troublesome insect that is bothering me. Tonight we are going to track down this miserable cockroach and we will squash it. We leave as soon as it is dark.'

There was no need to tell him any more. He had worked in his service long enough to know that all Abu Amir wanted from him was complete compliance.

As soon as the sun had set and the moon had started its watery climb into the sky, they set off for the home of al-Mughira. There was no time to lose. He had already heard rumours that the prince was gaining support from the populace. After all, the argument went, he was al-Hakim's brother, al-Rahman III's direct blood line and he was a just man. He had sworn to make al-Hakim's son his heir, instead of one of his own children. What could be fairer than that? It seemed all perfectly reasonable. How could anyone expect an eleven-year-old boy to rule a kingdom such as theirs? Better that a relative, his uncle in fact, should take over. Abu Amir knew that if people were already mouthing these sentiments, then it was only one more step before someone would put them into action. He could not let that happen.

They rode at a steady pace, Abu Amir leading the way on his favourite black stallion, Abbas at his side, behind them one hundred soldiers that the General had sent to accompany him. He had promised to resolve the situation with the prince, but he had not told the General exactly what he had planned to do. Abu Amir had trained as a lawyer and he knew the importance of keeping his plans close to his chest.

It did not take long to reach al-Mughira's home, which had been built on the lower slopes of the hills overlooking the Guadalquivir at the time when everyone who wanted access to the Khalifa's court, everyone with money or power, every sycophant and lackey, had deserted Córdoba for the new city of Madinat al-Zahra. It was a luxurious house built of stone with high walls and turrets, and the many lamps that lit it could be seen from a great distance despite the blackness of the night sky. As they rode up to the entrance, Abu Amir was alert for any sign of armed men but he saw none, instead the gates swung open to welcome them into the grounds. Was al-Mughira expecting him? Was this a trap? He urged his horse forward cautiously, but could see no threat to himself or his men.

A serving man in full livery stood at the steps of the house, waiting to greet the visitors. 'Welcome to the home of Prince al-Mughira,' he said. 'Who is it that wants to see him?' His manner was polite, and if he was surprised that a group of armed soldiers had arrived at his master's door, he did not show it.

'Tell your master that Abu Amir has come to visit him,' he said, then turning to his company of men, added, 'Abbas, and you two men, follow me. The rest of you stay here.'

The dogs in the yard, suspecting that something was not right, set up a loud baying, and before the manservant could summon his master, the door to the house opened and a tall, muscular slave stood barring the entrance.

'What do you want?' he demanded, his hand moving down to the scimitar that was tucked into his belt. 'Who are you? Why have you brought armed men to the home of Prince al-Mughira?'

Abu Amir did not reply but stood to one side while Abbas stepped forward and deftly slit the slave's throat before he could make another sound. Abu Amir watched the body slide silently to the floor and stepped over it.

'What's happening?' cried a frightened voice. A young slave girl stood trembling in the passage way, the bells on her ankles and wrists tinkling with her fear.

'Sit down and be quiet and nothing will happen to you,' he said to the slave, his voice like ice. 'Where is your master?'

The frightened girl pointed to a room at the end of the passage. 'In his harem,' she stuttered. 'He is with his family.'

The two soldiers pushed past her and burst into the room. Al-Mughira, although a young man, was of a corpulent build, with rolls of fat around his neck and stomach, his beard and hair were cut short and displayed the tell-tale red hue that he had inherited from his father. He was reclining on a mound of silk cushions, surrounded by his wives and concubines, while two small children were playing close by with a pet monkey.

'What is the meaning of this?' he demanded, indignation blazing in his blue eyes as he struggled to get up. 'These are my private quarters. No man is allowed into my harem, no man. You will die for this intrusion.'

He stopped, the words drying in his mouth. A look of terror had come into his eyes. 'Abu Amir? Is that you? Why are you here? What do you want from me that means you break into my house and assault my servants in this way?' he managed to say at last, his voice cracking with fear although his words were brave enough. He struggled to get up, looking around wildly for his sword.

'Good evening, Prince al-Mughira. Here, let me help you,' Abu Amir said, but instead of helping him, he pulled the prince along the ground, dragging him towards the soldiers. 'Al-Hakim is dead. May Allah receive him in his heaven. Rejoice in our new Khalifa, al-Hisham II.'

As the unfortunate prince tried to stagger to his feet, two of the soldiers pushed him back down and pinioned his arms to the floor.

'What do you want? Tell me. I am a rich man. Only let me go free and I will reward you well,' he said, his bombastic tone now replaced by a pleading whine.

'When you are Khalifa, you mean?' Abu Amir said.

'Yes, exactly. You can be my right-hand man, Abu Amir. I have heard good things about you. You can be my Grand Vizier or Head of the Armed Forces, any position you want. Just choose the post you would like and its yours. Just say what you want,' he babbled, his voice becoming shriller and shriller as he struggled against his captors.

'And if I want to be Khalifa?'

At these words Prince al-Mughira's face dropped. 'Just let me and my family go. I beg you. I will disappear. You will never hear from me again. I promise. Just let us go.'

'Enough of this. Prince al-Mughira, you are a traitor. Abbas.'

Abu Amir's slave stepped forward and kneeling down, put his hands around the prince's throat and squeezed. Although al-Mughira tried in vain to break free from Abbas's iron grip, he was powerless. He struggled and kicked, writhing wildly on the floor, but the slave was too strong for him. The prince's face turned red then blue, his eyes began to bulge as though they would pop from their sockets, but still Abbas held his grip on his neck. The women were screaming now, pleading for him to release their master. Their cries of terror mingled with those of their children, who had run to the far end of the room and were cowering in the corner. Abu Amir stood, expressionless, watching the man's struggles grow gradually weaker as his life drained from his body until, finally, he was still. Al-Mughira was dead. He lay there on the floor, his face waxen and his blue eyes staring wildly at nothing. Abu Amir lifted his gaze from the dead body to look at the women. The monkey had climbed up onto a pillar and was agitatedly bouncing up and down, screaming cries of alarm. The children were crying hysterically now and their mothers had gone across to comfort them, picking up the smallest ones and rocking them in their arms. He pointed straight at the terrified women and said, 'If you value your lives, remember that you saw nothing tonight. You saw nothing and you know nothing. Is that clear?'

He waited a moment and then, satisfied that the women had understood him, he turned to follow his men. He did not like to kill women and children. He was not a murderer. Nevertheless, he liked to believe that he was a man who did not pull back from an unsavoury act when it was necessary for a greater good. Killing al-Mughira would not have been necessary if the prince had not threatened the throne and the stability of the caliphate.

'You know what to do.' he said to Abbas.

'Yes, my Lord.'

The two soldiers carried the body outside into the garden and tied a noose around al-Mughira's bruised neck. Next they flung the rope over the branch of an olive tree and hauled him up. He dangled there, his silk robes torn and flapping sadly in the evening breeze, with one slipper missing. His turban had been knocked off in the struggle and now his auburn hair hung loosely about his head, hiding the grimace of death that marred his once noble face.

CHAPTER 4

Subh could not relax. She had heard nothing from her lover since their meeting with Ghálib and Mushafi. Why had he not come to her last night as usual? She had lain awake all night expecting to hear his tap at her door.

'*Sayyida*, have you heard the news?' her maidservant asked, pulling aside the curtains and tying them back with a silken rope. Afra was flushed and more agitated than normal. Her headscarf had slipped and her hair spilled untidily onto her shoulders.

'What is the matter, woman? You look as though you've run all the way here. I hope you're not going to bother me with some silly gossip from the women's quarters.'

'No, *Sayyida*, nothing like that. It's about Prince Mughira.'

'What about him?'

'He hanged himself. Last night. In his own courtyard. The news is all over the city.'

'The prince is dead?'

'Yes, *Sayyida*. Dead by his own hand. Why would he do that? Hang himself? He will spend all eternity suffering the same fate.'

'Stop all this flapping about and go and bring me my dark blue robe. I must speak to my son.'

'Yes, *Sayyida*.'

Subh went out onto her patio and sat down by the fountain to think about what she had just heard. This was Abu Amir's doing. She was sure of it. She dipped her hand into the cool water, lifting it and watching the drops catch the sunlight as they fell back into the pool. He had removed the threat to the throne in one swift blow. Brutal but effective. Not for one moment did she believe the prince had committed suicide. It was expressly forbidden by the Prophet, one of the gravest sins a Muslim could commit. No, al-Mughira would never have hanged himself. And why would he? He had his eyes set on the Khalifa's throne. Why would he throw all that away? And besides, he was a soldier, a brave man who had fought for his country. He would never have taken a coward's way out. No, this was what Abu Amir had meant when he said he would take care of it. She felt a thrill of pleasure that her lover had done this for her and her son. He said she could rely on him and now he had proved it. Now, she in turn, would do whatever she could to help Abu Amir. He deserved more than that measly post as administrator of the Khalifa's fortune. She smiled. That was how she had met him, almost ten years before. Al-Mushafi had sent him to her when she was looking for someone to administer her sons' wealth because they were too young to do it themselves and she was not eligible to do so because she was an ex-slave. She had needed someone reliable, efficient and influential to help her maintain their social position. Abu Amir had been all of that. Already known for his austerity and methodical work in the law courts, he was perfect for the job. And for much else besides she soon found out when they became lovers.

'Is this the robe you wanted, *Sayyida*?' Afra asked.

A blue winged magpie, startled by the maid's appearance, flew up into the trees, cawing raucously. The servant had tidied her appearance, pulling her hair back under her cap and adjusting her scarf so that it draped around her neck and over her shoulders. She waited for her mistresses instructions, the robe over her arm.

'Yes, that one will do.'

Subh stepped back into her room and stood patiently while her maid removed her night clothes for her and made her ready for the day. She usually took great care with her appearance but today she did not want to flaunt her position as *al-Sayyida al-Malika*, the new Queen Mother, rather she wanted to look demure, like someone who bowed to her son's wishes, like a wife in mourning for her husband. She sat while Afra combed and brushed her long blonde hair, still almost completely free of any grey, and then braided it into a long plait which she wound around Subh's head and covered with a white, mourning veil.

They had buried al-Hakim the day before. Like all funerals it happened immediately after the death and was according to their custom. She and the other women in his harem had washed his poor contorted body, closed his eyes and lips and tied up his chin with a silken sash. They had anointed him with myrrh and covered him with a simple shroud of pure cotton. They had removed all his jewellery and sat praying for his soul while he was placed in a shallow grave, lying on his right side with his head pointing towards Mecca. The only thing that distinguished this from any other burial was the thousands of people who came to the graveside to pay their respects and offer their prayers for his soul. He would have wanted it no other way. At heart he was a simple man and he would have wanted a simple funeral, but he had been a popular Khalifa—as had his father before him—and the people of al-Andalus wanted to offer their homage to a family that had kept their land at peace for so long. The crying and wailing from the women lasted well into the night and all the following day. Subh had come home exhausted from it all.

'Bring me some breakfast, Afra. I feel faint,' she said.

'Yes, *Sayyida*.'

Sayyida, it sounded so much grander than Princess. She was *al-Sayyida al-Malika* now and the most important woman in the kingdom. Who would have thought that her life would turn out like this? It certainly hadn't seemed like that the day they raided her village and stole her away. Subh had worked hard to get where she was but even she could not forget how lucky she had been when she had first come to Córdoba as a hungry, frightened child.

***

Clara was woken early the next morning by the repetitive chanting of a voice from somewhere outside. She peered out from under the wall of the tent and gazed at the winding river that separated her from the city before her. Cormorants flew low across the water, looking for fish, swooping down, skimming the surface and then diving to catch their prey; the lucky ones, with a wriggling eel or a fat carp hanging from its beak, alighted on the parapets of the bridge to swallow their breakfast. The voice and the chanting seemed to be coming from the tower at the far side of a massive building. Later she would realise that the voice was that of the *imam* calling the faithful to prayer and that the building was the famous holy mosque of Córdoba, a building that she would come to know well, but for now she was more interested in what the men - pirates, bandits or whoever they were - were going to do with her.

'Time to get up. Here, eat this before we leave,' the man with the gold earring said. He tossed some small loaves of bread on the ground beside them and the children fell upon like famished wolves.

'Where are you taking us?' Clara asked, her mouth full of the dry bread, but all she got in reply was a slap around the head. She bit back her tears and tried to swallow. The bread stuck in her throat but she was hungry and by now she knew that she could not rely on when she would next eat.

The children were still roped together. The rope that was entwined around her waist had got wet when they had jumped into the river and ever since it seemed to be growing tighter and tighter and was now rubbing her skin raw. There was no good complaining to Gold Earring because that would only earn her another slap.

'Hurry up. We haven't got all day,' the man with the strange accent said. 'The slave market opens at dawn.'

So they were going to the slave market. Did they mean to sell them as slaves? It seemed so. An icy feeling gripped Clara's stomach. If she was to become a slave then she would never find her way back to her family and she would have to live here in this strange city forever. She knew what it was like to be a slave. Her own family had slaves, who slept in the sheds with the animals and only ate what was left on the table after everyone else had eaten. She had seen her father beat one of their slaves once for stealing a loaf of bread and the man, who was so badly beaten that he could hardly stand by the time her father had finished, looked as though he would die. Was this to be her life, half starved and treated worse than a dog? If so, she would sooner be dead.

***

The slave market was on the edge of the city, not far from the Roman bridge and to get there they had to pass the city's holy mosque. By the time they had crossed the river the sun was already over the horizon, and as they walked past the Great Mosque she marvelled at its magnificence. It was far more beautiful than the churches at home, and huge by comparison. It towered above them, a terracotta monument of towers and cupolas and minarets. The walls, covered in hundreds of geometric designs, had windows flanked by small marble pillars, not just empty spaces to let the light enter, but with networks of interlaced stone struts, each one different, each one topped by horseshoe arches of red and white. The huge doors to the mosque were of beaten brass, bejewelled with a thousand studs and above them, a series of ornate arches, finely decorated in gold and red and blue, all of which glinted and glimmered in the early morning sun. Surely nothing bad could happen to her here in this lovely city.

'Hurry up. Can't you make them walk any quicker,' snapped Gold Earring.

One of the men tugged at the rope and the children stumbled forward. The girl in front of her was sobbing loudly and people passing by stopped to stare at them.

'Shut up that noise or I'll give you something to cry about,' another of the men said and slapped the back of the girl's head, which only succeeded in making her cry all the more.

Then all at once they had arrived. They were in a wide open space just like any other market except, instead of stalls selling herbs and vegetables, sweet cakes and leather shoes, there was a raised platform in the centre. Instead of tethered animals for sale there were people, dirty, ragged, starved men and women, some clinging to their children, all looking terrified, all in chains and all for sale. A burly man with a whip in his hand was dragging a young boy across the platform, encouraging him to turn and stretch and bend with spiteful flicks of the whip. Someone in the crowd shouted, 'I'll give you ten.' Then another said, 'Twelve.' At last the bidding stopped at fifteen and the boy was handed over to a withered old man in a brown cloak for a handful of coins.

'Right. Get the rope off the first one and smarten her up a bit,' Gold Earring said.

Clara had already decided that he must be the boss because everyone did as he told them. One by one the children were put up for auction. Some went for five dinars, some for ten and one girl, a pretty red-haired girl of about fifteen, was sold for twenty dinars. Clara wondered how much somebody would pay for her and who would want to buy her. It was strange to think about it. It was like when she had bought a puppy in the market at home. She had chosen the smallest one, the one she thought needed most looking after. Clara was one of the smallest girls here, so maybe someone would want to look after her.

***

She trotted along behind the woman who had bought her. She had paid three dinars for her, the least of all of them, but Clara didn't mind because the woman had a kind face not like the spiteful face of the man who had paid five dinars for her friend Ana. Ana had cried when she was handed over to him and had to be carried away, kicking, and screaming for her mother. Clara had felt like crying too but she swallowed hard and refused to let a single tear fall from her eyes. Her mother always told her that when things didn't go well she must always be brave and then they would get better. She hoped her mother was right.

'Try to keep up child. It's not far now,' the woman said in Castilian, a language not unlike her own.

She had a basket full of vegetables and fruit on her arm but she didn't ask Clara to carry it. She just strode along, chattering away to Clara as if she had known her all her life. Most of what she said Clara did not understand but it all sounded friendly. She wondered who she was. Was she the mistress or another slave? If she was a slave then she was well dressed. She wore a blue dress with a brown cloak over it and a small crocheted cap in the same blue was perched on top of her thick brown hair.

They walked through a maze of narrow streets until they eventually stopped outside the entrance to a two storey house.

'This is where you will live,' the woman said, gesturing towards the house and then pointing to Clara. 'You will work for me, in the kitchen. I do the cooking and you will help me.' She spoke slowly and rather loudly, pointing first to the vegetables in her basket and then to Clara again. Maybe the woman thought she was deaf.

'What is your name, child?' she shouted.

'Clara,' she replied as loudly and clearly as she could.

'We will call you Subh. My name is Ulla.'

Clara swallowed hard to fight back the tears. So, not only was she to lose her family and her friends, she was also to lose her name and with it her identity. She was no longer to be Clara, daughter of Maria Garcia and Fernando Alonso, sister to Pedro and Juanito, instead she was to become the slave called Subh. She was to be a nobody. Well maybe they could take away her name and erase her identity but she would still be the same person inside. Nobody could take that away from her.

Ulla opened the gate and led Subh into a paved courtyard surrounded by high walls. There was a sense of tranquility about the place. A fountain bubbled with clear water, a steady sparkling stream that spilled into a small pool edged with painted tiles and on which floated white water lilies and leaves the size of dinner plates. A flash of gold told her there was a fish in the pond and she longed to run forward to see if she could touch it but fear made her stay where she was. So far she did not know what was expected of this new slave called Subh so she would have to tread carefully. Cautiously she looked about her. The walls of the courtyard were hung with earthen pots, each one set one above the other in serried rows and each filled with plants of every colour and hue. The flowers hung down like garlands, covering the walls and filling the air with their perfume. Never had she seen anything like it. A tabby cat lay stretched on its back, playing with a leaf, its paws patting it back and fro. It lifted its head and regarded her solemnly through its tawny eyes and then lazily resumed its play.

'What's the matter child?'

'Is this where I'm going to sleep?' Subh asked anxiously, looking for a shed where there might be shelter or even some animals' quarters.

'No, of course not. You will sleep in the house with the rest of the servants. Now come along. We need to get you washed and smartened up before the mistress gets home.'

So Ulla was not her mistress. She was just the cook. Subh followed her into the house and through to another small courtyard where there was a large wooden tub, pitchers of water and, instead of flowers, rows of pots filled with herbs and vegetables. In one corner there was an earthenware oven and a collection of cooking pots. A vine grew up the side of the wall and stretched its tendrils across the beams, providing the space with overhead shade. Unripe grapes hung in huge bunches from its branches.

'This is our patio,' Ulla said. 'You will work out here, tending the herbs and preparing the vegetables for lunch. This is where we wash the clothes and prepare the food.'

'But I don't know anything about plants,' Subh whispered, staring at the pots of herbs. 'I have never had to work before.'

'Well, you have to work now. But don't worry child. I will show you what to do. Now before you do anything else, wash yourself in that water,' she said, pointing to the tub in the corner. 'Here's some soap and make sure you get yourself really clean. The mistress is very keen on cleanliness. I will go and find you something to wear.'

She left Subh looking about her in amazement, but by the time she returned with a pile of clothes over her arm, Subh had washed and dried herself thoroughly. How wonderful it was to feel the sweet smelling soap against her skin. At home she usually only bathed once a month like everyone else but the last few weeks had made her realise how disgusting it was to be really dirty and she had grown to hate the foul odour of the other bodies around her and of her own. She had longed for the chance to get rid of the stench that even the river could not wash away. Now, at last, she was clean again. She slipped out of her torn slip and pulled on the undergarments that Ulla had brought her then put on a brown robe.

'Here, these slippers should fit you. They belonged to Badra when she was small, but she's far too big for them now.'

'Who is Badra?' Subh asked.

'She's the mistress's only daughter. She's at school today. Then there are four sons, all grown now and working, nice boys all of them and clever too. The master is a school teacher. He is a kind man but very strict, so keep out of his way unless he sends for you.'

Subh nodded.

'And the mistress?'

'The mistress runs the home. She too used to be a teacher but now she stays at home and writes poetry. She is very clever. There are many books in this house but make sure you do not touch them because they are very precious.'

'No, Ulla.'

What would she want with books? She couldn't read. The only book that had been in her home was a prayer book. There wasn't even a Bible, although she had seen one in the church when she went there with her mother on a Sunday. It was a big black book and the priest read from it in a strange language. Juanito said it was Latin, the language of the clergy.

'Am I the only slave? she asked.

'Goodness no, child. There is plenty of work to be done in this house There are four of us. I have lived here for twenty years, and then there is Abdul, he was originally from somewhere in the north, Saxony I think he said, and he has been here even longer than I have. Then there is Tarub, who looks after the mistress. She's a merry soul. You'll like her. And then there's you. The mistress is a kind woman. She knows I'm getting old and my legs aren't as strong as they once were so she gave me some money and told me to go and look for someone to help me in the kitchen. I knew you'd be a good little worker the moment I set eyes on you.'

She smiled at Subh. But Subh did not believe her. She had bought her because she was the only one left and she was cheap. If Ulla had waited longer the men would probably have given Clara away just to be rid of her and be on their way.

'Ulla, is that you back from the market?' a woman's voice called from inside the house.

'Yes, *sayeda*. I have bought the new slave.'

'Oh excellent. Where is she?'

A tall, slim woman in a dark red robe came into the courtyard. Her black hair was pulled back from her face and held in place by a small embroidered cap. She smiled at Subh and said, 'Ah, so you are the new girl. What is your name, child?'

'Clara. Oh no, sorry, Subh,' she replied.

'Clara? Subh?'

'I gave her the name, *sayeda*. As she arrived here in the morning, I thought it was appropriate.'

'Of course, how delightful. Subh, "of the morning". Yes, I like it. Well Subh, I hope you will be happy here. Do as Ulla tells you and you will get along well.' She turned to leave then stopped and asked, 'Do you like poetry, Subh?'

'I don't know. I can't read,' Subh said, feeling for the first time in her life that perhaps this was something she ought to be able to do.

'Oh. And I don't suppose you can speak Arabic either. Well we will have to school you in both. Ulla, you tell me when the child is free and I will see to it. I feel in need of a distraction.'

'Very well, *sayeda*.'

'Give the child something to eat. She must be starving.'

'Yes, *sayeda*.'

'The master would like some fish for his lunch today. Can you see to that?'

'Of course, *sayeda*.'

Subh watched as the woman swept back into the house. How grand she was. How beautiful. She was so unlike Subh's own mother, a small, plump woman who bustled about after her children, making sure they had done their chores and were not getting into mischief, who wore a wide, white apron over her morning dress and fixed her hair on top of her head with big tortoiseshell combs.

***

The door to Subh's room opened and, instead of the maid with her breakfast, it was Hisham.

'Good morning my son. I hope you slept well,' she said, remembering to bow to the new Khalifa.

'No, Mama. I did not sleep well. I am frightened. Nobody has told me what I must do. If I am to be the Khalifa I must learn how to do it properly and how can I do that if no-one will teach me?'

'Don't worry, my child. Today you will meet with the men who will guide and instruct you. You are a clever boy. You will soon learn how to be a ruler.'

The boy started to cry, silently, the tears running down his face and onto his clean white robe. She looked at him in despair. How was he going to rule a country as disparate as al-Andalus, with its mixed population of Arabs, Mozarabs, Berbers, Jews and Christians, with enemies both on its northern borders and across the Straits in North Africa, with threats from the Christian princes and the Fatimite Muslims?

'What is it, my son? Why are you so upset?'

'I have no-one now, Mama. They are all dead, my brother Rahman, grandfather and now Baba. Who will help me? Who will teach me?'

'Hush child; someone will hear you. You are the Khalifa now. You cannot cry like a baby. You must be a man. And remember you are not alone. I will not leave you and I will make sure that you are surrounded by men who will help and protect you. Together we will rule this country, until you are old enough to do it alone.'

The boy wiped his sleeve across his eyes and tried to smile at his mother. 'You promise, Mama? You'll never leave me?'

'Of course not. Now come and sit here with me and we will have breakfast together, just like when you were little.'

For a moment she felt sorry for her son. As the second son, he had never been intended to succeed al-Hakim. It was Rahman, her first-born, who should be sitting on that throne. She sighed. He would be nearly fifteen now - still not old enough to rule, but more suitable for the task. He had been such a lovely child, intelligent, inquisitive, full of fun and sensitive, just like his father. Al-Hakim had named him abd al-Rahman after his grandfather, expecting him to be a great ruler too, but when he was only eight-years-old he had caught a fever and no matter what the doctors did to help him, he weakened and died. She had been heartbroken, as had al-Hakim. Even now her eyes filled with tears when she remembered his little wasted body and her own feelings of helplessness.

So now the crown had passed to al-Hisham, poor little Hisham, still a child. She was all he had. He would never know anything about her family because nobody ever gave a thought to a slave's family. Hisham would never even think to ask her if he had any uncles or grandparents.

How strange that she had been thinking of her mother this morning. She wondered if she was still alive. Had she died that day of the raid or had she found somewhere to hide and managed to survive? And what would she say if she knew that she was now the grandmother of the Muslim Khalifa, al-Hisham, their most hated enemy?

977 AD

CHAPTER 5

Amina had cooked the lamb with rosemary, garlic and honey. The smell filled the room and reminded al-Jundi that he had not eaten since the morning. The young Khalifa had spent most of the day in the throne room, receiving petitions and listening to grievances and al-Jundi had stood at his post, watching and waiting. There was never anything of importance as all matters of state were dealt with by the Triumvirate, in particular, the lawyer Abu Amir. The boy sat there looking bored and telling his fawning subjects that he would give their complaints his immediate attention. Instead a slave took note of it all and passed it on to the Grand Vizier, where it was either seen to or not. Al-Jundi had no idea what happened next. There were grumblings from the people that nothing was being done and their petitions were being ignored; they were used to the old Khalifa's method of dealing with them. On the first day of every week al-Hakim had given an audience to his subjects, allowing them to come to him with their grievances and dealing with them there and then. Sometimes he would dismiss a complaint, sometimes he would punish the guilty party but either way the matter was resolved for once and all.

It was a sham. A year had passed since al-Hakim had died and still nobody was teaching the young Khalifa anything. Even his mother was spending more and more time in Córdoba and the court was drifting back to where it had been before Madinat al-Zahra had been built.

'The food is ready,' his wife said, ushering the children to the table.

'This looks delicious,' he told her and sat down beside his children. 'Have you all washed your hands?'

'Yes, Baba,' answered Asim.

'It's your mother's recipe,' Amina said.

'Ah, so that's why it smells so good,' he said, smiling at his mother. 'And how are you Mama? Are you well?'

'I am well, thank you, my son,' Fatima replied.

They were all there, even his son Qasim who was training to be a doctor and often could not get home in time to eat with them. He looked at his sons; they were good boys, all of them. Boys? Apart from little Asim, they were men now. It wouldn't be long before they would be married too, like Durrah, his little pearl. She had married the year before and still he missed her merry little voice around the house. Soon she would be producing babies herself and making him a grandfather. Perish the thought; he was too young to be a grandfather.

'Baba, we had a new delivery of Barbary falcon chicks today. Grandfather bought them from some North

African traders. They are still very small but they will be real beauties when they are grown,' said Ahmad.

'Your grandfather will be busy then?'

'Yes, we all will. But Grandfather spends a lot of his time in Córdoba these days at the court so there's more work for us.'

By us, his son meant him and the rest of the assistant falconers, the minor falconers and numerous avian vets, all who helped to run the falcon house. The Khalifa owned thousands of birds. Some were gifts from visiting ambassadors, some were captured in the mountains, some brought down from Valencia and even the island of Mallorca and the best, according to his son, came from Lisbon on the far western coast.

'Why do you keep buying them? Why don't you breed them? Pick the best and breed from them?' Rafiq, his second son asked his brother.

Rafiq was a soldier in the Khalifa's army. He had followed his father into the profession and never regretted it. He was the most practical one in the family, always looking for the simplest and quickest way to solve a problem.

'It's been tried but they just won't breed. They don't like captivity,' explained Ahmad.

'Well if that's the case how do you train them?'

'The birds have to be young. The adults are very difficult to train. Anyway hunting is something that is natural to them.'

'Yes, but not handing over their dinner for someone else to eat,' his brother said with a laugh.

'Has the Khalifa been to inspect his birds recently?' asked al-Jundi.

'The new Khalifa? No, I don't think he has ever been. Why?'

'Do you ever take any of the birds to the palace for him to see?'

'I don't think so. Do you want me to find out?'

'No, it doesn't matter. Leave it with me.'

'What is it, Makoud?' his mother asked. 'What are you thinking?'

'Nothing, really. I just think that the boy should understand the importance of owning falcons, understand why visitors from other lands bring them to him as gifts. It is part of his heritage. It is a symbol of his absolute power.'

'Don't you think his father would have explained all that to him?' asked his wife.

'Maybe. But sometimes I think his father was too absorbed in his books to worry about his falcons. He understood their symbolic importance, how it told the world that he was part of a strong and powerful family, part of the Omeyyad dynasty, but he might not have conveyed that to his son.'

'So what are you going to do about it?' his wife asked, as she dished some more lamb onto his plate.

'I will talk to your father. Maybe he will have a good suggestion, after all he is the man in charge, the Grand Falconer.'

'Yes, and my boss, so don't upset him Baba, please,' said Ahmad.

'No lad, I won't upset him.'

***

It was some days later that al-Jundi found the opportunity to talk to his father-in-law. The palace had been in a state of turmoil because there was news of trouble on the northern marches with the Christian princes. The Grand Vizier had been dithering about what to do and now Abu Amir had stepped in and said he would take an army of men and ride north to sort it out. Al-Jundi had been astonished at this suggestion as Abu Amir was no more a soldier than the Grand Vizier was, but he was from sound Arab stock and that seemed enough to convince the populace that he was the man for the job. They had left that morning amid cheers and cries of 'death to the Christian princes'.

Al-Jundi was becoming more and more suspicious of Abu Amir. The whole thing seemed to be an exercise in increasing his own popularity. True he was a charming and generous man, always polite and attentive but there was something about him that al-Jundi didn't trust. He was far too close to the Khalifa's mother for one thing and he had heard rumours that they had been lovers for years, even when al-Hakim was alive. Then there was that manservant of his, Abbas. He was not someone you would want to meet on a moonless night. No, there was more to Abu Amir than met the eye.

He found the Grand Falconer in his office in the palace, talking to another of the city magistrates.

'Come in Makoud; I have almost finished,' he said, removing the papers from his desk and placing them in a box.

'*As-salama alaykum*, father-in-law,' al-Jundi said.

'*Wa alaykum e-salam*, my son,' his father-in-law replied. 'What can I do for you?'

'I wondered if I could talk to you about the falcons.'

'Of course. That is my job after all.' He smiled at him and gestured for him to sit beside him. 'Will you take some tea?'

'Yes, with pleasure,' al-Jundi said, even though he was not thirsty. His father-in-law was a very formal man and al-Jundi was careful never to offend him.

'So tell me, what you would like to know?'

'You remember that al-Hakim made me promise to serve his son, the Khalifa, when he no longer had need of me?'

'Yes, I know that. You are with him at all times, I believe.'

'I am and I cannot help noticing that he has little to do. The Regents are taking care of everything for him, which I understand is how it has to be until he is older but …' he hesitated.

'But what? What is the problem?'

'The problem is that he has nothing to do. I have sons. You too. You remember how easily they can get bored if they are not kept occupied? I think al-Hisham needs an interest, something to keep him busy.'

'Like a hobby?'

'In a way but something that is part of his birthright and with which he should be very familiar. I think he needs to learn about the falcons.'

'Do you indeed? And how do you propose we do that? I am far too busy with my work in the Falcon House, maintaining discipline, training not just the young birds but overseeing my assistants and ensuring that they follow all the protocols, and that's not to mention the hours I spend here on the magistrate's duties.'

'I understand. I wasn't thinking that you would do anything yourself. The other problem, as I see it, is that the Khalifa has no friends. He is alone most of the time. True he has his amusements and his slaves but what he needs is a friend.'

'Ah, now I understand. You want me to tell Ahmad to spend some time with him. Well, I don't know about that. Ahmad is a very promising assistant and I am extremely pleased with his progress. To be honest with you, I need him where he is.'

'But this is the Khalifa we're talking about. Nobody else seems to care about how he feels or what he is doing. He has become a machine for stamping seals on official documents, documents that he never reads and would not understand if he did so. We can't interfere in matters of state, I understand that, but surely we could do something for him. He is still a boy after all.'

The Grand Falconer sighed and stroked his long beard. He was an imposing man, not unlike the birds with which he spent so much time. His nose was large and hooked and his sharp eyes darted about, missing nothing. He leaned forward and stared at al-Jundi.

'If anyone else had suggested such a thing I would have thought they had some ulterior motive, but I know that you have only the child's welfare at heart, so I will consider it.'

Al-Jundi was not surprised at his reply. He knew that his father-in-law would not give him an instant answer. He was a cautious man. Working with raptors had made him so. One careless move could cost you a finger or an eye and he had the same attitude to all his business.

'Thank you, *sayyad*. Now I must be going as I am due to be on duty in a short while.'

'Have you heard about the campaign?' his father-in-law asked, rising to wish his son-in-law farewell.

'Yes, may Allah watch and guide them.'

'And bring us victory.'

'*Ma'a salama*, my father.'

'*Alla ysalmak*, Makoud.'

***

Two days later Ahmad came rushing into the house. 'Mama, Mama, is Baba home yet? I have some news for him.'

'I'm here, Ahmad. What do you want?' asked al-Jundi. Had the Grand Falconer made his decision so soon? It seemed that he had.

'I have been given a very special job to do, Baba. Grandfather has asked me to take one of the baby peregrine falcons to give to the Khalifa. He says I must show him how to take care of it and then, when it is big enough, we are to train it together.'

'That's very interesting, son. And what do you think about it? Would you like to see the Khalifa and teach him about falconry?'

'Oh yes, father. He is the ruler of all al-Andalus. I know he is just a boy like me but he is Khalifa.'

'What about the rest of your work?' al-Jundi asked, hoping that his strange request was not going to jeopardise his son's future.

'I am only to go there in the afternoons and I must go to the Falcon House every morning as usual to continue with my duties. I'm so excited. Grandfather says I must start tomorrow. He will go with me to explain to the Khalifa who I am.'

'Just as well,' said his grandmother. 'You don't want to get your head chopped off, do you?'

'Well I am very pleased for you. Please remember one thing, Ahmad, you will see me in the palace but you are not to speak to me. I might look as though I am not doing anything but I am always on duty when I am with the Khalifa. Do you understand?'

'Yes, father. I understand. I will pretend you are just any old Palace Guard, not my beloved Baba,' he said and threw his arms around al-Jundi.

Ahmad was almost sixteen and had been working for two years now but sometimes, when he was excited, he seemed to be just a young child again. He hoped that the two boys would become friends It would be good for the Khalifa and it wouldn't hurt Ahmad to have such an influential companion.

CHAPTER 6

The campaign to León had been his first incursion into enemy territory. Abu Amir was not a battle- hardened soldier like Ghálib but he had put his lawyer's mind to the tactics of battle and it had worked. They had outflanked and out-manoeuvred the Christians and won a resounding victory. Others may have been surprised at his success but he had not doubted himself for one moment.

'We have Allah on our side,' he told his army, a multifarious collection of soldiers, although he had no doubt that the Christians were declaiming the self-same thing.

He knew it wasn't Allah who would win this war; it was Abu Amir and his army. His soldiers were not pure bred Arabs, like Abu Amir himself, whose ancestor had been part of the first invasion two hundred years before, or so he liked it to be known although the truth was much hazier than that. These men were mostly mercenaries, Berber volunteers from North Africa and Christian prisoners-of-war who chose to serve in the Khalifa's army, over life as a slave. Then there were also the conscripted troops provided by each of the provinces, reluctant soldiers, inefficient and unreliable, and finally the few who fought for religious reasons, who saw each and every opportunity to attack the Christians as a *jihad*, a holy war. His first task was to bring this motley collection of men together and mould them into a brave and steadfast army. He may have been new to soldiering but Abu Amir understood men. He knew that two things were needed to win their loyalty: success in battle and generous pay. If they had the first then the second would follow. He also knew that if he wanted to achieve the authority that he craved, he had to win wars. People fought for all sorts of reasons, ambition, greed, religious zeal, the list was endless but, as far as he was concerned, a successful campaign meant riches. With wealth would come power. It was as simple as that. True, he didn't want to be seen as a war mongering upstart who was trying to bypass the Khalifa and take the throne for himself. No, that would only encourage opposition either from those loyal to al-Hisham or those who wanted the power for themselves. He would have to be careful, gain allies, win over the people and, above all, secure the support of the army.

The campaign to Ledesma, near León, had been a great success. They had crossed the border and laid waste to the Christian lands, driving their enemy further north. They had sacked the churches and loaded their mules with gold, silver and jewels, taken two bishops for ransom and captured over a thousand horses. The bishops alone would bring in a great deal of money and there had been other high-ranking prisoners that they could sell. Yes, it had been a successful military operation. Until now he had not fully realised just how lucrative winning a battle could be. The slaying of prisoners was forbidden under Islamic law so, instead, there were over a thousand men to be brought back to al-Andalus to replenish his army. There was plenty of booty and, in accordance with the law, he saw to it that all the soldiers had their share of it and more. His generosity made him their hero and when he returned to Córdoba, riding at their head on his black stallion, and the people lining the streets began to chant 'Al-Mansur, al-Mansur, - The Victorious One,' the soldiers had joined in. He was everybody's hero now.

'You have done well, my friend,' General Ghálib said, when Abu Amir dismounted. 'See how they have re-named you. You will always be known as al-Mansur from now on, in recognition of this, your triumphant first battle. I congratulate you. You have shown what quick action and courage can do in a tight situation. Maybe you can teach a thing or two to our colleague the Grand Vizier.' He chuckled and nodded towards the unsmiling figure of al-Mushafi.

'Thank you, my general. I must speak to you later, in private. When would be convenient?'

'Come to my house tonight. My wife will cook dinner for us. She is a splendid cook.'

'I would like that, dear friend.'

'Tonight then, after prayers.'

'*Ma'a salama.*'

***

Al-Mansur knew exactly where Ghálib's house was, although he had never been invited there before. It wasn't far so he didn't bother to ride. It was on the hillside not far from the home of the murdered Prince Mughira. All the elite lived in that area, with its plentiful water supply and its views across the Guadalquivir and the fertile plain beyond. It was close to the court at Madinat al-Zahra and also to the bustling city of Córdoba. The general's house was more modest than Mughira's but built in the same style as they all were, with closed walls and a central courtyard, a design that guaranteed privacy and protection. He hesitated outside the main gate for a moment, to adjust his cloak. He had taken some pains with his preparations that night. His beard had been carefully combed and perfumed and his tunic, a shorter, horseman's version that suited a warrior better than his previous lawyers' dark robes, made him appear younger and, he hoped, more virile. Instead of wearing a *ghifara*, the woollen cap worn by most men, particularly those of Berber descent, al-Mansur, to emphasise his Arab heritage, liked to hide his long hair under a cowl-shaped turban. All this was to impress not Ghálib but his daughter, the comely Ismá. Al-Mansur was a handsome man, or so Subh was always telling him, with dark skin and a proud bearing. His nose was straight and his lips full but it was his eyes that most people noticed, so black that they seemed unfathomable, the eyes of a falcon, they said. He smoothed his beard one last time and knocked briskly on the door. A dark skinned slave in a short tunic opened the door.

'I am Abu Amir,' he said. 'I have come to see General Ghálib.'

The slave bowed slightly and replied, '*Ahlan*, welcome al-Mansur, my master is expecting you. Would you follow me.'

He led al-Mansur into a small reception room and said, 'I will tell the General that you have arrived. Please wait here.'

Al-Mansur did not have to wait long before Ghálib came to greet him.

'*As-salama alaykum,* dear friend,' the General said.

'*Wa alaykum e-salam,*'al-Mansur replied, embracing him warmly.

'*Ahlan*, welcome to my humble home.'

'*Ahlan wa sahlan.*'

'Come with me and we will eat. Later we can talk,' said the General.

He followed the General through another passageway and out onto an enclosed patio. A low table had been spread with a variety of fruits and vegetables. There were sliced aubergines in a sauce of honey and caraway seeds, whole asparagus, bright red pomegranates, sliced so that the juice ran out onto a plate, and a large plate of boiled artichokes. A pitcher of water stood cooling in the fountain.

'I hope you have an appetite,' the general said, indicating that al-Mansur should be seated.

Almost at once, a servant entered with a steaming plate of mutton cooked in turmeric and thyme which he placed in the centre of the table.

'May I present my wife, Ghazala,' the general said, as his wife joined them. She carried a basket of bread in her hands.

His wife bowed, greeting her guest in the accustomed way with '*Ahlan*, honoured guest.'

Then she sat down beside her husband. She was a short, plump woman with wide hips and an even wider smile. Her main resemblance to her daughter seemed to be her round, chestnut eyes which sparkled and shone as though saying, 'I was young once too.'

'*Ahlan wa sahlan.*'

He looked around him and said, 'Where is your daughter this evening? Does she not eat with you?'

Ghálib looked at his wife.

'She will be here directly,' she said. 'You know how she is, husband, always day dreaming.'

As she spoke the girl came in and slipped into her place next to her mother. Al-Mansur smiled. It was a true mark of friendship that the General had invited him to eat in the company of his wife and daughter. It should be easy to persuade Ghálib to give him his daughter's hand in marriage instead of giving her to the feckless son of al-Mushafi.

'Good evening, child,' he said, looking straight at her.

The girl murmured a reply but kept her head bowed; she seemed a modest, even shy young woman. That would suit him fine. He certainly didn't want a wife as feisty as his mistress. No, a quiet, comely young woman who would give him plenty of sons was just what he needed. The girl had the same wide hips as her mother, excellent for child-bearing and, although she was not very tall, she was sturdy. If only she would smile at him he could see what her teeth were like.

'I hope you are hungry,' Ghazala said, as she dished out the mutton. 'It is my own recipe, a version of an old Jewish dish that my grandmother used to make.'

So the General's wife was from a Jewish family. Interesting.

'I am indeed, very hungry,' replied al-Mansur. 'The meat looks and smells delicious. I am sure it is wonderful.'

He could see the General was pleased that he had complemented his wife although the truth was that he was not keen on *dhimmi* food. It lacked both the finesse and the spiciness of Arab cooking.

'Yes, it is very tasty,' he said, helping himself to a piece of flat bread and mopping up the gravy.

'I'm afraid I cannot offer you any wine,' the General said, 'I know that some Muslims have taken to drinking a little wine but we do not drink alcohol in this house.'

'I am happy to drink water,' al-Mansur said. 'It is against our religion to drink wine and that is a good enough reason for me.'

In fact it was not strictly true because, in his younger days, he had often drunk wine, but now he was well aware that it would not be good for his image. It was important that he was seen to be not just a valiant warrior but also a man of morals, someone who upheld the laws of their religion.

***

Later, when the General's wife and daughter had retired for the evening, he and Ghálib sat drinking mint tea and playing chess. It was a game he enjoyed. It stretched his mind and meant he had to anticipate his opponent's next move and, in that manner, it was not unlike politics, a game in which he was becoming very interested.

Before his first military campaign he had spent a few nights playing chess against ibn Farid, one of the chess professionals who had often played against the old Khalifa. He knew it would sharpen his mind for the battle. After all, chess was little more than an enactment of a battle where one side sought to defeat the other, two armies lined up opposite each other, the Red army and the Black. The chess pieces represented the four divisions of the military: the infantry, the cavalry, the archers and the charioteers and over these were the commanders, the King and the Minister. It was not a game of straight forward attack, instead it required strategy and skill. Sometimes it was necessary to outflank the enemy or to sacrifice men for the greater good, but always, whatever else happened, the King had to be protected.

He surveyed the board in front of him. This was a particularly fine chess set. The pieces were carved in red onyx and black marble and were smooth and cool to the touch. Each division was distinctive, as it would be on a real battlefield: the large, imperious King, his minister a little shorter, a little dumpier, then the four divisions, each reducing in size until they came to the foot soldiers, the smallest and most dispensable of them all.

'You are too good for me,' he said, surrendering his King to General Ghálib.

The General smiled. Like all good soldiers, he loved to win.

'So, my friend, you said you had something to talk to me about. What is it? Is it about our mutual friend, al-Mushari?'

'Not really, although your decision may anger him.'

'Since when have I been frightened of angering that old woman? Spit it out man, what is it?'

'I would like to marry your daughter? My first wife is dead now and I am not getting any younger. I feel it is time that I had a wife from a good family, who will give me many sons. I can see no-one I like better than your daughter. She is a lovely girl, quiet and well educated. I think she would make me an excellent wife.'

'Ismá? You'd like to marry Ismá? Well that is a surprise. But you are right; she would make anyone an excellent wife. However, there is a problem.'

General Ghálib stroked his beard and said no more for a moment. Al-Mansur waited. What would he reply? Would he think giving his daughter to al-Mansur was worth upsetting the third member of the Triumvirate? The General began to pack the chess pieces carefully into their carved ivory box but still did not speak. After a while al-Mansur began to feel that the General's silence was a slight to his honour and was on the point of leaving when the General heaved a great sigh and said, 'You do know that I am in the process of negotiating Ismá's marriage to al-Mushari's son?'

'Why would you give your daughter to that Berber family when she could marry a man who can trace his ancestry back to the invasion of Tarik?' he asked.

'I must admit that I am of the same opinion, but I do not want it to be thought that I am not a man of his word.'

'Has the contract been agreed?'

'No. You know al-Mushari. He is a good man but he does not know how to make a decision. I think that we have not seen this side of his character before because, in the past, we always had a strong Khalifa to make the decisions. Now it seems that the Grand Vizier is not up to the job. He is even dithering over the simple matter of his son's marriage.'

'I do not like to speak ill of our colleague but I know that I can speak frankly to you, my dear friend. His indecision at the time of the attacks from the north could have cost us the border. This time we were lucky and the Christians were pushed back but next time ...,' al-Mansur left it for the General to finish his words.

'Yes, next time the Christians could cross the Duero and take our lands. But there won't be a next time because people will want you to take control. You have proved your worth on the battle field and there's no way it would be left to that dithering Berber.'

'So, no marriage payments have been made?'

'No, that is the point we have reached. Al-Mushari thinks the dowry we are offering is too little. He wants me to give his son more.'

'He is a man who places great importance on striking a bargain, is that not so?' Al-Mansur paused, sipping his tea and then continued, 'Money is important to me, too, but making a good match is more important. I have told you why I want the hand of your daughter. Well what do you say? Will Ismá become my bride?'

'I take it you want an answer tonight?'

Al-Mansur nodded.

'Very well. I will draw up the contract tomorrow and you will be wed at the next full moon. Does that suit you?' the General said, with a smile at his future son-in-law.

'That suits me very well, my friend. Now I must leave you. I have many things to organise. *Ma'a salama.*'

'*Alla ysalmak*, my son-to-be.'

Al-Mansur felt very pleased with himself as he walked back to his home through the deserted streets. A reddish moon hung low in the sky, barely lighting his way. Al-Mushari would be angry when he heard the news. He would see it as an insult to his family. Yes, a marriage with al-Ghálib's daughter was an excellent strategy. In one move al-Mansur would gain a close ally, drive a wedge between the General and the Grand Vizier and gain even more popularity with the common people by marrying the daughter of a man who had started his successful career as a freed slave. People loved a rags to riches story. Yes, it had been a successful evening. Only when he was almost home did he stop to wonder what Subh's reaction would be to the news. He did not want to alienate her because he still needed her patronage, at least for now. She had just engineered his appointment as major-domo of the Royal Household, but he had his sights on something higher. He stopped and retraced his steps, cutting down a narrow passage and heading for the North Gate of the city. He would visit her now, this very night and tell her about his plans. He would be open with her so that she was aware that this was nothing more than a marriage of convenience, as so many were these days, and he would continue to see her as before. He smiled to himself. *Al Sayyida al Malika* was an extraordinary woman, perceptive and sharp. She would understand. He and she were so alike in many ways, both ambitious, both wanted power and neither of them hesitated to do whatever was necessary to get what they wanted.

CHAPTER 7

Subh stretched her arms above her head, feeling the silk sheets cool and soft beneath her naked body. Her lover had come to her last night and normally she would be happy and relaxed, remembering his touch, re-savouring his kisses, but this morning it was different. She could not erase the news from her mind. She had always feared this moment, the time when he would draw away from her and turn to someone younger. She could feel the jealousy eating away at her stomach, the bile rising in her throat as she thought about him being with another woman. It was ridiculous for her to feel that way; after all she had been a concubine, just one of many in al-Hakim's harem and she would still be a slave if she hadn't been fortunate enough to give him two sons. All Arab men of importance had more than one wife. Unlike the monogamous Christians, their religion allowed them as many as four. Al-Mansur was not her husband, only her lover and she was not his wife. She had hoped that one day she might have been, but he had made it very clear that it was not a good idea for either of them. Such a marriage would jeopardise their futures. There was nothing she could do to stop him marrying the girl but she would do all she could to bind him to her. She could not bear to think that he would never come to her bed again.

She rolled on her side, welcoming the delicate breeze that floated in from the garden bringing with it the scent of fruit blossom. She closed her eyes and let her thoughts drift back to the house in Córdoba, where she had learnt, little by little, of the ways of her new home.

***

The house was in darkness, shrouded in gloom since the death of Zaynab bint Zakariya. Her mistress, whom she had come to love as a mother, had taken a fever and nothing the doctors could do would cool her burning body. She had died a month before but still the house was in mourning. Al-Jali, her husband, had been distraught at her death and shut himself in his library, not even appearing for meals.

'Here child, you can go to the market for me this morning. It will give you something to do instead of mooning about the place with that long face. As if it's not bad enough that the master sits in his library all day with his nose in his books and barely eats anything I prepare for him, now you are behaving like a lovesick camel. Come now, I know you are sad that the mistress has died but life must go on. We all have to die one day,' Ulla said, handing her an empty shopping basket and adding, 'See if you can find any of those sugared almonds that the master likes. Perhaps I can tempt him to eat with some of them.'

'But it was so quick, Ulla. She was ill for such a short time.'

'Would you have preferred it if she had suffered?'

'Of course not. I just wasn't ready for it.'

'And neither was the master. I have never seen a man so changed.'

'I think he is angry with me,' said Subh, sadly. 'He never looks at me and won't even say good morning.'

'He is not angry with you, child. He is angry with Allah for taking away his Zaynab. He is grieving, that is all. Come, cheer us all up with one of your songs.'

Subh did not really feel like singing but she began to sing a traditional song that her mistress had taught her. She had lived in this house for ten years and during that time Zaynab had educated her in many things, how to sew, how to paint, to read and speak Arabic, and best of all she had introduced her to the poetry that she loved above all else. Subh had learnt by heart not just the poems that her mistress wrote but also those of the famous poets ibn Abd Rabbihi and ibn Faraj and would often sit at her mistress's feet reciting them to her. Her mistress's favourite was ibn Faraj's poem 'Chastity' which began with the lines:

'She came unveiled in the night,

illuminated by her face,

night put aside its shadowy veils as well.'

She was murmuring the words softly to herself when the door to the master's room opened and he stood there staring at her.

'Stop that noise at once. Do you have no respect for the dead? Get out, girl. Get out now.'

Subh had never heard him speak to anyone like that before. He was normally so correct in the way he addressed everyone in the household. She grabbed her cloak and ran. What did he mean? Just get out of his sight or was he telling her she must leave?

***

When she arrived back, her shopping bag overflowing with lemons, spinach, rice for the midday meal and a huge watermelon, the door to the library was once again closed and there was no sign of al-Jali.

'Ulla, I have what you wanted. I even found some sugared almonds for the master,' she said, going out to the patio where Ulla was sitting on a low stool, supervising her assistant as she chopped and diced vegetables for the lunch.

Ulla was old now; her hair was grey and her face was lined. She no longer did any of the heavy work around the house. Normally those jobs would have gone to Subh except for the fact that two years before, when Tarub left to get married, the mistress had taken Subh out of the kitchen and made her her personal maid. So she no longer worked with Ulla, who now had a new assistant to help her, little Zarqa, so called for her blue eyes, and who had been bought from the slavers just like Subh. She was a quiet child who did what she was told and hardly spoke to anyone. Unlike Subh, she would not have Zaynab there to help and educate her. Tears came into Subh's eyes as she thought of her mistress and all that she had done for her.

'Good. Put it down there. Zarqa will see to it in a moment. By the way, the master says you are to go to the library. He wants to speak to you. You can take him a plate of the almonds when you go.'

'What does he want?' Subh asked, nervously.

The master had never asked to speak to her before. She could not remember him ever sending for any of the servants because it was always the mistress's job to manage the household.

'I don't know. The mistress's brother is with him,' said Ulla.

Subh knocked gently on the library door and waited, her stomach churning with anxiety. Why had he sent for her? Was he going to send her away? She felt herself grow cold at the thought. She had been very happy here. She knew she would never again find a mistress as kind and thoughtful as Zaynab. She had not only taught her many things, she had helped her to believe in a better future. Subh was still a slave but she was not treated like a slave in this house, and her mistress had filled her head with ideas of a different life. She had explained to her how she could become a free woman if she converted to Islam or if she married a Muslim man. She told her that she was clever and talented, that she could do many things if she only put her mind to it. She explained to her that education was very important, not just for men but women too. And Subh had believed her. But her beloved mistress was dead, and who would help her fulfil her dreams now?

'Come in,' her master called from the dark recesses of his room. He sat at his desk. An oil lamp burning beside him shed a wavering light on the rows and rows of books that were piled beside him. A second man sat across from the master, an open book in his hand. It was her mistress's brother, Sulayman, who lived in Madinat al-Zahra.

'Come here, Subh,' the master said.

She walked towards them and stopped, self consciously.

'Ulla says would you like to try these sugared almonds,' she said, holding out the plate.

'Thank you. Put them down on the table.'

The table was covered with scrolls and pens and ink. Carefully she moved one of the scrolls aside and placed the almonds next to it.

'So, what do you think?' the master asked his brother-in-law.

'She is very pretty, in a boyish way. Lovely hair and those eyes, so blue. Yes, she will bring a fair price.'

A fair price? She though she was going to faint. They were going to sell her. How could the master do that to her?

'She is not just pretty, she is talented too,' the master said as though she were not there, as though she could not hear the cruel words he spoke. 'My wife, your sister, spent a lot of time on her education. She speaks Arabic, she can sing and recite poetry.'

He looked straight at Subh and said, 'Sing that song that my wife liked so much.'

She swallowed hard; her mouth was dry and she wasn't sure she could do as he asked. She took a deep breath and began to sing a song by the poet ibn Abd Rabbihi. When she finished no-one spoke. She waited, wondering if their silence signified good news for her or bad.

'Now, recite one of my wife's poems, please. Her brother would like to hear one.'

She began to recite the last poem that her mistress had composed, a sad story about two lovers torn apart by their families. The emotion she was feeling at that moment overspilled into the words she spoke and, when she had finished, she saw her master wipe a tear from his eye.

'She has a beautiful voice,' Sulayman said. 'I can hear my sister in those words. Yes, you are right, she is no ordinary slave girl. I think the Khalifa might well be interested in her.'

'You don't think she is too tall and too slim? She is nothing like as voluptuous as the women of Córdoba so it's possible she will not be to his taste.'

'The Khalifa puts a great value on the arts, especially poetry and prose. The fact that she can read Arabic must surely make her more attractive.'

'Yes, I agree.'

They both looked at Subh as though she were an item on a stall in the market. What would her mistress say to them if she were here? She would never have sold Subh into an uncertain future. Never. Subh was angry with the master. She had always been a good servant, loyal and obedient. Why was he getting rid of her?

'But why are you selling me?' she asked before she could stop herself.

Her mistress's brother looked astonished at her boldness, but the master just smiled, his old, patient smile and said, 'I'm sorry Subh but we have no need for you now. I know this must be a shock to you but you see, now that your mistress is no longer with us,' his voice wavered and then he continued. 'Now that your mistress has gone we do not require a lady's maid. However, my wife was very fond of you and had high hopes for your future, so because of that, I do not intend to just sell you to anyone. I will find you a place worthy of your talents. My wife would have wanted me to do that.'

Subh could not hold back the sobs that rose in her throat. She was being sent away. She would have to leave the place that had become home to her.

'Don't cry, my child. My brother-in-law will take good care of you. He is returning to Madinat al-Zahra today and you will accompany him. Run along now and get your things together. Tell Ulla to give you something to eat and be ready to leave as soon as we have finished our lunch.'

He turned away and started to talk about other things while Subh stood, tears streaming down her face, looking at him in bewilderment. After a minute or two he noticed she was still standing there.

'Hurry up now, Subh. It won't be so bad, you'll see,' he said, opening one of the scrolls to show Sulayman. 'Look at this, my brother; it's magnificent, some of the finest poetry ever written.'

It was no use. Her tears made no difference. The master had made up his mind. She was to leave today. Subh went straight to her room and threw herself on her sleeping mat. How could he do this to her? Her mistress would not have wanted him to throw her out. Of that she was certain. Now this man, her mistress's brother, was taking her to Madinat al-Zahra to sell her.

She had been to the city once before with her mistress, and on that occasion they had visited Sulayman's home and eaten with his family. That had been a nice day. The city was magnificent, smaller than Córdoba but very busy. It had been built on the lower slopes of the Sierra Morena, and the Khalifa's palace was situated so that it overlooked everything: the houses of the townspeople who lived below, the wide expanse of fertile plain that produced the food for the citizens, the roads that linked the city to Córdoba and beyond, the river that provided them with water and fish, the garrison of the Khalifa's army, the area where the artisans worked, potters, stonemasons, cobblers, blacksmiths and many more. That day they had walked around the perimeter of the *alcázar,* admiring it but not entering it. It was said to be more beautiful than anything that was in Córdoba, with four hundred rooms and the roof supported by four thousand marble pillars, but all she could see were high stone walls and imposing arches, similar to those she was used to seeing as she walked about Córdoba. Now she was going to live there, and from what the men had been saying, they intended to sell her to the Khalifa, al-Rahman III, an old man.

'Subh, my dear girl, I am so sorry to hear that you are leaving us,' Ulla said, coming into her room and putting her arms around her. 'Come with me to the kitchen and I will give you something to eat and a few things to take with you.' Her kindly face was lined with concern. 'We will miss you, Subh. We will miss your sunny smile and your happy songs.'

'Oh, Ulla, I don't want to go. I want to stay here,' she sobbed. 'Can't you speak to the master? Tell him you need me here. Please. Don't let them send me away.'

'If I could do anything my child, believe me I would, but the master's mind is made up. I don't think it is because we don't need you anymore; it has more to do with the fact that you remind him too much of the mistress. He can't forget how fond she was of you and how much she did for you. It hurts him to remember how happy those days were.'

'But that's not my fault. It's not fair,' she wept.

'Come now. Wipe your eyes and let me help you pack your things. It wouldn't do to make the men angry now, would it.'

Together they put her few possessions in an old carpet bag that the mistress had given her: her new slippers, her blue robe, a crocheted cap that she had made, some clean underclothes and her winter cloak. Then she followed Ulla into the kitchen for the last time.

***

Her mistress's brother was not unlike his sister in looks, and was equally as studious, but he was a quiet man and said nothing to her, except, 'Put your bag up here, on the donkey.' Then he led the way out of the city, through the west gate and out onto the Nogales Road that linked Córdoba to Madinat al-Zahra. It was a beautiful morning, fresh and cool; the sun was climbing slowly in a cloudless blue sky and swifts swirled overhead, swooping and diving after insects. Normally Subh would have been excited about going somewhere different but today she barely noticed her surroundings. Walking with her head down and her mind numb, she was oblivious to the shrill cries of the swifts and the steady clip-clop of the donkey's hooves on the paved road. With each step she was moving further and further away from all that she knew and loved, her friends, her books, her home. The mistress was dead and now everything was going to change again. What sort of existence was she going to have in Madinat al-Zahra? And for how long? The Khalifa might not want her and then where would she go? Even if he did decided to buy her, he was old and who knew what would happen to her when he died. Her life would be disrupted once again.

They walked in silence, stopping occasionally to sit by the roadside and drink from the water flask.

Tell me about yourself, child,' Sulayman asked at one point. 'Do you remember anything of your life before you went to live with my sister?'

She looked at him in surprise. That life seemed so far away now. She hadn't thought about her old home for a long time. 'A little,' she replied, shyly.

'And do you miss it?'

'I miss my mother sometimes,' she said and her eyes began to fill with tears. 'But it was a long time ago.'

'Indeed.'

'I sometimes wonder if she is still alive, my mother that is. And I wonder what happened to my brothers and sisters.'

'That's only natural,' he said and looked as though he wished he had not asked her about her past. 'Look, we're almost there.'

She saw the city before them, nestled in the green foothills of the Sierra Morena; it gleamed a brilliant, shimmering white in the midday sun. For a moment she felt her spirits rise; it was impossible to look at its splendour and not feel some excitement.

'Is that Madinat al-Zahra?' she asked.

'Yes, that's the city there, in the distance. It is less than half an Arab mile away, now. We will arrive in time for lunch, and then this evening I will take you to meet Yamut al-Attar, the Chief Black Eunuch.'

He must have seen the horror on her face because he laughed and said, 'Don't worry, child. He is not a fearsome man, quite the opposite. He is in charge of the Khalifa's harem and he is the one who will decide if you are suitable or not.'

'So I won't see the Khalifa?'

'No, not right away. It is Yamut who choses and buys the women. He is very experienced and knows exactly what the Khalifa wants.'

'But what if he doesn't like me? What will happen to me then?'

Sulayman shrugged and continued walking.

***

Sulayman's wife, al-Bayda, had taken her to the baths that afternoon. Subh had washed her hair and lain in the warm water, cleansing herself of the dust from the road and feeling the tiredness slip away from her. Occasionally, in Córdoba, she and Ulla had gone to the baths with their mistress, but usually she washed herself in a wooden tub on the back patio. This was luxurious. Al-Bayda was enjoying the baths as much as she was and, when it was time to get out, suggested that they both have a massage.

The slave girls rubbed sweet smelling lavender oil into their shoulders and backs then massaged their hands and finally their feet. Another girl came and combed Subh's wet hair then rubbed it dry and combed it again after sprinkling it with a light perfume.

'Do you know what is going to happen to me?' she asked al-Bayda, shyly.

'I only know what my husband has told me, which is not a lot - he is not a man much given to chatter - but he has said that this evening he is going to take you to the Chief Black Eunuch to see if he will buy you for the Khalifa's harem.'

'But what if he doesn't want me? They say I'm too thin.'

'It's a possibility, but I don't see why he wouldn't. Maybe the Khalifa is tired of all those voluptuous women in his harem. Variety is the spice of life they say. Anyway, that is why Sulayman has instructed me to make you as beautiful as possible.'

She looked at her critically and added, 'But you're right about being thin. I don't know what he thinks I can do about your skinny hips in just a few hours. You need weeks of fattening up to reach the standard of some of those concubines.'

Subh looked down at her firm body with its flat stomach and tiny breasts; her thighs were slim and her legs long. Al-Bayda was right; she was nothing like the other women in the baths, with their buxom bosoms and heavy thighs, their round stomachs and wide hips.

'Don't worry. I know for a fact that the Khalifa is very fond of northern women, especially blonde ones. His mother was a princess from Navarra, you know. She was captured as a young girl, just like you, and brought to Córdoba.'

Subh wasn't really listening. Her mind was racing with the possibilities of what would happen to her if the Khalifa rejected her.

'I can read and write,' she said suddenly.

'Can you, my dear? Well that is a definite advantage.'

'And I can sing and recite poetry.'

'All useful gifts.'

'My mistress taught me. She wanted me to be educated.'

'Of course, Zaynab was a wonderful woman. She always wanted the best for everyone. We will all miss her. Now come along. We must hurry because I still have to find you a suitable robe for this evening.'

***

Al-Bayda had chosen something from her own wardrobe that was now too tight for her, a robe of ivory silk. It fitted Subh perfectly. Then Bayda helped her arrange her hair in two long plaits which she fixed in place with a crocheted cap of the same colour.

'Perfect,' she said, standing back and looking at her handiwork. 'Demure but lovely, I think that will do.'

'Is she ready?' called Sulayman from the patio.

'Yes, here she is. What do you think?'

'She'll do. Come girl, let's get this over with.'

His cold tone made Subh feel she was being led to her death, but a wink from his wife brought a smile to her face.

'That's it. Remember to smile when you meet Yamut. You have perfect teeth and your smile brings out the dimples in your cheeks. I'm sure he will be delighted with you,' Bayda said, beaming at her in encouragement and obviously hoping that all her efforts would please the Chief Black Eunuch.

Subh walked a few paces behind the mistress's brother, along the paved road that led up to the North Gate and the entrance to the Khalifa's personal quarters. A guard stood on duty at the gate.

'We have come to see Yamut al-Attar,' Sulayman explained. 'My name is Sulayman ibn Zakariya and he is expecting me.'

'Very well. Go along that passage and wait in the room at the end. I will send a message to him that you are here.'

They did not have to wait long before a giant of a man, dressed in baggy white trousers and a loose robe of pale grey came into the room. His skin was like polished ebony and his head and face were completely shaved. She had never seen anyone like him before. So this was the Chief Black Eunuch, a man with many years experience in his work and who, according to Bayda, ruled the harem with supreme authority. Would he like her? She felt her stomach start to churn again and would have liked to have turned and run back to Bayda, but the Chief Black Eunuch was already speaking to Sulayman.

He bowed slightly and said, '*As-salama alaykum*. You wanted to see me?'

'*Wa alaykum e-salam.* I have brought the girl I told you about,' Sulayman replied, pulling Subh forward so that Yamut could see her clearly.

'She is originally from the north of Spain, Navarra I believe, but she is fluent in Arabic. She can sing, recite poetry and she can read and write.'

'She is very thin,' the eunuch said, taking Subh by the arm and turning her around so that he could get a good look at her.

Subh remembered what Bayda had advised her and looked at Yamut and smiled. If he noticed he did not comment but instead turned to Sulayman and said, 'I do not think she is suitable for the Khalifa. He prefers his women to be more rounded. I agree she is pretty but the harem is full of pretty women. This one is too much like a boy.'

Subh's heart sank. What was going to happen to her now?

'But she is very clever. She would be able to entertain the Khalifa with stories and poems,' Sulayman continued. He was determined to find her a home.

'What has she been doing since she arrived from the north?'

'She worked for my sister, Zaynab bint Zakariya in Córdoba. My sister has recently died and her husband is looking for a good situation for the girl.'

'What work did she do for your sister?' Yamut asked.

'At first she worked in the kitchen but for the last few years the girl was my sister's personal maid. My sister, who was a teacher, decided to make the girl her protégée. She educated her in all the arts, including calligraphy, and made sure that she learnt about Arab culture.'

'Well, as I said, I do not think she would suit the Khalifa. He is getting old and his tastes are very particular these days. However I think she would do very well in the harem of his son, al-Hakim.'

'Al-Hakim, the heir to the throne?'

'Yes. I have been given the charge of supplying women for his harem as well. Now the prince has his own preferences when it comes to the members of his harem, but I am sure he would welcome someone as educated and well versed as this young woman. What is her name?'

'My sister called her Subh.'

'Very well. Now to business. How much are you thinking of asking for this woman, Subh?'

She did not follow the rest of the conversation; her head was spinning with questions. Was it true? Was she to be part of al-Hakim's harem? She had heard her mistress speak of him often; she had admired him greatly for his wisdom and learning. She said that he loved books above everything else and was building his own personal library. So far he was said to have collected over 300,000 books. He sent agents to all parts of the East to buy him rare books and, if he heard of a book that was not for sale, he paid for someone to copy it out by hand and bring it to him. He employed scribes to translate books from Latin and Greek into Arabic and he commissioned learned men to write new books. It was a passion, but he was not just a collector, he was also a reader and that was what her mistress had admired most of all.

'Then it is settled.'

'Thank you, *sayyad*,' Sulayman said, with a slight bow. '*Ma'a salama.*'

He put the purse of coins into his pocket and turned to Subh. 'You will be well looked after in the harem of al-Hakim. Allah has looked down on us today, my child. My sister would be very pleased with the deal we have made. *Ma'a salama*, child. May God go with you.'

'*Alla ysalmak.* master.'

'Come with me girl. I will take you to the *zenana* where the other women will take care of you,' Yamut said, striding away further into the labyrinth of passages that led to the Khalifa's quarters.

It had begun. Her new life had begun. Something told her that this time it would be different. She would never allow herself to be sold again.

***

A gentle tap at the door woke Subh from her memories. She sat up with a start. Now was not the time to be idly reminiscing about her past. There were important decisions to be made and she had to be sure she was part of them. Al-Mansur was an ambitious man but was he ruthless enough to usurp her son? She thought not but could she be sure? They had an agreement but would he stick to it? Surely he must realise that his influence was stronger with her by his side. Still she would need to keep alert if her position was to be secure, and if her son was to be kept safe. She had not come all this way just to have the prize stolen from her at the last moment. Her son was now the Khalifa and she was *al-Sayyida al-Malika*; together they were invincible.

CHAPTER 8

The boy picked up a round pebble from the flower beds and rolled it around in his hand; it was just the right size for a sling shot. He lifted his arm and threw it as hard as he could at the bird. The peacock let out a shrill scream and lunged forward on its ungainly legs, its long tail dragging in the dust. It was a female with none of the colourful splendour of the male; its feathers were grey and drab by comparison. The boy had the urge to look over his shoulder to check that his father had not seen him but stopped, saddened when he remembered that Baba was never going to reprove him for anything again. He missed his father, especially the hours that he had spent with him in this very garden. It was his garden now, his palace, his servants. He was the new Khalifa and he was bored. He was bored and lonely. A year had already passed since his father had died and still he was not sure of his duties. No-one had been to instruct him in the things that were the responsibilities of the Khalifa and when he had asked the Regents they told him to go away and play. They said he was too young for matters of state, that he should just enjoy himself and not trouble his mind with such things. It did not seem right. His father had spoken to him of the importance of being a just and strong ruler. He had told him how easy it was for a country to fall apart if the Khalifa was weak or corrupt. Baba had been neither of those things. He had ruled the country well; everyone said so. If only Hisham had listened more carefully when his father had spoken of these things then maybe he wouldn't be feeling so confused now. He picked up another pebble and threw it after the peacock, but the bird was wary now and hurried into the bushes out of sight.

'Excuse me, Your Highness. There is a messenger from the Grand Falconer,' a slave said. He was accompanied by a skinny young man not much older than Hisham.

'Yes, what is it?' he asked.

At last here was someone other than the slaves and the soldiers who guarded him day and night. It was good to see a different face. Even his mother hardly came to see him these days. She said she was working hard to secure his future but he did not know what she meant. Surely his future was secure; he was the ruler of al-Andalus.

The boy approached, bowing low so that his forehead touched the ground. Hisham liked it when people bowed before him; it was the only time he really felt he was the Khalifa.

'Who are you and what do you want?' he asked.

The boy stood up. He had a small box in his hands and he offered it to Hisham. 'The Grand Falconer thought you would like to have one of these new falcon chicks,' he said, carefully opening the box.

Inside was the angriest little bird that Hisham had ever seen; its white feathers were fluffed out in rage, its dark beak open in protest and it stared right at Hisham with beady, black eyes. He stepped back nervously.

'What is it?'

'A young Barbary falcon. We have just received them from North Africa. The Grand Falconer thought you would like one to train.'

'Train? How could I train that?' The bird continued to squawk at him, never removing its eyes from his face. 'It looks as though it will bite me.'

'They are fierce birds, it is true Your Highness, but they are easy to train, once you know what you are doing.' The boy continued to hold out the box to al-Hisham. He seemed unsure of what to do next.

'Very well. Gassan, you can leave us now,' al-Hisham said to the slave. 'You, come with me.' He took the box from the boy and led him down the steps into the garden. The peacocks had retreated to the far corners of the palace grounds, still screaming their annoyance. Close by, a pair of collared doves roosted in the olive trees, cooing softly.

'So, the Grand Falconer thought I should have a falcon,' he said.

'Every great ruler has falcons. It is a symbol of their power,' the boy explained.

'Of course. I know that. My father, al-Hakim II told me all about that,' he said, feeling that his words were probably the truth, although he could not remember anything specific that his father had said on the subject. He had seen falcons displaying their skills at public events and special celebrations and sometimes, when a visitor from overseas came to see his father, he brought him a rare falcon as a gift, but the truth was that Hisham had not paid much attention to any of it. Many men went hunting with their falcons but, as al-Hakim had not been particularly interested in hunting, he had never encouraged his son to participate.

'Actually it was my father who thought you would like to learn more about falconry and the Grand Falconer agreed. My father said you were probably bored, being all alone in this big palace,' the boy said, looking about him. He seemed overawed by the splendour of the gardens.

'Bored? How dare you? The Khalifa is never bored. He has far too many things to do. How dare you speak to me like that.'

The boy looked frightened. He bowed to the ground and muttered, 'Please forgive me Your Highness. I did not mean to be rude.'

'Who are you anyway?' Hisham asked. 'What is your name?'

'My name is Ahmad ibn Makoud. I am an assistant falconer. My father is Makoud ibn Qasim, your bodyguard.'

'Al-Jundi? He is your father?'

'Yes, Your Highness.'

Hisham liked al-Jundi. He felt safe with him watching over him. His father had said he was one of the soldiers you could trust; he could not be bribed with money nor promises of power. So this was his son. How strange, it had never occurred to him that al-Jundi had any children. In fact he had never thought about al-Jundi's life at all. He had no idea where he went when he left the palace or whom he went to see.

He opened the lid of the box carefully and immediately the falcon began to squawk again. 'It is a very angry little bird,' he said.

'He's hungry that's all. When we feed him he will calm down a bit.' Ahmad took a scrap of meat out of his pocket and offered it to the chick, which instantly swallowed it, its white throat rippling as it forced the food down its gullet.

'Have you ever visited the Falcon House?' the boy asked him.

'No. We will go now. Gassan,' he called. 'Gassan. Tell al-Jundi that I am going to the Falcon House.'

'Yes, Your Highness.'

'What do you want to do with the chick?' asked Ahmad.

'You look after it. You will be my falconer. I think I will call it Daruj because it will be the fastest falcon you have ever seen.'

This was fun. Already he could imagine himself strutting about, the hooded falcon sitting on his gloved hand. How impressive he would look.

***

The Falcon House was outside the palace but still within the walls of the *alcazaba* so it took only a short time to get to the *rabad al-Bayyazin*, the district of the falconers. Ahmad carried the chick carefully and walked a respectful distance behind the Khalifa.

'This is where all the birds, your birds, *sayyad*, are kept. They are fed, trained and exercised by the falconers.'

'This is a very big place. How many falconers are there?' asked al-Hisham, looking about him.

'I don't know exactly but a lot of people work here: there are the assistant falconers and minor falconers who look after the birds, then there are the officers who record details of the falcons' nesting and breeding habits in the agronomic calendar. They know the areas where the best falcons breed. I'm sure the Grand Falconer will advise you of all this, and of the taxes raised.'

'Taxes? What taxes?' al-Hisham asked.

'They are your taxes, Your Highness; they go to your treasury. Many farmers want to hunt with their falcons and so there is a 5% falconry fee which comes out of their normal taxes.'

'You seem to know a lot about it,' al-Hisham said, annoyed that this boy knew more about the royal falcons than he did.

'Assistant falconers have to learn a little of everything. The Grand Falconer says that falconry is not just about prestige it is also an important economic activity for the country.'

This is something that the Regents should have told him. They should have sent the Grand Falconer to him to explain it all. If it hadn't been for al-Jundi he would still know nothing about it. It was annoying how they ignored him, annoying and insulting. He would speak to his mother about it.

'What's that over there?' he asked, pointing to a rectangular stone built building with a low roof.

'That's the hospital where the doctors who specialise in avian diseases keep the sick birds.'

'Sick birds? Why would a bird need a doctor? If the bird is ill then why not kill it?' al-Hisham asked in astonishment.

'These birds are very valuable, Your Highness. I have not explained myself very well. I apologise. You see, it is impossible to breed falcons in captivity so each bird has to be tracked to its breeding grounds where we locate the nests and capture the chicks. That is why it is important to keep records of their nesting habits. We only capture the birds when they are young, like this one,' he said, indicating the falcon chick in the box - it had been quiet since he had fed it. 'Then they are easier to train. So you see, if a falcon is sick, the falconers want to save it. Some birds, the best, are very difficult to capture and therefore they are greatly prized. You have many very rare birds in your Falcon House. They are a symbol of your wealth.'

The young Khalifa opened the door to the building; it was gloomy inside but cool and there was a strong smell of dried straw and manure.

'Oh. So what illnesses do they suffer from?'

'There are many but mostly they suffer from diseases of the digestive system. If we see any signs of this then we take the bird directly to one of the doctors before it can spread to the other falcons.'

Al-Hisham stopped by a large wickerwork cage and stared at an enormous bird sitting on a perch, one of its legs tethered with a leather thong.

'Will Daruj grow up like this one?' he asked. 'It doesn't look very tame to me.' The bird appeared to be looking at him as if he were to be its next meal.

'No. This is a goshawk. She is recovering from an injury to her leg. See she has yellow eyes. Daruj has black eyes. Goshawks are hard to train but they are good hunting birds, powerful and strong. They fly low over the ground looking for small animals to kill, so they are very popular with the townspeople who use them to catch rabbits and small deer. My brother hunts with a goshawk, but his is a male and a bit smaller. The Barbary falcon, on the other hand, usually hunts other birds. Their flight is high and fast and they catch their quarry in mid-flight. They are wonderful to watch.'

'I want to see one,' the Khalifa said. 'Show me an adult Barbary falcon hunting.'

'I can show you one here, in the Falcon House, but we will have to wait until this evening to see one hunt,' Ahmad replied. 'The birds only hunt in the early morning or just before sunset.'

'Well this evening we will go hunting, then,' al-Hisham said, tearing his eyes away from the goshawk, whose golden eyes followed him wherever he moved.

They stepped out of the hospital into the bright glare of the sun, and for a moment Hisham could not focus.

'We will go back to the palace now,' he said.

As they made their way back, they passed a pen full of hunting dogs which, not recognising the Khalifa for who he was, began to bay loudly. Ahmad, who still seemed to be trying to answer all the Khalifa's questions, said, 'And of course there are also the men who care for the animals, the greyhounds and the horses. There are almost as many animals to be fed and watered as there are birds. So, yes, a lot of people work here.'

***

When Hisham got back to the palace the first thing he did was go to his mother's quarters in the *zenana*. 'Where is my mother?' he shouted at a slave. 'Where is *al Sayyida al Malika*? I demand to see her.'

'Your Majesty, she is with the other women,' the slave stammered.

'Well get her then. Now.'

He was angry when he thought of what was being kept from him and his anger grew even stronger when he realised that there could be many things about which he knew nothing and never would unless someone instructed him. If the law said he was too young to rule, then so be it, but that didn't mean he was too young to be kept informed. What would happen when he was eighteen?

Or twenty? Or thirty? Were they going to keep him in the dark forever?

The slave girl came scurrying back and bowed low before him.

'The *Sayyida* says you are to come with me,' she said, leading him into the innermost part of his mother's quarters.

'Mama. I need to speak to you. It's important,' he said.

His mother was sprawled on a low couch, drinking a sweet smelling infusion from a glass. She looked up at him and lifted her hand languidly.

'Hisham, my darling. What is the matter? I could hear you shouting at that poor slave girl from here. That is no way for the Khalifa to behave.'

He stared at her. Even his mother was not taking him seriously. He was thirteen and she still spoke to him as if he were a child. Well he was no child; he would soon be a man. Already his body was telling him of the changes that were taking place. He would not be treated like a child any longer.

'And is that the way for *al-Sayyida al-Malika* to greet her Khalifa? I remember that you always bowed before my father and spoke to him most respectfully. I am the Khalifa now. I am no longer a child and I want the same respect.'

Slowly his mother rose from the couch and then bowed before him. She smiled and sat down again, saying, 'I am sorry my son. You are quite right. The Khalifa deserves respect, no matter what his age. Now don't be angry. Come and sit beside me and tell me what is troubling you.'

Her smile was warm and inviting, and he realised, with a pang of pain, just how much he had missed her.

'You never come to see me, Mama. I sit alone all day and no-one comes to see me. Why don't you visit me anymore?'

He felt like crying and would have liked to sit next to his mother and let her put her arms around him and comfort him, but he forced his face to be still and he pushed his loneliness away from him. He remained standing, waiting until, reluctantly, his mother also stood.

'I am sorry, my son. I have been very busy. You do not realise that I have a lot to do to ensure that you stay safe. I will try to come to see you more often.'

'I do not understand you, mother. What is it that you do? Why am I not safe? I have my palace guards. The *alcázar* is surrounded by soldiers and I have al-Jundi. Nobody could be safer than I am. So what is it that you do, and why does nobody come to instruct me?'

'Dear boy, you do not understand the intrigues of the court. Yes, you are safe here, inside the *alcazaba*, surrounded by soldiers, but a khalifa always has enemies, people who would like his power, who lust after his wealth. Sometimes those enemies are obvious, like the Christian princes in the north or the Fatimite tribes in North Africa, but other times they are people who pretend to be your friends but who think that they have more rights to your throne than you do. It is my job to identify those enemies and get rid of them.'

'But when will I learn about the taxes and how much money I have? I am thirteen now. It is time that I knew more about my duties.'

'But darling, that's why there is a Regency, to make all those decisions for you. You are still a child in the eyes of the law. Enjoy your childhood while you can.'

'I am not a child. Tell the Regents that I want to see them. Tell them that the Khalifa has sent for them.'

'But they are very busy men,' she said.

'Tell them, mother. I want them here, tomorrow morning.' He felt like stamping his foot to emphasise the point, as he used to do when he was a young child.

'Very well, Your Majesty,' she said, bowing before him and staying like that until he had left.

He felt quite pleased with himself until he got back to the throne room. Then he realised that she had not promised to spend more time with him.

***

Just before sunset Ahmad arrived at the palace and was shown into al-Hisham's presence.

'Good, you are here,' Hisham said.

He had been waiting all afternoon, hoping that nothing would interfere with the hunt. He had little idea what to expect but he was excited at the prospect of being out with men and their falcons.

'The Grand Falconer was not happy when I said we were going on a hunt,' Ahmad said. 'He says we must stay within the palace grounds. But don't worry; we will go back to the Falcon House and I will show you a peregrine in flight.'

'I want to go out with the others,' the Khalifa said. 'I am not a prisoner. I am the Khalifa. How can I go hunting if I am kept in here. Gassan, go and find al-Jundi and bring him here immediately.'

Ahmad looked very uncomfortable at the Khalifa's outburst but he said nothing. He had taken a leather jesse from his bag and was twisting it in his fingers.

'What's that?' Hisham snapped. His anger had returned.

'These are called jesses,' the boy replied. 'They're to tie around the legs of the falcon. See this ring, this is so that we can tie the leash to the bird.'

'Do they hurt them?' Hisham asked, his curiosity overcoming his anger.

'No. They help the falconer to hold the bird still until it's time to let it fly. And of course you need them when you're training your falcon. We all make our own. I made these for you,' he said, handing them to the Khalifa.

'For me?'

He accepted the gift and examined it carefully. The leather was soft and pliable and had been divided into two long, narrow strips; at regular intervals along each of the jesses small slits had been cut.

'See these slits. You place the jess around the falcon's ankle and then loop it back through the slit and pull it into place, then pull it through this second slit but not too tight. It has to be secure but it's also important to be comfortable,' he explained.

'Thank you,' al-Hisham said. 'Now all I need is a falcon and I think I'd like something bigger than that squawking chick.'

'Your Highness, you sent for me,' al-Jundi's voice broke through the still evening air.

'Yes. I want to go out on a hunt with your son, but the Grand Falconer advises against it. So you will go with me, to protect me.'

'If you are sure that is what you want to do, Your Excellency, I will accompany you. First I will organise your horse.'

He turned and left without a glance at his son. Hisham wondered if he was a strict father. He looked at the boy, who seemed worried. What was the matter? Was he frightened about something happening to the Khalifa or was he worried about the falcons? The falcons most likely.

'What is it? Are you not happy that we are going on a hunt?'

'Yes, I am happy about the hunt. It is the most exhilarating experience. I am sure you will enjoy it, although you will not be able to handle the birds.'

'But next time, when I have learnt what to do, then I can fly my own peregrine,' he said. 'So, if it is not the hunt, what is it then?'

'Well, Your Highness, we are now at the end of April and very soon the birds will begin to moult.'

'So?'

'We do not fly the birds when they are moulting. The moult lasts until the end of August, when we are able to fly them again. There is a strict calendar that we work to: the birds nest in January, in March they lay their eggs which hatch in April and then it takes the chicks about 30 days to get their plumage. You could see that from the one I brought you. So after tonight we will not be able to hunt with the peregrines again until August.'

Hisham felt a stab of disappointment. Finally he had found something that had captured his interest and now this lad was saying that he could not do it for another three months.

'So what's the point in going out now?' he snapped, rather petulantly.

'Well it would give you a chance to see what it's all about and to experience the thrill of the chase. Three months will pass very quickly. After all you have a lot to learn if you want to hunt with your own falcon this autumn.'

The boy was right. He had no idea how to control one of those enormous birds, never mind fly one. He had a lot to learn.

'You speak well, Ahmad. We will go this evening as planned and then tomorrow you can start to teach me all that I need to know.'

'It will be an great honour, Your Highness.'

'My Lord, al-Jundi has your horse ready,' Gassan said.

CHAPTER 9

Al-Mansur was not happy. The boy khalifa had sent for him and the other two regents. He had considered sending him a message to say that he was too busy to attend but decided that it was too risky. It was far too soon to reveal his true feelings for al-Hakim's useless son, better to wait until his own position was more secure and there were others who shared his belief that al-Hisham would never be a competent ruler. He had to take it step by step and the first step was to remove that tiresome al-Mushafi. Maybe he had been a good vizier when al-Rahman III was alive but he was getting too old for it now. He didn't understand that peace on its own was not enough. The peace would only hold if the ruler, in this case the Regents, demonstrated their power from time to time. Their next mission should be to retake the fortress of Gormaz but he couldn't get the support of the Grand Vizier, and the General was reluctant to go against him.

'*As-salama alaykum*, my friends,' he said to al-Mushafi and General Ghálib, both of whom had arrived before him and were already waiting in the *Dar al-Wuzara*, the Hall of the Viziers.

'*Wa alaykum e-salam*, my son,' said the General. 'Do you know where the Khalifa wants to meet with us?'

Al-Mansur noticed that the Grand Vizier did not return his greeting and seemed intent on ignoring his presence. 'How are you al-Mushafi?' he asked.

'Well enough, thank you,' he said and turned away again.

'You, slave. Tell your master that we are all gathered here waiting for him,' al-Mansur said to one of the men standing by the entrance to the Hall of the Viziers.

The slave bowed and left. A few minutes later he returned and said, 'The Khalifa would like you to meet him in the Hall of Abd al-Rahman III.'

The three men rose and followed the slave.

'The Rich Hall. Well he must be trying to impress us,' the General whispered to al-Mansur. 'Perhaps he'll be sitting on his throne.'

'He's an utter nuisance. Why can't he just play with his toys like other boys.'

'Perhaps it's because he is not like other boys. After all he is the Khalifa,' said al-Mushafi. 'Maybe it's time we started to involve him more in the government of his kingdom instead of ignoring him.'

Al-Mansur would have liked to strike the Grand Vizier, he was so angry with him, but he contented himself with giving him a look which said so much more than words.

'So you don't agree, how surprising. How is your daughter, General Ghálib? Is she happy to be married to this autocrat? I suppose she is used to taking orders, being the daughter of a general,' the Grand Vizier continued.

So that's what it was all about. Al-Mushafi had heard about his marriage to Ismá and he was angry. Well he knew he would be.

'My daughter is very well, thank you my lord Grand Vizier. She has always been a good obedient daughter and now I expect she will be a good, obedient wife.' The General was about to say something else but they had arrived at the Hall of Abd al-Rahman III.

They climbed the steps from the garden, skirting the ornamental ponds brimming with golden carp, and entered through a richly decorated horseshoe arch. This was the most impressive room in the palace and normally used only for ceremonial occasions or important visiting dignitaries. Meetings were normally held in the *Dar al-Wuzara*. By inviting them here, the boy was trying to assert his authority. Al-Mansur hoped he wasn't going to be a problem.

The young Khalifa was seated on his throne and the three men bowed and approached him in the traditional manner.

'Your Highness wanted to see us?' al-Mansur asked, assuming the role of leader, despite the fact that he was the youngest member of the Regency. 'What can we do to help you?'

'Good day gentlemen. It is not what you can do to help the Khalifa, Abu Amir, it is more what I can do to help you. It has occurred to me that you have forgotten that I exist. I am alone in these rooms all day and I have nothing to do. My father worked hard to rule his kingdom and I want the opportunity to do the same.'

'Of course, Your Majesty,' said General Ghálib. 'We understand but we thought that maybe you should wait a few years until you are older. Until then, rest assured we will look after the kingdom for you.'

'I have no doubt that you are doing a good job and I know that I am young and have no experience, but how will I gain any experience if nobody instructs me?' al-Hisham answered.

Al-Mansur was impressed with how the boy was handling himself. The child was more mature than he had realised. This was worrying.

'I have sent you many papers to sign, Your Majesty,' the Grand Vizier said. 'You have an important role to play, even now, in the running of this country. You are, after all, the ruler of al-Andalus.'

'And as such I want to know more about my duties.'

'Of course, of course. Maybe you could attend some government meetings, to see what happens. Although I fear you will be very bored as they are extremely dull,' added al-Mansur.

'Tell me now what has been happening in my country? I need to know. I want to know about the taxes.'

'Taxes? Why do you want to know about taxes? Is there something you need, Your Highness? You only have to say and anything you want will be brought to you,' al-Mushafi said.

'I am the Khalifa. I want to know how much money I have in the treasury.'

'Well, Your Highness, that is not something I can just tell you without consultation,' the Grand Vizier replied. 'Is there a particular reason why you want to know this?'

There was something in his voice that made al-Mansur pay closer attention; the Grand Vizier looked nervous. It seemed that the Khalifa's question had hit a nerve. He watched al-Mushafi pull out a square of cloth and wipe his brow. Yes, he would have to look into this further. Had al-Mushafi been helping himself from the Khalifa's coffers?

'Yes there is. I need to know where my money comes from. I am the Khalifa and I should know about these things. They tell me that the people pay many taxes and I want to know more about them. Why do they pay them? How much money do they pay me? What happens to that money? That's what I need to know.'

'Well that is very easy, my lord. I can tell you about the taxes and how we collect them,' the Grand Vizier replied, with a sigh that seemed to the lawyer like an expression of relief. Yes, al-Mushafi was definitely hiding something.

The Grand Vizier began to explain to the boy about the taxes paid by the *dhimmi* - Jews and Christians who preferred to worship in their own faith - and about the taxes paid by the farmers and the merchants. His voice droned on and on. If anyone was going to instil a profound dislike for government in the new khalifa, it was al-Mushafi. Al-Mansur smiled to himself. He need not worry about getting rid of al-Hisham; the Grand Vizier would kill him with boredom. He watched the Khalifa, who at first listened carefully to what he was being told, but, bit by bit, let his attention waver until al-Mansur could see that he had lost interest.

'Maybe that is enough information for the Khalifa this morning,' he said, smiling at the boy. 'Perhaps we should take a break, Your Highness.'

'Yes, that is a good idea, Abu Amir. Thank you all for coming. Next time I would like you to tell me about my army, General Ghálib.'

'I would be delighted to do that, Your Majesty.'

The Khalifa stood up and the men bowed low and waited while he gathered up his long robe and walked back to his quarters.

'Excuse me, gentlemen, I must leave you. I have much to do this morning,' said al-Mushafi, scurrying off in the direction of the Mint.

Once he was out of earshot, al-Mansur turned to the General and said, 'I suppose he's gone to check up on the accounts. I swear he was about to shit himself when the Khalifa asked how much money he had. Something's going on there and I'd like to know what it is.'

'Do you think so? I agree he was not behaving normally this morning but I put that down to his displeasure over your marriage. You think he has been embezzling public funds?'

Al-Mansur smiled. The General was a brave soldier but he was no politician. Al-Mansur had already struck a wedge between the two men with his marriage to Ghálib's daughter, now he would sow a few seeds of doubt in his mind.

'I'm not saying that. No, of course I wouldn't accuse a man of al-Mushafi's stature of being dishonest, but maybe he knows of something irregular that has happened and doesn't want to share it with us.'

'So what do we do?'

'We could wait and watch and maybe catch him with his hands in the money sacks or we could go to the judge and ask for someone to check the treasury accounts.'

'What if we are mistaken? Maybe we should wait. After all we don't have any evidence that he has done anything wrong.'

'You are probably right. Though I did wonder how he could afford to buy that big house on the Nogales Road. And, I hear, he has given very generous dowries for all three of his daughters, but that could just be because they are not the most beautiful of women and maybe it was hard to find them husbands. No, you're right. It could be all coincidence. Yes, we will wait and see what happens.'

By then two men had arrived at the North Gate.

'I must leave you now, my son,' said Ghálib. *'Ma'a salama.* Give my daughter a kiss from her father.'

'I will. *Ma'a salama,* father-in-law.'

Al-Mansur had no intention of waiting to see what would happen; he already had a plan. He headed back into the city, in the direction of the offices of the judiciary. He knew many of the judges personally from his days as a lawyer in Córdoba. It would be easy to convince one of them to open an investigation into al-Mushafi's finances. After all it wouldn't be the first time that a government official had stolen from the public purse, and he was sure it wouldn't be the last.

***

That evening al-Mansur decided to visit Subh; he had not seen her alone for some months. His new wife was a delightful girl, very willing and obviously very fond of him. He was glad he had married her. Already her body was swelling and it wouldn't be long before she gave him a child and, if Allah was looking favourably on him, a son. Life was looking good for him. His meeting with the judge had gone better than he expected. It seemed that he was not the only one who would be happy to see al-Mushafi disgraced, the Grand Vizier had made many enemies over the years. The only disquiet that al-Mansur still had was regarding al-Hisham; he did not know what to do about the young Khalifa. He had no intention of letting him rule; no, this was al-Mansur's opportunity to wrest the caliphate from the Omeyyads and establish his own dynasty. He expected to have some resistance from the Khalifa and certain members of the court in the future, but, by the time that happened, he would have his own followers and then he was in no doubt who would win. However he hadn't expected to face that problem so soon; now here was a thirteen-year-old boy already questioning him and the other regents. He was going to have to move quickly and establish himself as the true leader of al-Andalus before the boy grew much older.

That was one reason for visiting Subh. He could not continue to neglect her; he needed her too much. She was angry about his marriage that was obvious. It was just female jealousy; it didn't mean anything. He was sure he could depend on her; the *Sayyida* was a shrewd woman and she relied on her role as the mother of the Khalifa to maintain her own position in court otherwise she would become a nobody again. She would be happy to compromise and if he promised to let the boy retain the title of Khalifa she would help him put his plan into place. Of course once he was the supreme ruler then he would get rid of him, but Subh must never know that. The *Sayyida* would never agree to the murder of her own son, no matter what al-Mansur promised her.

His heart began to beat more rapidly as he thought of his mistress. He imagined her lying on a low couch, wearing a robe of pale blue muslin, the light from the lamps playing on her golden hair, hanging loosely about her bare shoulders. She had silver sandals on her feet, silver bangles around her dainty ankles and garlanding her arms while outside music was playing, a lute, a gentle voice singing. The air smelled sweetly of incense and roses. She looked at him and smiled, her kohl-rimmed eyes dark with seduction, her red lips parted in anticipation, her arms held out to him, waiting for his embrace. Yes, he had stayed away too long.

CHAPTER 10

The Khalifa's mother was feeling very pleased with herself. Al-Mansur had visited her again last night. He came every week now, sometimes more than once. He was already tiring of his new wife, as she knew he would. He was a man who needed a real woman, not a young virgin who would just lie there with her legs apart. After all who could compare an inexperienced girl with a woman who was once the concubine of the Khalifa of al-Andalus? She had been trained in all that a woman should know about the ways of pleasing a man and she certainly had pleased her lover last night. She smiled to herself when she remembered how nervous she had been when she had first entered the harem of the Khalifa's son; she too had been a virgin then.

***

Yamut had taken her into the *zenana* to meet the other women of the harem. She could not believe the beauty of the rooms she passed through; all the floors were of marble and covered with brightly patterned carpets. The walls were hung with tapestries, richly embroidered with designs of animals and plants; at the windows delicate curtains floated to and fro in the fragrant breeze that came in from the gardens, bringing with it the scent of roses and jasmine and honeysuckle. Young women lounged on low sofas, or sat on silk cushions, chatting quietly to each other; one or two looked up and smiled as she passed, others were reading, others painting; one young girl was playing the lute and another was painting an intricate pattern on her feet with henna. Everyone seemed happy.

Eventually Yamut found the woman he was looking for. 'Zahr. This is a new member of al-Hakim's harem. Her name is Subh. You will look after her and tell her what to do,' he said and turned and left.

Subh looked at the woman. She was short and very plump; her skin, smooth and silky, was the colour of honey and gleamed in the wavering lights of the oil lamps.

'*As-salama alaykum*,' Subh said, shyly.

The woman smiled at her and said, 'Come with me and I will find you some new clothes. You can't wear those in here.'

Subh looked down at the new robe of ivory silk that her mistress's sister-in-law had given her and wondered what she meant by that. This was the nicest dress she had ever owned. What was wrong with it?

'This is Afra,' Zahr said, waving at a young black slave, a girl no more than eight or nine-years-old. 'She will be your servant. She will help you to bathe, she will dress you and do your hair. She will also teach you how to make yourself more beautiful, to blacken your eyes with kohl and ripen your lips with carmine.'

'My servant? Help me to bathe?'

Subh could not believe that she would ever have a servant, just like a lady. Nobody had ever helped her to bathe or dress before, not since she was a very small child and her mother had cared for her. Those had been her duties as a maid to Zaynab. Now someone, albeit a tiny girl, was going to do the same for her.

'But I am a concubine, not a lady. Why would I have a servant?'

'I can see you have a lot to learn. While Afra is preparing your bath, I will explain a few things to you. First of all, you are not a concubine, yet. You may become one after you have been to the school and learnt all that they can teach you. A concubine is not just a pretty woman; she is someone who can sing, tell stories, dance and recite poetry. She must learn to play a musical instrument and she must learn what it is that pleases her master, in your case the Khalifa's son.'

'Are you a concubine?' Subh asked shyly.

'Yes, I graduated from the school a few years ago but al-Hakim only sent for me once. I had been here for five years and was beginning to think I would never get the chance to see him when I heard he had asked for me. I was so excited but, in the end, it wasn't a success. I know I did well. I danced perfectly; it was a dance I had been practising for weeks and I knew every step. I thought he was pleased. Then he thanked me and asked me to sit down and recite some poetry for him. I was well prepared and again it went well. He had tears in his eyes by the time I had finished. I thought everything was fine and that he would next ask me to undress but instead he just wanted to talk to me about the poem I had recited and asked me what I thought about the poet. Well I wasn't prepared for that so I didn't know what to say. In the end he sent me away. I was very upset that he didn't even try to make love to me. I cried for days. But then I discovered that I wasn't the only one he had treated like that. Every so often he sends for one of the concubines but all he does is listen to them playing the lute and then he asks them to read to him. Can you read?'

Subh nodded.

'Good, because that seems to be all he is interested in. In a way it's not so bad; we have a comfortable life here. But everyone wants to be the one to have his child. Even if you have a girl child, your life improves and you are given your own rooms and treated really well. Of course if you have a boy, an heir to the throne, then you have made it; you will no longer be a slave. The mother of the heir to the throne can never be a slave, so you become known as *al-Sayyida al Malika*, the queen, the most senior of the women in the harem. That's what everyone wants to achieve. But how can that be possible when the Khalifa is now old and his son prefers books to women?'

While Zahr talked, the maid Afra led Subh into the sunken bath and washed her body with soap that smelled of rosemary. The bath was like the *hammam* that al-Bayda had taken her to but a smaller version and was built out of marble instead of stone; the cold water gushed out of silver taps and the hot water was brought to them by silent eunuchs, who left the basins on the floor and backed away without looking at them.

'They do say,' Zahr continued, sitting by the edge of the bath and dropping her voice slightly, 'that he prefers boys to girls. I have heard that there is a separate part to the harem, where only Yamut has been; that's where he keeps young men for al-Hakim's pleasure.'

Subh looked at her in surprise. Why would he prefer boys? And if he did, then why was she here? Something that Sulayman had said the first time he had seen her came back to her; he told the master that she looked like a boy. Had he been planning to sell her to al-Hakim all along?

'So where are you from, Subh? How did you come here?' Zahr asked.

'Originally I am from the north,' she said, her voice wavering. 'My name was Clara and I was captured and brought to Córdoba and sold to a family. They were very kind to me; the mistress taught me to read.'

'So why did they sell you to the Khalifa?'

'The mistress died and they didn't need me anymore,' she said, the words almost choking her with the pain.

'Did they name you Subh?'

'Yes, the cook called me that.'

As she thought of Ulla and her mistress, tears came into her eyes; she had been so happy in that house. What sort of life was she going to have here?

'Subh is a nice name. My name is Zahr al-Riyad; it means flower of the garden. Before I came here my name was Adaeze. I am from Africa. I was a princess,' Zahr said. 'My family were slaughtered and I was brought here as a slave. It was a long journey; we walked through the desert for weeks until we came to the sea and then we sailed for many days before we arrived here. I don't remember much about it; it was a long time ago and I was very young.'

'The man that brought me here, is he in charge?' asked Subh.

'Yamut? Yes, he runs the place but the person who's really in charge is al-Hakim's mother, the Khalifa's chief wife. She's a real dragon; some say she's a *djinn* because she always knows what people are thinking. She blames us for the fact that her son still has no heirs. That is why she told Yamut to look for someone different, someone who could converse with her son but could also seduce him.'

She looked at Subh's naked body and continued, 'I expect that was why he chose you. You look more like a boy than a girl.'

'But I'm not a boy,' Subh protested. 'I'm just a bit thin.'

'Well I can't see that it will make much difference anyway. But as I say, be careful what you say in front of the Royal Wife; she has the power to make life very difficult for you if she wishes.'

***

The sound of her maidservant opening the shutters to her windows brought Subh back to the present. She sat up, blinking in the bright sunlight that spilled into her bedroom, illuminating the rumpled bed and the spilt wine on the rug.

'It is late,' she said, slightly accusingly to the maid.

'It was very late when your friend left last night; I thought you would like to sleep a little longer than usual,' said Afra. 'He left this behind.'

She handed Subh a leather scabbard suitable for a curved knife. Engraved into the leather was an Arabic inscription: *'Allah is my only judge.'* It was Abu Amir's old family motto, but since his recent successes in battle he preferred to have *'al-Mansur bi-llah'*, 'Victorious by God', engraved on his personal accoutrements.

Subh smiled. Afra never referred to Subh's lover by name, only as her 'friend'. She was very discreet and very loyal. She had been Subh's personal maidservant since the day she first entered the harem and she understood her well. In fact she was the only person that Subh could truly rely on.

'Thank you, leave it with me. Now I must get up. I want to visit my son.'

'I have some news for you, *Sayyida*.'

'More gossip?' If Afra had a fault, it was that she loved to make a drama of things.

'Al-Mushafi is in prison,' the maid said, and waited for her mistress's reaction.

'The Grand Vizier is in prison?'

'Yes, *Sayyida.*'

'And do you know why he is in prison?'

'They say he has embezzled the Khalifa's money; he is accused of peculation. There are many who say he is not fit to be one of the Regents.'

'When is the trial?'

'Today, *Sayyida*. If he is convicted he will be disgraced and stripped of his rank and wealth. His poor children will have nothing.'

'That is grave news. Come, let us hurry; I have an urge to be with my son this morning.'

***

Al-Hisham was sitting in the garden, a young hawk on his hand. He looked up and smiled at her.

'Mother, come and see this,' he said. 'This is Daruj; he is a peregrine falcon. I have been training him and soon I will be able to fly him. Isn't he beautiful?'

'He is indeed very handsome, my son. The peregrine is the perfect bird for a Khalifa.' She sat down beside him and stretched out her hand to stroke the bird but it edged away, sensing she was a stranger despite the hood that shielded its eyes.

'Has anyone been to talk to you about al-Mushafi? Has General Ghálib been here? Or al-Mansur?' she asked.

'No, Mama. Nobody has been here today, only you.'

'Al-Mushafi, your Grand Vizier, has been accused of peculation. His trial is today. They say he has been stealing money from the treasury and selling favours. If he is convicted he will go to prison and then of course he will not be able to advise you.'

'But I thought al-Mushafi was a good man. He was my friend. Why would he steal from me?'

'I don't know my son. Sometimes people are not what they seem.'

'Does that mean that someone else will become the Grand Vizier?'

'Yes, of course; it is the most important post in the government, after that of Khalifa.'

Already she was thinking what Abu Amir would do. She was sure he would not give the position to anyone else; he would keep it for himself. It was what he was after all along. He was, of course, the obvious choice; he had experience from his early days as Inspector of the Mint, one of his first government posts and, since then, he had gained great experience in the Treasury and other positions within the court. She was sure that somehow he had engineered the disgrace of al-Mushafi so that he could be Grand Vizier. She feared for her son. Although she loved Abu Amir with all her heart, she did not trust him. When she was not with him, not bound by his magnetic charm and his sweet tongue, she saw in him a ruthless man, someone for whom ambition had no bounds.

'I hope it's not Abu Amir,' her son said, looking away from her and stroking his falcon.

'Really, my son, why is that? I thought you liked Abu Amir. He is a very able man and a brave soldier.'

She wondered why her son never called Abu Amir by his new name. Did it worry him that his minister was called 'the victorious one'? Did he see him as a threat?

'He frightens me. I heard that he had a soldier beaten to death for some minor misdeed, and it's said that it was his own son.'

Subh had heard the rumour too. She knew Abu Amir had sons from his first wife and that one of them had gone into the army. Surely it wasn't his own son that he had ordered to be beaten so cruelly. The next time he came to her bed she would ask him if it was true.

'I expect it is just a rumour. Don't worry about it. Anyway what can Abu Amir do to you? You are the Khalifa.' She took his hand and kissed it. 'So where is your young friend today?' she asked.

'Ahmad has to work in the Falcon House in the mornings; he will come and see me this evening. He has taught me a lot about falconry but I still have much to practice.'

'I'm pleased for you, my son. A khalifa needs to know about his falcons. Your father was not very keen on hunting but he loved the birds and he knew how important it was for his prestige to keep a well stocked Falcon House.'

The young Khalifa nodded wisely.

It was true; she was happy to see him taking an interest in something other than his toys, but she was worried about the future. What exactly were the Regents planning for her son's future? Or, more importantly, what was Abu Amir planning and would he confide in her? Already he had cut the Regency to two. How long before he was in sole command?

'Would you like me to ask Abu Amir to send someone to teach you more about the administration of the country?' she asked. 'Someone from the law courts perhaps?'

'No mother, not at the moment. I still have much to learn about my birds. Maybe later.'

'Very well, my child. I will come and see you tomorrow.'

Subh walked back to her rooms. Since she had born al-Hakim two sons her life had changed dramatically. Her mother-in-law had been retired to a splendid house in the country, leaving Subh the most important woman in the harem. Now there was no-one who could tell her what she could or couldn't do.

***

Subh was not unhappy with her life in the harem. She enjoyed the company of the women, some of whom had become close friends, but it was a strange existence without the presence of men. Many of the women had formed close bonds and, she was sure, practised illegal sexual acts together. One woman, who had been a concubine for many years, had taken a special liking to her and spent a lot of time talking to her and helping her learn about the ways of the harem. She would sit beside her and stroke her hair and sometimes put her arms around her. At first Subh had enjoyed the attention, but then she realised that the woman was in love with her and she became frightened. Zahr warned her to distance herself from her before Yamut found out.

'Just keep away from her,' she said. 'There are many women like her in here. It is only natural. There are no men so they take their lovers from the women, but it is strictly forbidden and they do so at the risk of severe punishment. Do not have anything to do with her or any of the other lesbos. You must keep yourself a virgin for the Khalifa.'

'But when will he send for me? I have completed my course at the school. I have been here for four years now, and so far no-one has noticed me except that woman.'

'It will happen. don't worry. Yamut will make sure it happens.'

A few days later she was sitting in the garden practising the lute when Afra came running towards her.

'Subh, you must hurry. The Royal Wife wants to talk to you. You are to come with me at once,' she said.

The Royal Wife, that did not sound good. She was not aware that the Royal Wife even knew of her existence so why would she send for her? She followed her maid through the labyrinth of passageways until they came to the innermost part of the *zenana*.

'She is in there,' Afra whispered. 'You must go in and bow, then wait until she tells you to approach.'

Subh's stomach was churning with anxiety. What was going to happen? Was she being sent away again? Had they decided that she was unsuitable after all? She entered the room, keeping her eyes firmly on the ground before her, her head bowed low.

'Ah, you must be the new girl, Subh,' a gentle voice said. 'Come closer so that I can see you.'

Subh lifted her head and looked at the Royal Wife, mother of al-Hakim. She was a lot older than she expected but, although heavily lined, she was still beautiful.

'Don't be shy, child. Let me see you.'

Subh moved closer until she stood directly in front of her.

'So you are the one Yamut thought might tempt my wayward son. Yes, I can see what he means. With some different clothes and a haircut you could easily pass for a boy, a very handsome boy I must admit but a boy nevertheless.'

Subh said nothing.

'You must be wondering why I have asked you to come here. Well I will tell you. My husband is old and on his deathbed, and my son is his heir to the throne. All is as it should be, you might say, but there is a problem. My son has no heirs. He has no wives. He is not interested in marrying and he is not interested in having any children. That is not a normal situation for a khalifa. Usually the khalifa has so many offspring that they are fighting amongst themselves for the throne. That is not the case here. I am his mother. It is my duty to help to resolve this situation and that is why I wanted to talk to you. I realise that you are a young woman, with very little experience of life, but Yamut tells me that you have been in the harem of al-Hakim now for four years and you are ready to be presented to my son. Please do not be offended by what I am going to say to you.' The Royal Wife paused. She looked genuinely concerned as she said, 'The thing I want most, with all my heart, is for my son to have a child. I have prayed to Allah for this to happen but now Allah has shown me that I must do something to help. That is where you come in. I have heard that you are a very well educated young woman, that you can read and write in Arabic, that you are familiar with our songs and our poetry, that you have a beautiful singing voice. My son will welcome you into his quarters but that alone will not be enough to get into his bed. You have heard no doubt - it is impossible to stop the gossip in a place like this - that my son has a predilection for pretty young men. There is nothing I can do about that, but it does mean that unless he can be tempted to go to bed with a healthy young woman we shall never have an heir to the throne and it will go to one of his bastard cousins.'

'What do you want me to do?' Subh asked, hesitantly. She was still unsure if the Royal Wife wanted her to do anything at all or if she was just expressing her own concerns.

'I want you to seduce him, in any way you can. If it means dressing like a boy, having your hair cut, whatever it takes I want you to do it. The important thing is that you become pregnant. I don't need to tell you what will happen if you do have the Khalifa's child because I'm sure the other women will have told you already how it will change your life.'

Subh did not know what to say. For a start she had no idea what things men did to each other. After all she had only just learned the female arts of seduction and nobody had mentioned anything about what men did together in bed.

'Yamut will help you. You will not be alone in this. Think about my son and what he likes and first of all make him your friend. Bit by bit you will gain his confidence and then you might entice him to make love to you.'

'Yes, *Sayyida.*'

'Go now, my child and think about what I have said. May Allah look down on you and bless you in your task.'

Subh bowed and backed away, out of the heavily perfumed room and back into the passageway.

'What did she want?' Afra asked. 'What was she like? Was she angry with you?'

'No, she was very kind. She is old but she is beautiful. She wants me to give her a grandchild,' she said, a plan already forming in her head.

The Royal Wife was a clever woman; she had ruled the Khalifa's harem for over forty years and still her mind was as sharp as ever. She knew that although al-Hakim was well aware of the importance of producing an heir, he was incapable of doing so. Unless they could find a woman capable of arousing his ardour, the succession would not be secure. For some reason, which Subh did not think was very flattering, the Royal Wife thought that their best chance lay with her.

It would not be easy. She knew little of these things but her very innocence could be to her advantage. She had already formed a clear idea of the approach she would take and, as the Royal Wife had suggested, the first step was for al-Hakim to accept her as a friend. She would learn all she could about poetry, not just how to recite it - that she could already do - no, she would read about the poets and their lives, try to understand why they wrote what they did. She would learn how to converse with al-Hakim about these things and she would look to him for advice. Then she would move to stage two. She would be outspoken and speak about the need for him to have an heir, ask why he had no wives and then maybe suggest a solution. It sounded easy when she looked at it like that but it was fraught with danger. What if al-Hakim was offended and had her beaten for being so outspoken? Would the Royal Wife be able to protect her? Would she want to? She might wash her hands of the whole plan and leave Subh to rot in some dungeon.

'Bring me some parchment and a pen,' she told her servant.

Later that day she sent Afra with a note to give to the Royal Wife. In it she asked for someone to go to the house of her old mistress and borrow some books about the lives of the poets Ibn Abd Rabbihi and Ibn Faraj. She knew al-Hakim had many books but she did not want to ask to borrow any of them until she was better informed about her subject. First she had to impress him and then, maybe, he would suggest that she read one of his books. It would take time but the prize was worth waiting for. The Royal Wife had made that very plain.

PART 2
978 - 979 AD

CHAPTER 11

Al-Jundi couldn't believe the news. The Grand Falconer and most of his men were moving to Córdoba. A new Falcon House was being constructed to house the birds and bit by bit they were being transferred to their new home.

'What's the matter?' asked his wife, as she placed a bowl of fruit on the table. 'You've hardly touched your food.'

'It's nothing. I'm not hungry,' he said. Everything was changing, and a bit too fast for his liking.

'Well, I've some good news for you,' she said. 'Something to bring a smile to your face.'

'Indeed? What is it?'

'Your little girl is going to be a mother. Durrah is going to have a baby,' she said, beaming at him in delight.

'What our little Durrah? That's wonderful news. May it please Allah that she has a son.'

'And you will be a grandfather,' his wife said.

A grandfather already. He could not believe that so many years had passed and now his own baby girl was to become a mother.

'Have you heard about the Falcon House?' his son, Ahmad, asked, patently uninterested in all the chatter about babies. 'They are moving everything to Córdoba, all the birds, everything. Has Grandfather said anything to you? Do you know what will happen to me? Does this mean the Khalifa is going to Córdoba too?'

'You have a lot of questions, son, but I do not have the answers. Don't worry. I'll speak to your grandfather and find out what is going on.'

'The Khalifa has never said anything about moving. He is talking about what we will do in the autumn, how we will take the new bird out hunting. I don't think he knows anything about it.' Ahmad sighed and continued, 'The birds won't like it, you know. They don't like to be moved. It will take them a long time to settle in to their new home. Has anyone thought about that?'

Ahmad's long, thin face was sad and, once again, al-Jundi was reminded of his brother Omar. Where was he now? Was he even still alive? His brother's love for a concubine had meant exile for him, and death if he ever returned. Al-Jundi had done what he could to keep his little brother from the executioner's axe but he still felt guilty that he had not done more for him.

Al-Jundi was a straightforward man, a humble soldier, no good at politics and intrigue, never had been and never would be. That was what worried him. He could see that his son was unhappy about the effect that moving to Córdoba would have on the falcons, but al-Jundi wasn't worried about the birds; he was more concerned about the political manoeuvring behind the relocation. Why move the Falcon House to Córdoba, when the Khalifa still lived in Madinat al-Zahra? He had a bad feeling about it. Everyone knew that the country could not be held together by a young boy; a coup was possible at any moment. A strong ruler was needed for a country as rich as al-Andalus, especially now. Uncertainly hung in the air like a dark cloud. There was talk of the Fatimites moving troops to the North African coast, just a few Arab miles across the sea from them and, worse still, rumours that Ramiro III of León was thinking of annulling the peace treaty that al-Hakim had made with him. But surely that was why there was a regency, to rule the kingdom until al-Hisham came of age, to give stability to the people. Al-Jundi had no head for politics and although his instinct told him that al-Mansur was planning something, what it was he could only guess. However, what he did know was that he would have to remain vigilant if he was to ensure the young Khalifa's safety.

'Maybe you should mention it to the Khalifa,' he said. 'Tell him about the move and see what he says. Perhaps only some of the birds are being moved. As I said, I'll have a word with your grandfather. He must be the one who has given the order, so he should know all the details.'

'Birds, birds, birds. Will you two stop chattering and eat up your food,' Fatima said. 'And is that your eldest son, late again? You should tell him his food will be given to the dog, next time he's late.'

'He can't help it, Mama,' said Amina. 'He gets held up at the hospital.' Al-Jundi's wife put an extra plate on the table for Qasim, who had just arrived, hot and flustered.

'Sorry I'm late, Teta, Mama, Baba. I was called out to see to a man who had fallen down a gully and hit his head.'

'Is he all right?' al-Jundi asked.

'He was unconscious for a bit but I think he'll be fine. He'll probably have a headache for a few days but that's all.'

'Who is he?'

'That's the strange thing, nobody has come forward to claim him and I can't find anyone that recognises him. He has nothing on him to say who he is, and he doesn't want to talk to us.'

'Is he a foreigner?'

'I don't think so. He looks like a soldier, but not one of the Khalifa's soldiers. He has no uniform, only a bow and some arrows and a dagger, all of which he keeps close to him. Another thing about him, he has this long scar down the side of his face, just the sort of wound you'd get in battle, from a curved sword.'

'Do you want me to take a look at him?'

'What good would that do? We'll keep him in the hospital for a bit to keep an eye on him and then he'll go on his way, carry on with his journey to wherever he was going when he had the accident - if it was an accident.'

'Do you think he was attacked?'

'It's possible. Either that or he was drunk.'

'Well he probably isn't from around here, otherwise somebody would know him. Nothing much happens in this place without someone knowing about it,' he said bitterly, thinking once more of his exiled brother.

***

Later that day al-Jundi went in search of his father-in-law and found him, as usual, in his office at the palace. He was directing two of his clerks on how to pack up the mountain of documents that had been compiled during his years as magistrate in Madinat al-Zahra.

'*As-salama alaykum*, father-in-law.'

'*Wa alaykum e-salam*, my son. Have you come to help me with all these damn files?'

'So it's true, you are moving to Córdoba?'

'That has been the order. Pack up and move to Córdoba. As though it were that simple. It's not an easy task to move thousands of birds and all the men, just like that. But that's what has been decided.'

'Who has decided it?' al-Jundi asked.

'The Regents of course. Al-Mansur, in particular, says it will be easier to administrate from there. Personally, I can't see why. The court has functioned perfectly well all these years here in Madinat al-Zahra. Why go to all the expense and trouble to move? The Mint has already gone, you know.'

'But why? Do you think he has an ulterior motive?'

'Ah, my son, who knows. I am not a politician. There is talk of al-Mansur building a new palace on the east side of the city. Maybe he wants to have everything close to hand, where he can control things. He certainly was quick enough to move the Treasury.'

'And the Khalifa? When does he go to Córdoba?'

'Now there's a curious thing. I haven't heard anything about him moving away from Madinat al-Zahra.'

'Maybe they're waiting until everything is ready.'

'You could be right, but I don't think so. The rumours have it that he is to stay here until he is of age.'

'That won't be for a few years yet. Surely al-Mansur doesn't intend to leave him here alone?'

'Perhaps the Khalifa will move in to the new palace when it's finished,' his father-in-law said, packing more files into a wicker basket and stacking them with the others.

This was looking more and more like the preparation for a coup. With al-Mushafi in prison, the Regency had been reduced to just two. Now that had been a strange incident. Why had they suddenly decided to investigate al-Mushafi's accounts? It seemed that whoever had suggested it - and he wouldn't mind betting that the suggestion originated from al-Mansur - had been right. Al-Mushafi had embezzled some money - there was no doubt about it. He would remain in prison for a few more years yet and by then the Khalifa would be able to rule.

Al-Jundi looked through the open doorway to where his father-in-law's two clerks were loading the panniers onto a pair of donkeys; the animals waited patiently, heads down, in the shade of an old olive tree.

'When do the birds go?' he asked.

'Some have already gone, but it will take a while for them all to be moved.'

'I'm confused, don't the falcons belong to the Khalifa?'

'Of course.'

'So why are they going to Córdoba and he is staying here?' al-Jundi asked.

'He's just a boy. If the court is in Córdoba then the birds have to be there too. They are as much a symbol of the court as the Khalifa. They'll be needed for pageants and ceremonies, for hunting, especially when there are visiting dignitaries at court. So you see, it's important that the birds are close to hand. Of course we will leave some of the falcons here in Madinat al-Zahra, for the Khalifa's personal use.'

'So al-Mansur will preside over the court as though he is the supreme ruler?' al-Jundi said, lowering his voice so that no-one else could hear his slanderous words. He trusted his father-in-law, so he continued, 'Do you think this is the first stage of a coup? If the Khalifa is isolated in Madinat al-Zahra, what's to stop al-Mansur taking the throne?'

'Don't let anyone else hear you saying such things. He may only be the Grand Vizier, but al-Mansur is a powerful man. See what has happened to al-Mushafi, a man previously thought to be above suspicion and now neatly tucked away in the prison dungeon. I'm telling you, you don't want to cross al-Mansur. That man is as treacherous as he is ambitious.'

'So you think al-Mushafi was innocent?'

'I don't know. I'm just saying that I think it is very suspicious that someone would suddenly think about checking the Treasury accounts.'

'Leaving the way for al-Mansur to take over the role of Grand Vizier,' al-Jundi continued along his father-in-law's line of reasoning.

'Best to leave it, my son. Think of your family.'

'Speaking of which, what about Ahmad? Will he have to move to Córdoba?'

'He will stay with the Khalifa, for now. From what I hear they seem to have formed a close friendship.'

'Yes, that's true. But what of Ahmad's future?'

'Have no fear, my son; he will continue to learn all there is to know about his trade and, when the time is right, there will be a job for him in Córdoba, if that is where the court remains. It's hard to say what will happen these days. We are in uncertain times.'

'All the more reason to look after the Khalifa and his future,' al-Jundi said rather brusquely, as though he blamed his father-in-law for moving the court to Córdoba.

'You worry too much, my son. The Khalifa will be safe here in the palace and when he comes of age, he will take his rightful place as ruler.'

'I hope you are right.'

***

As al-Jundi walked back to find the Khalifa, his thoughts were on security. To an outsider the palace and the Khalifa were well protected; Palace Guards were stationed around the perimeter of the *alcazaba* and at every entry point in the high stone walls. No-one could enter the *alcázar* without being seen by one of them, but how many of them could be trusted? This was al-Jundi's concern. The majority of the Palace Guard was made up of Slav mercenaries or freed slaves; there were few that were like him, battled hardened and loyal to the throne. If al-Mansur, or anyone else for that matter, made a move against the Khalifa, how many of them would stand firm? He needed to get together a band of soldiers who had been loyal to al-Hakim and would extend that loyalty to his son, and he needed to do it quickly. He would go and talk to his old commander ibn al-Rashid. He was retired now, but he could advise him on whom to approach.

The two guards on the door to Khalifa's private quarters, stood to attention as he approached.

'At ease, soldiers,' he said. 'Where is the Khalifa?'

'He has not left all morning. I think you will find him in the garden.'

Sure enough, when al-Jundi entered the room he could see the doors to the garden were open and al-Hisham was sitting by the fountain reading.

'*As-salama alaykum*, Your Highness. How are you today?'

'*Wa alaykum e-salam*, al-Jundi. I am well. I am reading about my falcons. Your son has brought me this list of all the birds that are in the Falcon House and where they originated from. It is very interesting. Do you know I have a pair of eagles that have come from the Zagros Mountains in Persia. Do you know where that is?'

'No, Your Highness. I have never travelled outside of our beautiful country.'

'It is a long way away, further than Baghdad. It says here that the eagles are twenty-three years old. I must ask Ahmad to take me to see them.'

'Has anyone been to see you today, Your Highness?'

The boy looked up from his scrolls and frowned. 'No. No-one has been, not even my mother. Why do you ask?'

'No reason, my Lord. And yesterday? Did the Regents come to see you yesterday?'

'No. They haven't been to see me for weeks. Sometimes they send a messenger with something they want me to sign, but I haven't seen any of the Regents in person for a long time.'

'So you are not aware that some of the falcons are being transferred to Córdoba?'

'My falcons? Why are they moving them to Córdoba? What will happen to my Falcon House?'

'I don't know, Your Highness. I have just left the Grand Falconer and he told me that they are moving some of the birds to a new Falcon House.' He couldn't bring himself to tell the boy that most of them were going. 'But Ahmad will be staying here to look after your special birds, and to help you.'

'When is this happening?'

'It has already started, Your Highness, but it will take some months to complete the move. Apparently it is not an easy task.'

'Does Ahmad know about this?'

'He only learned about it today, Your Highness, as did I.'

'So what can we do to stop them, al-Jundi? There must be something we can do. We will ask the Grand Falconer to stop it.'

'The Grand Falconer said he had received orders from the Regents. There is nothing he can do about it.'

'How can they do that, without my permission,' the young Khalifa shouted, throwing down his book and storming inside, leaving al-Jundi standing there in the garden alone.

***

Al-Jundi knew where to find him; the ex-*quaid* had taken a modest house on the edge of the town, close to the *Bab al-Sura* gate. His old friend was sitting outside his house, dozing in the early evening sunshine. He looked older than al-Jundi remembered him and, without his uniform, seemed somehow diminished.

'*As-salama alaykum*, dear friend. How are you?' al-Jundi asked.

'*Wa alaykum e-salam*, soldier. It is a long time since I have seen you,' al-Rashid replied as he stood up to embrace him.

'You are well?'

'As well as can be expected for a soldier who has outlived his fighting life. I survive. And you? I hear you are the bodyguard to the new Khalifa. What's it like to be a baby-sitter?'

'The Khalifa is young, it is true, but that is all the more reason for me to take care of him. I made a promise to his father and I intend to keep it.'

'Of course, of course, no need to get on your high horse with me, al-Jundi. I've known you too long. Now will you come inside and have a glass of tea with me or shall we stand here in the street arguing?'

'I'll come inside, of course.'

He ducked through the doorway and followed his old commander through to the inner courtyard, where rows of pots were filled with sweet smelling lilies, jasmine, rosemary and marjoram; there were other flowers and herbs but al-Jundi was not familiar with them. The effect was one of being in an enclosed garden.

'This is what I do now,' al-Rashid said. 'I grow things and then I sit and look at them.'

Al-Jundi recognised the slight edge of bitterness to his words and nodded sympathetically. This was no life for a man of action. His friend had no wife and no family, whether from choice or whether it was because of being a soldier all his life, al-Jundi did not know. He had probably not expected to live so long; a soldier's life was usually short and his death bloody. Now here he was, in his seventieth year and living alone.

A young maidservant appeared as if by magic, carrying a silver tray with a tea-pot and two glasses. She set it down on a low table and the men sat next to it. Then she disappeared as silently as she had appeared. How different this was from his own noisy, bustling home, with his mother wanting to know everything that was going on, Amina singing all day long while she cooked and looked after the house, little Asim with his ceaseless stream of babyish questions, and the constant comings and goings of his three older boys.

'So, how do you enjoy looking after the boy Khalifa?' al-Rashid asked.

'It is my job. It's better than being away on campaign after campaign, as I was when I was younger. This job suits an older man. Anyway I have a family now and it's nice to be able to see them grow up,' he said, thinking of the friends and comrades he had seen hacked to death in battle.

'But the Khalifa would have given you any promotion you asked for as a reward for saving his son's life.'

'Yes, but I think I was tired of a soldier's life, and even if he had made me a general, I would still have been on active duty. They were good years that I spent by the side of al-Hakim. If they hadn't been I would not be here now, trying to ensure that his son lives long enough to become the ruler of our country.'

'You think something will happen to him?'

Al-Jundi sipped the sweet tea before replying. 'I honestly don't know, but all I can see is the potential for danger. He is young and vulnerable and, as far as I'm aware, there is no-one by his side except me.'

'He has a castle full of guards and an army of men. What could possibly threaten him?'

'For a start, he is left to his own devices all the time. No-one is bothering to train him in his duties; his mother hardly ever visits him and the Regents ignore him. It seems to me that everyone would just like him to disappear.'

'Surely not. He is the Khalifa. Are you sure that you are not exaggerating the situation?'

'Maybe. But my job is to prevent any harm coming to him. So what if I take unnecessary precautions? Better to be safe than sorry.'

'But the Regents are running the country. Surely they will protect him.'

'It is the Regency that worries me, in particular al-Mansur; his power and his popularity are growing all the time. Now I hear that, bit by bit, he is moving the court back to Córdoba. The Treasury has already gone and soon it will be another department, then another. Madinat al-Zahra will become a ghost town.'

'But that doesn't constitute a threat to the Khalifa.'

'Maybe not, but there are no plans for him to leave Madinat al-Zahra; he is to stay here in the palace, surrounded by his guards. Now do you see my concern?'

'Yes, you may have a point and, as you say, it's always better to be safe than sorry. No campaign was ever won without careful planning, as we well know. So, why have you come to visit me? And don't say, it was to see how I was. Busy men do not make social calls. You want something from me, so go on, spit it out.'

Al-Jundi smiled at his friend's outspokenness; he had always been so. That was one of the many things that had made him a good commander; everybody knew exactly what was expected. There was never any confusion over their orders.

'I need to build a team of dependable soldiers, loyal to the Khalifa above all else. You know the sort of unscrupulous, mercenary foreigners that we employ in the Palace Guard these days. How can I rely on them to protect the Khalifa when I am not there? I want my own men, men I can trust. I haven't been on active service for many years so I have lost touch with the men I fought alongside. Now I need you to recommend some good soldiers to me.'

Al-Rashid picked up his glass and stared at the clear green liquid for a few moments, then he said, 'Very well. We will go through a list of them together and then I will go and speak to them on your behalf.'

CHAPTER 12

Al-Mansur strode across the bridge towards the mosque; the air was cool and a low mist clung to the surface of the river. Overhead, swallows swooped and dived, chasing clouds of insects that swarmed up from the grassy banks and, coming from the towering minaret before him, the call of the *muezzin* reverberated through the air, calling the faithful to prayer. Al-Mansur was a pious man, but no-one could call him a fanatic. Born into the faith, he followed the rules and observed all the Muslim festivals, but he had never given much thought to what it all meant. Now he realised that his religion could be the key to his success. An important part of his plan was to convince the people of al-Andalus that he was a man entitled to be their new leader, maybe even their new Khalifa and he had to demonstrate this by leading a blameless life, show them that it was he who was worthy of being the spiritual head of Islam, not that puny boy. Not only that, but he would show them that it was he alone that could lead them to victory against the infidel. The Christian princes were a niggling thorn in his side so he would declare a *jihad* against them. It would bring him a two-fold success, uniting the country against the enemy of their religion and, more importantly, bringing him new riches in the shape of spoils of war.

That was why, with the sun barely above the horizon, he was going to pray in the Great Mosque instead of in the privacy of his own home; here his devotion would be on show to everyone. He had other plans too. Al-Hakim had been a greatly respected khalifa; he was a religious man who had strictly enforced the laws of Islam and often quoted from the *Haddith*. He had been particularly opposed to the drinking of wine, even going so far as wanting to have all the vineyards burnt to the ground in order to remove temptation from his people. He had eventually been dissuaded from such drastic action on economic grounds - the export of wine was a profitable business. Al-Mansur would continue with this policy and he would be ruthless in his punishment of any departures from the orthodox faith, be it drinking wine or adultery.

The Great Mosque was already almost full when he arrived; men were washing themselves in the Courtyard of the Orange Trees prior to entering the holy place, others were talking and waiting for the *muezzin* to finish his invocations, some were already inside, bent over their prayer mats, deep in contemplation. Al-Mansur went first into the courtyard and washed himself carefully, then made his way to the front and chose a place close to the *mihrab* to place his prayer mat. He had noticed some men looking at him and speaking amongst themselves; they had recognised him. He knelt, forehead touching the mat and waited for the *imam* to arrive and the service to begin.

But his thoughts were not of Allah, nor of paradise; they had taken a more sinister turn.

What was he going to do about al-Hisham? The boy would soon grow into a man and then he would expect to take his rightful place as ruler. If Al-Mansur waited until that time came it would be too late to do anything about it; he had to act now. He had wrestled with this problem night after night, tossing and turning as he tried to find an alternative solution to the inevitable, but in the end he knew that the only conclusion was to eliminate him. After all, what was the point of getting rid of al-Mughira if he was going to leave the Khalifa alive? Of course it would have to look like an accident. Nothing must be traced back to him. Luckily Assab knew who to contact; he had told him of a man, an assassin who was said to be both ruthless and discreet. For the right fee he would do whatever was asked of him and keep his mouth shut. It was said that he'd even slice the throat of his own mother if the price was right. It would cost, naturally; once the man knew who his target was, he'd expect to be paid handsomely. Money was not a problem; the next campaign would bring him plenty of riches. Of course he did not really expect the man to keep quiet, despite what people said of him, not over something as important as this; he would talk to someone sooner or later, a casual comment in a bar, a veiled hint over a glass of wine, the urge to tell someone how it was he who had changed the course of their world; a slip of the tongue could reveal all. No, once the deed was done, he'd arrange with Assab to make him disappear and then his secret would be safe. If he was lucky he might even get his money back.

The *imam* intoned the last of the prayers and the service was over. One by one, the men rose and began to file out of the mosque. More heads were turned in his direction as news of his presence spread. Al-Mansur walked slowly to the main door of the mosque. It had been originally built by Abd Rahman I, two hundred years previously, then as the city grew it had been extended by Abd Rahman II and finally by the previous khalifa, al-Hakim II. He turned and looked back at the rows of double horseshoe arches, red and white, supported on marble pillars and illuminated by hanging brass oil lamps that cast creamy pools of light on the red earth floor; it was a magnificent sight but already it was too small for the growing population. He resolved that, when he became ruler of al-Andalus, he would double its size; that would be his legacy to the city where he had grown up.

***

Al-Mansur could see from his expression that the General was not pleased and it didn't take much imagination to know it was to do with the next campaign to León.

'*As-salama alaykum*, father-in-law,' he said. 'What brings you here today with a face like a constipated camel?'

'*Wa alaykum e-salam*, son-in-law. I need to talk to you, urgently,' General Ghálib replied, ignoring the remarks about his mood.

'Of course, please take a seat and I will send for some lemon tea to refresh you.'

'I do not need tea. I need to know why you have decided to declare a *jihad* against the Christian king in León? We have lived in peace with these people for many years, ever since the reign of Rahman III. True there has been the odd skirmish with some of the rebellious princes, but they were never sanctioned by King Ramiro. He has always kept the peace. What is the point of stirring up trouble now, by declaring a *jihad*? Surely peace is better for our country than war?'

'The Christians are on our borders, infidels that threaten our religion, our way of life. We must annihilate them before they destroy us,' Al-Mansur said, standing up so that he towered above the little general. 'I am surprised that you cannot see that. There have been rumours for some time that they are preparing to attack us. King Ramiro cannot be trusted to keep his word, no Christian ruler can. We must take the initiative.'

'Rumours? Silly washerwomen's gossip, I say. There is no substance to them and even if it were true, surely diplomacy and negotiation would be better than plunging the country into an expensive war again?'

'What has happened to you, my father-in-law? You sound like that scoundrel, al-Mushafi; he had no taste for battle either. Have you lost your battle-lust? Do you no longer have the nerve to face cold steel? Would you prefer to spend the rest of your life behind a desk, ruling from the comfort of the palace? Well, I can tell you, unless we show these Christians that we mean business, there will be no safe haven for you in the palace or anywhere else.'

The General sighed and sat down, his expression one of resigned compliance. 'Very well. Tell me what you want me to do,' he said. 'But I am not convinced that this is a good idea.'

'I need fifty thousand men,' Al-Mansur said, sitting down beside him. General Ghálib opened his mouth to protest but Al-Mansur held up his hand to stop him. 'Ten thousand of those will be *jinetes*, ten thousand will be archers and the rest will be skirmishers, infantrymen. We leave at the next full moon.'

'That's a lot of soldiers, my son. Can we afford to pay so many men?'

'Promise them the usual booty and a bonus on the heads of all the Christians they bring to me, on top of their regular pay. You will have plenty of volunteers, you'll see. Send someone to north Africa and recruit some more Berbers; they are excellent horsemen. When they know we ride to victory, they will come. After all, where there's victory there're riches.'

'Very well. You do realise that this is the third campaign this year?'

'It is the first in our *jihad*, our holy war. The people are fed up of the Christians on our borders; they will welcome this. We are fighting for Islam, remember, not just for al-Andalus. The Christians will come to know this land as *Dar Djihad*, the land of the *jihad* and they will come to fear us.' Yes, and he would become known as the scourge of the Christians.

'What about the Palace Guard? I heard a rumour that you were planning to disband them. Tell me it's not true.'

'Yes, you are well informed. The Khalifa has 3,750 men in his bodyguard, all Slavs. First of all, I think that is too many. Why does he need so many Palace Guards when we are moving the court to Córdoba? We can protect him and his palace with ordinary soldiers. In the second place, I don't trust them; we call them Slavs but most of them were recruited from León, anyway. Christian mercenaries. Not the most reliable people to have as bodyguards for the Khalifa, wouldn't you agree?'

'Have you forgotten that you are not the only person in this regency? Three men were appointed to the task of administrating the country until al-Hisham comes of age. Do I have to remind you that you are not in sole charge?' Ghálib was spluttering with rage. 'It is one thing to declare a *jihad* against our enemies - that is bad enough - but now you are interfering in matters of the Khalifa's safety.'

'We are but two now, my dear father-in-law. If you remember, our colleague is languishing in prison for embezzling the Khalifa's money. It is up to the both of us to carry out the duties of the Regency. If I have offended you by being precipitous in this matter, I apologise. I was, after all, merely trying to be reasonable. The boy does not need nearly four thousand guards to protect him. That's a small army, for heaven's sake.'

'The Khalifa has always had a strong Palace Guard.'

'And he will continue to do so, but without employing quite so many men and certainly without using Slavs.'

'So when were you going to inform me of this?'

'This very morning. You just didn't give me the chance to bring up the subject.'

The General let out a sigh of exasperation, but al-Mansur could see that his words had mollified him slightly.

'You know it is my sworn promise to guard the Khalifa from all danger. I would not have anything happen to him,' the General continued.

'And nothing will. Do you really think I do not have the young man's safety at heart? I am doing all this for him, so that when he comes of age he will inherit a rich and peaceful kingdom.'

'Yes, well, I had better go; there is much to organise,' Ghálib said, preparing to leave. 'By the way, how is my daughter?'

'Ismá is well. Pregnancy agrees with her.'

'My wife thinks she should come and stay with us until the baby is born. You will be away on the campaign and she will be alone. It is not a time for a woman to be without her family. I hope you have no objection.'

'None whatsoever. I will ride more easily if I know my lovely Ismá is with her mother. I will tell her to prepare to move to your home as soon as I leave.'

'Thank you, my son-in-law. *Ma'a salama.*'

'*Alla ysalmak*, General.'

Once the General had left, al-Mansur went into his office. If he could arrange for the assassination of al-Hisham to happen while he was away on the campaign, it would mean that no blame would be attached to him and, when he returned, triumphant from battle, to a country with no ruler, he would be able to step into the role with ease. Yes, it could all work out very well for him.

He summoned Assab to him. 'Assab. Go to the Jewish quarter. Close to the synagogue you will find a cobbler's shop. Go in and ask for Isaiah. Give him this note. Wait while he reads it and do not leave until you see him burn it. He will give you a message for me. Is that clear?'

The slave nodded his head.

'Then come straight back here and give me his reply.'

Once more the slave nodded.

Al-Mansur handed the note to him and turned back to the task in hand. He spread the maps in front of him and began to plan his campaign. After all, declaring a *jihad* was not enough; he had to win. The Khalifa's army was divided into five corps, each under a general. General Ghálib would lead the infantry, General Yushabi, an Ethiopian as black as night, would lead the archers and slingers on the right wing and the young, as yet untried, General Adnan, the left wing. He, as *Amir*, their Commander-in-chief in the field, would lead the cavalry in the centre and that would leave the last General, ibn Musa, to bring up the rearguard. Each man would have ten thousand soldiers under his command, and each corps was split into five contingents of two thousand men under the command of a *quaid*. The contingents were divided further by five into groups of four hundred men each and then into sections of eighty until they reached the smallest unit in the army, the squad of sixteen men. All the sub-divisions of this mighty army had their own flags to distinguish them in battle, with the exception of the squads, which were led into battle by their *nazir*, with a pennant tied to his lance. New as he was to battle, Al-Mansur had taken immediately to the strategy of warfare. It was so logical, so precise, so easy to plan; it appealed to his ordered mind. Once the battle started, of course, things were different. When their blood was up soldiers were apt to do anything; their instinct was to kill or be killed. However, by dividing the chain of command down to the smallest unit, the chance of controlling these battle-crazed soldiers was greatly increased.

There were two generally used methods of fighting the enemy, either by repeatedly attacking and retreating or by charging at close quarters. Whichever was used, both relied heavily on the policy of retrenchment, whereby, after each prolonged encounter, the soldiers at the front withdrew, allowing soldiers from the rearguard to move up for a new encounter, thus providing a constant flow of fresh soldiers on the front line.

If they could meet their enemy on a level battle field then he would start with the first method. He would line up the foot soldiers in the vanguard, under the command of Ghálib, who had used this method of attack many times before. The infantry, with their long, heavy lances, shields and razor sharp javelins would partially kneel, their lances dipped and touching the ground, their shields raised before them. The archers would stand behind them and then, behind them, in the centre, al-Mansur with the cavalry. When the Christians advanced, the infantry would remain in position until their enemy was within range then they would throw their javelins, the archers would fire their arrows, then the infantry would cut into them with their lances. At this point, the lines of infantry and archers would open up, some moving to the left and others to the right, leaving a void in the centre so that the cavalry could charge through and cut down the enemy. It was so effective and so simple.

***

On the morning after the full moon, al-Mansur's greatly increased army marched through the arches of the Grand Portico in the palace of Madinat al-Zahra and lined up on the parade ground. From his viewpoint on the terrace above, the Khalifa could review his troops, row upon row of armed infantrymen, their shields and armour gleaming in the sun, men who stood tall and straight, red capes on their backs, their lances in their hands and swords tucked into their belts. Behind them stood the bowmen and slingers, their weapons by their sides and, on the right, the *jinetes,* the daring, dashing cavalry that were the mainstay of any battle. Al-Mansur sat astride his favourite stallion, which fidgeted and pawed the ground impatient to be off, and waited for the Khalifa's blessing. It mattered little to him personally, but to leave without it would be a bad omen and that could affect the men's morale. All eyes were raised expectantly, watching the terrace that overlooked the parade ground for any sign of their young ruler. At last their wait was rewarded as the slight figure of the Khalifa, dressed in the military uniform of Supreme Commander, stepped into sight. His mother, *al-Sayyida al-Malika*, stood by his side. The boy held a document in his hand and, after staring at the men waiting patiently for him to begin, read something from it, but his voice was too weak to carry his words and what did reach the waiting soldiers drifted away on the wind. It did not matter. It was enough that he was there and he was giving them his blessing. Now the men would fight, knowing that Allah was on their side. Al-Mansur's hand went automatically to the copy of the *Quran* that he always carried into battle. He let it be known that he had copied the entire book himself but the truth was that one of his scribes had written most of it.

Al-Mansur watched as the boy raised his right hand and slowly let it fall again; that was the signal to leave. He wheeled his horse to the right and rode out through the arches of the Great Portico, his men marching behind, first the foot soldiers, a motley collection of mercenaries, Berbers, negroes and freed slaves, some who fought with swords, some with lances and others with slings and bows and arrows. Next came the *jinetes*, riding their immaculately groomed horses, their legs hanging loose at the horses' sides, with gleaming helmets, resplendent in coats of mail and red capes, some carrying heart shaped shields, some round, some with short bows and others with javelins, then came the stream of provision carriers, the donkeys and camels laden with tents and food, the cooks and blacksmiths, the grooms, the slaves, the doctors, the lumbering great siege engines, the catapults, the naphtha throwers and their tubs of naphtha with which to ignite the arrow tips of the archers, the drummers with small drums for calling men to battle, the wagons heavy with arms: arrows, swords, lances, spare armour. There was excitement in the air. It was always like this, despite the long journey that they all knew was before them and which separated them from the moment they lived for, that exhilarating moment when the battle began, when the air was alive with the screams of men, and the drumming of the drums reverberated in everyone's blood, urging them forward, to death or glory.

CHAPTER 13

Al-Hisham was impatient for Ahmad to come; today was the day when they were going to fly his hawk. His stomach was churning with excitement. He was ready for this; Ahmad had said so and even al-Jundi had agreed that he could join the hunt.

He had learnt a lot in the past few months. Ahmad had started by teaching him the special terms that were used in falconry; it had its own language and, he said, al-Hisham would look stupid if he said 'wings' instead of 'sails', or 'claws' instead of 'pounces' and he was to remember that the bird's tail was called a 'train'. These terms were far more descriptive and they showed an understanding of the hawk and its life. The male was referred to as a tiercel because it was a third smaller than the female. This fact he found strange; surely the female should be the smallest but Ahmad had said not. Some of the terms made sense to him but others seemed to have no reason to them; for example young birds were called 'eyasses' and old ones, 'passagers'. Then there were words for the actions they did; when they wiped their beaks on the ground or on a branch they were 'feaking'; when they defecated they were 'muting' and when they pulled themselves to their full height and shook themselves they were said to be 'rousing'. All this he had to know, according to Ahmad, in order to understand what the falconers were talking about. He needed to take note of the signs that the bird would display when it was in the mood for the kill, how its crest feathers would rise and its toes would tighten on the glove; he needed to recognise when the bird was nervous by the way its head sank down on to its shoulders, how the narrowing of its eyes meant that it was happy and when it looked distant it was probably tired, how when it held its feathers tightly to its body it was frightened and when they were loose, the falcon was relaxed. There was so much to remember.

They had spent the summer teaching Daruj to fly to his hand. He would leave him sitting on his perch and step away with food hidden in his glove, each time a little further, and each time the bird flew straight to him. It was wonderful this feeling he had for Daruj, how his heart leapt when the bird took off and flew at him. He knew it was the food that attracted him, of course, but he couldn't help feeling that a bond was growing between them. When he mentioned this to Ahmad, he said that it was very possible. Hawks were intelligent birds and capable of forming an attachment to their owners, but to always remember that they were, at heart, wild creatures. They could be tamed to a certain extent with the lure of food and easy hunting but they were used to flying free. They would return to the glove if they were trained well with kindness; if not they could fly off and never return.

His mother had told him that hawks were messengers between this world and the next. He hoped it was true and then he could send a message to his father and tell him how much he missed him. He would tell him about Ahmad and Daruj; he would tell him of his loneliness and how empty the palace was without him; he would tell his father that he remembered all he had taught him and that he would try to be a worthwhile successor to him and, finally, he would tell him that he loved him. All these things he would whisper in Daruj's ear and hope that, somehow, his words reached his father.

'The young man from the Falcon House is here, Your Highness,' said Gassan.

'Bring him to me.'

'Very well, Your Highness.'

Within moments, Ahmad was by his side, panting heavily, as though he had run all the way from the Falcon House.

'I am sorry I'm late, Your Highness,' he said. 'We can go as soon as you are ready. Everything is prepared. We are going out onto the plains below the city of Córdoba. It is excellent land for hunting.'

'Good. Let's go.'

'My father is waiting with your horse, Your Excellency. Come with me.'

Al-Hisham followed the boy through the palace and into the courtyard where, only a few weeks before, he had bestowed his blessing on the troops setting off to the north. That had been fun. He had enjoyed looking down on that enormous army, watching it march off to war and knowing that they were his men and they were fighting for him and his kingdom. His mother said that they were sure to be victorious and they would come back with gold for his treasury and slaves for his army. He was to pray for their success each day when he went to the mosque.

Al-Jundi was waiting in the courtyard; he had some forty soldiers with him. They weren't the usual Palace Guards, dressed in green and gold, but ordinary soldiers, with helmets and red capes over their chainmail shirts. All were on horseback and all were armed. For a moment he felt as if he too were going to war, and a thrill of excitement ran down his spine.

'Here is your horse, Your Highness,' al-Jundi said, leading a young, brown mare towards him. 'She is the finest in the stables and has been hunting many times. She will not scare when your hawk returns to your hand.'

'Are you going to hunt as well, al-Jundi?' al-Hisham asked.

'No, my Lord; at least I hope not. We are here to ensure your safety.'

***

The ride out across the plain was exhilarating; Ahmad had explained that there would be plenty of hares and rabbits hiding in the stubble left from the harvested corn and maybe even some partridges. They had stopped first at the Falcon House to collect their hawks and to join up with other falconers who had young birds to fly. The Falcon House seemed rather empty; many of the falcons had already been transferred to their new home. At first al-Hisham found it awkward riding with Daruj on his gloved hand, but after a while it felt completely natural. The hooded bird was quiet, patiently waiting for the moment it would get the chance to fly. Ahmad had helped him tie the jesses to Daruj's leg and attach the long creance which would prevent the bird from flying away. Al-Hisham knew that the key to training Daruj well was patience, that and the ability to watch and wait, and above all to be quiet; too much chatter disturbed the bird. They had spent weeks just getting him to sit on al-Hisham's gloved hand without bating to be free. He had been frightened that his bird would injure itself as it took headlong dives at the ground, thrashing his wings in anger, but Ahmad had explained that it was because Daruj was frightened and that all Hisham could do was repeat the process time and time again until the bird began to feel secure; great patience was required. Al-Hisham had to become invisible, the falconer said, and, no matter how boring he found it, he had to keep repeating the exercise, each time reinforcing it by giving Daruj titbits of food and, eventually, the hawk would settle on his fist as calmly as in a tree. Al-Hisham hadn't found it boring at all; he loved every minute he spent with this wild creature whose enormous black eyes seemed to see into his very soul. Al-Hisham stroked the soft leather hood that covered Daruj's head and whispered a little nonsense to him. He was glad that he did not have to let him fly free this evening; he could not bear it if Daruj did not come back. Ahmad had said it was too soon for him to fly without a creance, but one day he would have to.

There were about forty of them in the party; ten from the Falcon House and thirty soldiers. They were heading for the edge of the fields, where the flat expanse of fertile plain turned into the woody foothills of the Sierra Morena. The falconers reined in their horses and dismounted.

'This is a good spot to begin the hunt,' Ahmad explained. 'The birds will be able to range over both the plain and the woods; it will be good hunting for them.'

Al-Hisham was getting impatient to start and Daruj, sensing this, began to hop from foot to foot.

'Wait and watch what I do first, then you can fly Daruj,' Ahmad said. 'You wanted to see how fast they can fly, well watch this one; she's a beauty.'

He had a two-year-old female peregrine falcon on his glove, her black wings folded by her side, her white throat fluttering slightly with anticipation. Al-Hisham felt that he could see her heart beating beneath the black and white banded feathers that covered her breast. She was a beautiful bird.

'We don't need the creance for this one. She'll come back to the glove with no problem,' Ahmad said.

One of the falconers, a big man, with a ruddy face and hands the size of shovels, opened a basket and let out a blue rock dove, which instantly flew up into the air, happy to be freed from its confinement. It flew fast and straight, sensing the danger it was in. Ahmad waited for a moment then, having removed the hood from his falcon's head, raised his arm with the bird still sitting motionless on his hand. The falcon flexed its wings and looked around, taking in everything, the waiting horses, the falconers with their birds ready for the hunt, the soldiers, standing to one side, not sure where to position themselves so that they did not interfere with the young Khalifa's pleasure, the wide expanse of stubble where potential meals could be hiding, and there, within easy reach, a fleeing rock dove. The dove was fast but not fast enough to outstrip the falcon which left its young master's hand and flew up and after it like an arrow from a bow. The rock dove knew the chase was on; it changed direction, twisting and turning to avoid the raptor; it dived slightly then soared again but the falcon was too fast for it and flew straight into the dove, knocking it from the sky in mid-flight. It dropped to the ground, dead or stunned, al-Hisham did not know which, and instantly the peregrine was upon it. It tore at the dove with its deadly beak, ripping the feathers from its body and tossing them to the wind, and then settled down to eat it. Before it could eat too much of its kill, Ahmad had run over to it, picked up the dead rock dove, cut off one of its legs and used it to lure the falcon back to his glove. The rest he put in his bag. It was all over in a flash.

'He is fast,' al-Hisham said in admiration. 'The dove didn't have a chance.'

'Yes, he's a good hunter, this one, and he's learned quickly. I'm going to take him out hunting cranes next week.'

The other falconers were busy with their own birds. One man had already removed his falcon's hood and had launched him into the air. The bird wheeled above them, its tail spread like a dark fan behind it, its triangular wings wide as it scanned the ground for signs of its quarry.

'See how high he flies. He's looking for hares,' Ahmad said. 'There are loads of them down there in the stubble. The dogs will scare them out and then he'll be able to catch one.'

Sure enough, two of the dogs were working their way through the corn stubble, weaving back and forth, their handlers whistling and calling to them all the time.

'Look, the falcon's spotted something,' said Ahmad. 'Watch carefully.'

The peregrine falcon was circling high over the cut corn then, before al-Hisham could even register what was happening, it had dived straight for the ground. Its speed was breathtaking.

'Yes, he's got it,' Ahmad cried in delight. 'That will make a nice meal for someone tonight.' He watched the falcon's handler run over and relieve the bird of its kill, tucking it into the canvas bag which hung over his shoulder. One of the dogs, a rather skinny under-fed creature, ran up to him, barking and jumping up to try and take the hare. That was strange. He didn't recognise the dog; it wasn't one of theirs. All their hunting dogs were trained not to pick up the kill. They were all well fed and very obedient. No falconer would have brought such an unruly animal on the hunt. Now one of the men was calling the dog, but the dog ignored him. No, he certainly wasn't one of their hunting dogs.

'What's the matter with that dog?' the Khalifa asked. 'And who is that man?'

'I don't know. I've never seen him before today, but he seems to know ibn al-Attar. Perhaps he's a friend of his.'

'It's my turn, now,' the Khalifa said, impatient to try out his own bird.

'All right, today we'll see if Daruj will go for a pigeon. Are you happy to do this?'

'Of course. It's what we have been training for, isn't it Daruj,' he whispered to the bird.

'All right. Now slowly, take off his hood and let him look about him. In a minute I will give the signal for them to let out one of the pigeons.'

Al-Hisham, his heart thumping with excitement, did as he was told. Daruj looked at him with his black shiny eyes then swivelled his head and looked around at the sun glinting through the trees, at the pale sky that would soon turn dark, at the fields of stubble that disappeared into a golden blur that was the horizon.

'All right, I'll give the signal now,' Ahmad said.

Another basket was opened and a pigeon flew out, fluttering upwards, a slow lumbering bird compared to the falcon that shot off al-Hisham's glove like an arrow, straight towards it. Daruj whirled and wheeled in mid-air and snatched the pigeon before its flight to freedom had even begun. Then he came to the end of his line and dropped to the ground, the dead pigeon still in its pounces.

'Good. He did very well. Now you have to retrieve the pigeon before he eats it all. Remember he has to look to you for food; that is how you control him. Here take my knife and cut him a slice and put the rest in your bag.'

He reached across to give the knife to al-Hisham, but his hand was still sticky from the blood of the rock dove and the knife slipped from his fingers and fell into the lush grass at their feet.

'Don't worry. I'll get it,' al-Hisham said, swinging out of the saddle and dropping to the ground.

In that instant an arrow flew past his head and struck Ahmad, who uttered a low groan and dropped from his horse. Al-Hisham looked at the young falconer, lying by his feet. What had happened? Why had someone shot Ahmad? Before he could do anything, his soldiers had surrounded him, cutting him off from any further attack. Everyone seemed to be talking at once, shouting orders and counter-orders; horses were pawing the ground with excitement, birds, frightened by the sudden commotion began to bate and scream, dogs started to bark. Al-Hisham heard one of the soldiers shout, 'Attack. We're under attack. Someone has tried to kill the Khalifa. Over there, in the trees. The arrow came from there.'

'You men, find him. Bring him back alive,' ordered al-Jundi riding across to al-Hisham. 'The rest of you stay here to protect the Khalifa.'

The soldiers galloped off into the woods, swords in hand.

Al-Jundi turned to the Khalifa and asked, 'Are you hurt, Your Excellency?'

'No, no, but someone has shot Ahmad. You must help him, al-Jundi. See to Ahmad. Is he dead? Tell me he's not dead.'

Al Jundi bent over the supine body of his son. The arrow was embedded just below his collar bone and there was a lot of blood on his tunic but otherwise he looked unhurt.

'No, he's not dead. He's still breathing.'

'But all that blood.'

'Don't worry, Your Highness. I don't think it's fatal. I've seen this type of injury before; if no infection sets in then he will recover.'

He lifted the boy into his arms and cradled him against his body. 'Ahmad, speak to me. Ahmad, open your eyes. Speak to me,' he said.

The young falconer groaned and looked up into the concerned face of his father.

'Baba? What happened? Aahh! I've been shot.' His fingers touched the flight of the arrow and he grimaced in pain.

'Hush, my son. We are taking you to get help. Leave the arrow where it is until we will find someone to remove it.'

'The Khalifa? Is the Khalifa all right?' Ahmad asked, his voice coming out in short gasps.

'He's fine.'

'We must get him to a doctor,' al-Hisham said. 'Straight away.'

He was frightened. What if Ahmad did not recover? He felt sick at the thought, and realised that, more than anything else, he did not want Ahmad to die. He was the only friend he had. His life would be unbearable if Ahmad was not there.

'Of course, I will send two of my men straight back to the palace with him,' said al Jundi.

'Take him to Abu al-Zahrawi. He is the court physician. He will know how to remove the arrow. And tell him that I have sent you. He must do everything he can for Ahmad. He must not let him die.'

'Yes, Your Highness. I know the man. He served your father well.'

Suddenly al-Hisham remembered Daruj. Where was he? The line was broken; the creance no longer tethered him to his hand; instead it hung loosely on the ground. He climbed onto his horse and looked to where he had last seen the falcon. Daruj was no longer bent over the dead pigeon, tearing it apart. He was nowhere to be seen.

'My hawk. Where is my hawk?' he cried. 'Daruj, Daruj.' He whistled and held out his hand and whistled again and again. 'Daruj. Daruj.'

His desperate calls rang out through the clearing and then, suddenly, a rapid descent, a whirring of wings and a thump as the falcon grabbed his glove. He was back. Al-Hisham could not believe it. He had come back to him. Quickly he caught hold of the trailing jesses and pulled a titbit of meat out of his bag to reward the young hawk. He stroked his head and whispered words of love to him while he slipped the hood over his eyes, the hood he had made from the finest leather and embroidered with the letters H and D. Hisham and Daruj. Now he felt that they were truly a team. His hawk had had the chance to fly free and yet he had come back to him. On his first flight.

'Look, al-Jundi. My hawk came back to me. He was free and yet he came back to me.'

'We must go back to the palace now, Your Excellency. It is not safe for you to be out until we find and apprehend that assassin,' al-Jundi said, positioning himself by his side. 'We will give your hawk to one of the falconers to take back to the Falcon House.'

'No. Daruj comes with me. I will look after him in the palace.'

'Very well, Your Excellency.'

Al-Hisham could feel his blood racing. The once tranquil hunting scene, with men and their birds, moving quietly across the fields, their dogs setting up a partridge, a pigeon, flushing out rabbits and hares, all so that the hawks could pursue and catch them, had been shattered. Now al-Hisham sat, with his hawk on his fist, within a cordon of protecting soldiers. The rest of his guard had galloped off into the trees, in pursuit of the assassin. The falconers had hooded their hawks, called their dogs to their side and were turning towards home. The hunt was over for today. A riot of feelings whirled inside al-Hisham: excitement at the attack, surprise that anyone should try to kill him in broad daylight, disappointment that the falconers were heading back to Madinat al-Zahra, delight with his hawk, concern for Ahmad, and fear that this was what being a Khalifa meant, that he would always live in danger of an attack on his life.

CHAPTER 14

Ahmad couldn't think straight for the pain in his shoulder. It radiated down his arm and across his chest. Someone had slung him onto the back of a horse and now they were galloping towards Madinat al-Zahra as fast as they could, and with every stride the arrow seemed to dig deeper into his flesh. He gritted his teeth but he couldn't hold back his groans of pain. He felt confused. It had all happened so quickly. One moment he was talking to the Khalifa and the next he was on the ground, screaming in pain. He felt a twinge of embarrassment at how he had cried out, like a child, but it was the unexpectedness of it, he told himself. He wasn't a coward. The galloping horse leapt over a low hedge and the pain in his shoulder intensified. God, but it hurt like hell. He screwed his eyes shut to hold back the tears. What would the soldier think of him if he saw him crying.

'Hang on in there, lad,' the soldier said. 'Not far now.'

He must have cried out when they jumped the hedge. How embarrassing. Thank goodness Baba wasn't there to see what a baby he was.

After what seemed an endless journey, the horse slowed to a walking pace as they entered the North Gate and then began to canter gently towards the hospital. By then his shoulder was on fire and he knew it would get worse because they still had to remove the arrow.

'Here we are,' said the soldier, reining in his mount and leaping down. 'Hey you, boy. Run and find Abu al-Zahrawi. Tell him the Khalifa has commanded that he come and attend to this man, right away. And you over there, take this horse to the stables.'

The soldier lifted him off the horse as though he weighed no more than a sack of chicken feed and carried him into the hospital.

'This way,' said a young man in a grey tunic. 'Put him down on that mat. The doctor will see to him as soon as he can. He is very busy today.'

'I don't care how busy he is. The Khalifa's orders are that this man should be seen immediately and by Doctor Abu al-Zahrawi and no-one else.'

The soldier laid Ahmad carefully on a low bed, alongside other injured patients. It was such a relief to be lying down and still. The pain in his shoulder had dulled to a persistent ache, a red fire that dug deep into him instead of the exploding white bursts of torture he had felt on the ride to the hospital. Ahmad closed his eyes and was about to drift off into sleep when a familiar voice said, 'Ahmad. What the hell has happened to you?'

He opened his eyes to see his brother, Qasim, staring down at him.

'How did this happen?' his brother asked.

'I don't know. One minute I was teaching the Khalifa how to take the quarry away from Daruj and the next I was on the floor with an arrow in me.'

Qasim bent over him. 'This doesn't look too bad but we need to remove it carefully, in case it's nicked an artery.'

'We are waiting for Abu al-Zahrawi,' said the soldier. 'He will attend to him.'

'But he isn't here at the moment. He's lecturing to some students.'

'Then tell him that we are waiting. It is the Khalifa's command.'

'I will send someone to tell him but, in the meantime, at least let me clean up my brother's wound a little and give him something for the pain.'

Ahmad knew the soldier would refuse. He had his orders and he would stick to them, regardless whether Ahmad bled to death waiting for this doctor to appear.

'Look, it was Abu al-Zahrawi who taught me. I will only do what he would do. I am a qualified doctor,' Qasim continued.

'You are a young man. He is a famous surgeon. His fame is known throughout the country and in other lands. He is the Khalifa's physician and he must come and treat this boy, himself. Those are my orders.'

'Very well. Just hang in there, Ahmad. I will be right back.'

Ahmad closed his eyes and tried to will himself to ignore the pain, which had now returned with relentless intensity.

***

He must have passed out because the next thing he knew someone was by his bed.

'This is the patient?'

'Yes, *sayyad*. He is a falconer and he was hunting with the Khalifa when he got shot,' said the soldier. 'The Khalifa wants you to treat him.'

'So, I see.'

He cut away Ahmad's shirt and bent down to take a closer look at his wound. 'Well, young man, I expect this hurts, doesn't it? You seem to have lost a lot of blood but you were very lucky, a little lower and the arrow would have gone right through your heart.'

The doctor was an imposing figure in a white turban and white robes. He had a thick black beard and a narrow moustache covered his top lip. His eyes were clear and piercing but his voice was gentle and he smiled at Ahmad when he said, 'So you are Qasim's brother. Well you are very fortunate to have such a good doctor in your family. Qasim was one of my better students.' He looked across at Qasim, who stood at a respectful distance, watching and waiting. 'But don't worry, young man, your injury doesn't look too serious. I will remove the arrow and stitch up your wound, and you should be as good as new in a few days.'

He turned to Qasim. 'We will take him into the operating room. Arrange that please, while I get ready,' he said and walked out.

Operating room? Ahmad felt sick. What was he going to do to him? Why didn't he just pull the arrow out and bandage him up?

'Hey, don't worry, little brother. He knows what he's doing. He has treated thousands of wounds like yours. Once, it would almost certainly have been fatal if you were shot in the chest with an arrow, either from the trauma of removing it or from blood poisoning, but Doctor Zahwari has developed a special technique for removing arrow heads without causing damage to the patient. You're lucky that he is here to help you. Now do you think you can walk?'

'Yes, of course,' Ahmad said, pushing himself up, although his legs felt as though they would collapse under him.

'Good. Here, lean on me. You know Mama will be furious when she hears what you've been up to.'

'It wasn't my fault I got shot. I was just doing my job.'

'I know. But she won't see it like that.'

His brother walked him slowly into a large airy room, with a fountain of fresh water in the centre. Beds covered in white sheets were lined up in two rows, one either side of the room and about half of them were occupied with patients, all wearing identical long white shirts. Ahmad could hear some gentle music coming from the garden, although he could not see the musicians. There was an air of calm about the room, accentuated by the scent of the fragrant herbs that grew in pots outside the open windows: lavender, lemon balm and valerian were among those that he could recognise from his mother's small herb garden. Inside the room an orderly was going from bed to bed handing the patients bowls of food.

'It's meal time,' Qasim explained.

He led him out of the room and down a passage into a smaller room, where Doctor al-Zahrawi was waiting for him. The doctor had changed out of his white robes and now wore a simple grey tunic. Another man, also in a grey tunic was setting out some metal instruments on a table. Everything was very clean and smelled of something Ahmad could not place, but was so astringent that he could feel his eyes watering.

'Drink this, young man. It will calm you while I am removing the arrow,' the physician said, handing him a glass of reddish-brown liquid.

Ahmad drank. It was not unpleasant, tasting a little of anise and lavender.

'Have you washed the table down with a solution of calendula?' he asked his assistant.

'Yes, Doctor.'

'And prepared the hare's blood?'

Ahmad was startled. What on earth was that for?

'Don't worry,' whispered his brother. 'We always sprinkle that on the wound at the end, to help it heal.'

'Right, then let's get him on the table where I can get a good look at him,' the doctor said.

Ahmad felt rather light headed. The pain in his shoulder did not seem so bad anymore and he wanted to say that he was all right and could go home now, when there was a sudden sharp stab under his collar bone and he felt the arrowhead being pulled out. It made him feel sick.

'Oh. Is that it?' he asked, drowsily. 'Can I go now?'

'In a little while. We have to stitch you up first. You don't want to bleed all over my clean hospital, do you?' the doctor said, soothingly. 'Qasim, pass me the yarrow; we need to stop this bleeding. The arrow head was deeper than I thought but we seem to have got it out cleanly. Yes, that's better. Right, now let's stitch him up.'

Ahmad watched as his brother passed a needle and some silk thread to the surgeon, who began straight away to sew up his wound with small neat stitches. He felt he was watching all this from far away. It was like watching his mother sewing clothes for the baby. The needle went in and the needle came out, the needle went in and the needle came out. He was so tired. He couldn't keep his eyes open any longer.

'Has he passed out?' he heard Qasim ask and his voice seemed to be a long way off.

***

When Ahmad woke he was lying in one of the beds in the large room and he was wearing a white shirt, like all the other patients. He tried to sit up but the pain in his shoulder gripped him like a vice and held him down.

'You're awake at last,' his brother said. 'I thought you were going to sleep for a week. How do you feel?'

'Sore. I feel as though I have been chewed up by a wolf. I hurt more than I did when I arrived. Is that right? Shouldn't I feel better now?'

'Patience, my little brother. You need time for the shoulder to heal. A couple of days and you'll be out of here.'

'A couple of days? Why can't I go home now? Mama will take care of me.'

'Doctor al-Zahrawi says that you need to stay. We want to make sure there are no complications and that the wound doesn't become infected.'

'Did you really sprinkle me with hare's blood?' Ahmad asked with a smile. 'Or was it just one of your silly jokes?'

'It's no joke. But it's not what you're thinking. We don't cut up hares and drip their blood all over you. The hare's blood has been dried and ground into a fine powder. It's very good for stopping an infection and speeding up the healing process. We use it all the time and nobody has died because of it, yet, little brother.' He bent down and hugged Ahmad.

'Hey, that hurts,' Ahmad said.

'Sorry. It's just that I'm so glad you're going to be all right,' Qasim said, looking serious for a moment. 'Look, I have to go home now but I'll come back in the morning.'

'What will you tell Mama?'

'That you've got into trouble again, of course.'

Ahmad lay back and looked up at the plastered ceiling above his head. It had been designed to represent the night sky and was covered with thousands of tiny diamond shaped stars that twinkled in the light of the oil lamps that were now being lit, one by one. He could hear the music quite clearly now and as he listened he felt himself growing sleepier and sleepier. Only one question remained in his head. Who had shot him and why?

CHAPTER 15

Subh was worried and angry. How had this attack on her son happened? What had al-Jundi been thinking of, to let the Khalifa go out on a hunt, with only forty men to protect him? She had sent for him. She wanted to hear his side of the story. All she could get from al-Hisham was a load of gibberish about his damn hawk. Who was behind it? Her immediate thoughts were al-Mansur, but he was away on the *jihad* against the Christians. She sighed. Her feelings for this man were becoming more and more complicated. She needed him in more ways than one; her position and the safety of her son depended on his protection and her love for him was turning into an obsession, but still she did not trust him, not completely. Each day he became more and more powerful and certainly more popular. His campaigns brought new riches to the country. He had convinced the people that he was the man who would save them from the Infidel, despite the fact that the country had lived in peace with the Christians on their borders for as long as she could remember. He had convinced them that he was a pious man who followed the laws of Islam religiously. He had convinced both them and her that he was doing all this for the Khalifa and that one day her son would become the sole ruler. This was what she hoped but, every so often, doubts about al-Mansur's true ambitions made her wonder. He was no longer the quiet, young man who had come into her bed filled with gratitude for her help and avowing undying love for her; he was more confident now, more arrogant, more powerful and, what still caused her breast to burn with jealousy, he was married to a beautiful young girl.

'*Sayyida*, the soldier al-Jundi is here to speak with you,' said Afra, taking the opportunity to remove the uneaten bowl of fruit from the table by Subh's side.

'Send him in.'

Now here was a man she thought she could trust. He had been by her husband's side for many years. She had been so sure he would take care of al-Hisham for her. She was disappointed.

'Your Highness, you wanted to speak to me?' al-Jundi said, bowing low before her.

'Yes. I want you to tell me how it was possible that an unknown assassin managed to shoot an arrow at my son, while he was on a hunting trip.'

'I am profoundly upset about what happened, *Sayyida*. My men are searching for the assassin as we speak. He will not escape. We intend to catch him alive and to find out who is behind this outrageous assault. An attack on the Khalifa is an attack on all of us.'

'So you think this was planned? Not just a random attempt on my son's life?'

'There was nothing random about it, *Sayyida*. It was most definitely planned. If the attacker was a stranger to the city, someone had to have told him about the Khalifa's movements. Someone is behind this and we need to find out who it is.'

'But how will you find this murderer?'

'Leave that to us, *Sayyida*. Just rest assured that we will find him and we will deal with him. Your son will come to no harm.'

'I rely on you, ibn Qasim, to protect my son. I will be spending more and more time in Córdoba and I need someone here that I can depend on.'

'Yes, *Sayyida*.' He paused and added, 'I see that some parts of the court have been transferred to Córdoba, already. When will the Khalifa be moving?'

'Oh, not for some time. He is too young at the moment. The Regents have agreed that it is best for him to stay here, where he is safe, and not to get involved in matters of state until he is old enough to understand them.'

A worried look flashed across the soldier's face as he listened to her words. One moment it was there and then it was gone.

'What is it? Is something worrying you?'

'No, *Sayyida*. It's just that when the Regents cut the number of Palace Guards stationed here I thought it meant that the Khalifa would soon be going to Córdoba.'

'They have reduced the number of Palace Guards? Why?'

'I do not know *Sayyida*. It is a strange that they would do that. And now there has been an attack on his life.'

'Do you think he is in danger, here in Madinat al-Zahra? Tell me.'

'No, *Sayyida*. He is in no more danger here than he would be in Córdoba. I merely thought that he would be taking up some of his duties soon.'

'He is only a boy. There is time enough for him to attend to duties. For now he can enjoy his childhood, play with his toys, his birds, amuse himself.'

The soldier's face was impassive now, as he stood before her in silence.

'Let me know as soon as you have discovered the perpetrator of this act. You have the arrow. Find out whom it belongs to.'

'There is nothing on the arrow to identify the owner, *Sayyida*. Nevertheless, we will find him. I promise you.'

'Very well. Keep me informed,' she said, waving her hand at him in dismissal.

She had not berated the soldier as she had originally intended because something in his old eyes convinced her that he would continue to protect her son, no matter what happened. She did not want to alienate a man like that. She had an increasing suspicion that her son was going to need all the friends he could get if al-Mansur's power continued to grow.

'Afra. Bring me an infusion of anise; my stomach is upset this morning.'

She lay on her couch, richly covered with blue satin and multi-coloured silks, the cushions adorned with scarlet tassels, and gazed through the open door at the peacocks greedily pecking up seeds from the lawn. This was her home now; all this luxury was hers. She would let nothing happen to take that away from her. She had earned it all; every gold plate, every silver bangle, every leather sandal, every tunic, every robe, every carved ivory jewellery box, every diamond ring, every emerald anklet, every tapestry on her walls, every rug that covered the floors of her splendid rooms had been given to her because of what she had achieved.

***

Yamut had been informed of the plan; the Royal Wife had seen to that. He promised to help Subh in any way he could. First he had obtained the books she requested and, for the last few months, she had been learning as much as she could about poetry. Yamut had even brought in an eminent scholar to discuss the poets and their works with her. Now she felt ready to meet the Khalifa and Yamut had already prepared the way for her. Tonight was the night. She was to go to his rooms and dance and sing for him, like any other concubine, but then she was to engage him in conversation. Her heart was beating fast. What if her plan went wrong? He was the second most powerful man in the land and, if she overstepped the mark, he could have her thrown out, or worse if he thought she was trying to manipulate him. She could hardly tell him it was all his mother's idea.

'Are you nervous?' Zahr asked her, as she adjusted the fine silk veil that covered Subh's face.

'What do you think? I've never been with a man before.'

'Don't worry; he probably won't want to do anything to you. I expect you'll just sit there and listen to him talk about his boring poets until he gets tired of you and sends you away.'

'If he isn't interested in women, why does he agree to have them sent to his room? Why doesn't he tell Yamut not to bother him?'

'I don't know. Maybe he thinks it is expected of him. Maybe his father insists on it. After all, having a harem of a thousand beautiful women is a sign of status; it tells everyone how rich you are and how important. It's like all those damned birds he has; it's all for show. They say he's as interested in hunting as he is in women, but one day he will be the Khalifa and it's important that he plays the part well. Some say he would as soon be left alone with his books and not have the responsibility of being a ruler, but his father has made it clear that al-Hakim is the one to succeed him when he dies, so he has no choice.'

'How do you know all these things?' she asked, amazed at the concubine's insight into the life of the Khalifa's son.

'You hear a lot of gossip in here; the eunuchs who guard us love to chatter about what's happening in court. So remember that; if you have any secrets be careful who you tell them to, otherwise they won't be secrets for long.'

Zahr laughed and added, 'And the Royal Wife is the worst of all; she knows everything that is going on.'

'Do I look all right?' Subh asked, smoothing her tight fitting tunic into place.

The Royal Wife had sent it to her and, instead of concealing her small breasts and skinny arms, they emphasised them. She was sure she looked more like a boy than ever. Her hair was not loose like all the other concubines but tightly plaited and wound around her head like a cap; the only relief to the severity of her look was the rich embroidery on the hem of her tunic and the gossamer veil that floated over her face and shoulders.

'You look lovely, different but lovely all the same. That is a beautiful tunic and it fits you so well. Don't worry. Remember you must smile when you are with the prince.'

Smile? Subh was so nervous that she doubted that she could make her lips move, never mind smile. She was trembling inside and her mouth felt dry. She would never be able to sing if she didn't relax.

'Here, drink this infusion; it will help you to loosen up,' Zahr said, handing her a glass of warm tea.

'What is it?'

'It's just a little tea made from *asafetida*. It will settle your stomach and help your nerves,' she said, then added with a smile, 'It's also an aphrodisiac.'

Subh laughed. 'In that case, shouldn't we be giving it to the prince?'

But she drank it down anyway and, almost immediately, felt the tension leave her and a calmness spread through her body. It was going to be all right; she could do this.

'Subh, are you ready?' called Yamut.

He stood in the doorway, wearing his best robe and a skull cap on his bald head. She could swear that he looked more nervous than she did.

'Now remember, just relax and do what you have been trained to do,' he said. 'The Khalifa will not even notice you at first; you will be just another concubine that has been sent to entertain him. You need to attract his attention and then keep it.'

'Yes, Yamut; I'm ready.'

She followed him through the winding passages that linked the harem to the prince's rooms until they came to an imposing doorway; two armed guards stood outside. They recognised Yamut and one of them opened the door to allow them to enter.

'Your Highness, I have brought the girl Subh to entertain you. She is a girl from the north but she is well versed in the songs and poetry of our land and has a sweet voice. I am sure you will find her company congenial.'

A man dressed in a loose robe of peacock blue silk, lounged on a bed of richly embroidered cushions; he looked at them and lifted his hand as a signal for them to enter. As she approached she saw that the prince was a good looking man, although rather older than she had imagined. His hair was a dark auburn, but streaked with grey and worn loosely about his shoulders. A short, neat beard covered the lower part of his rather pale face. He had the same northern blood in his veins as her and it was evident in his listless blue eyes. Even from where she stood she could see he was a man doing his duty not a man about to engage in a night of passion. She didn't know whether to be relieved or disappointed.

'You may leave us, Yamut,' he said, and his voice was warm and deep.

She listened to the heavy door shut behind her and stood, waiting for the musicians to begin so that she could dance, but there was no signal from the prince so they too waited; the silence weighed down on her and her nervousness returned.

At last al-Hakim spoke. 'Come here, girl. Sit by me,' the prince commanded.

Nervously Subh sat on the couch next to the heir to the kingdom of al-Andalus. She could not believe this was happening to her.

'Tell me your name.'

'Subh, Your Highness.'

'Well Subh, how are you going to entertain me tonight?' The prince was polite, but he could not disguise his boredom with the whole procedure.

'I can sing to you, Your Highness or I can recite some poetry.'

'Very well, recite me a poem,' he replied, stifling a yawn.

It was obvious he had no interest in her and her accomplishments, but she was not going to give up. The

Royal Wife had made it quite clear what the rewards were for anyone who could produce an heir and Subh was determined that she would be the one to do so. One way or another she would make this man desire her.

'I know many poems, Your Highness. Would you like something by Ibn abd Rabbihi? He was a favourite of my old mistress and she taught me many of his works.'

The boredom fell from his eyes and he leaned towards her. 'Ah, so you are familiar with the poet Rabbihi?'

'Of course, my lord; he is a son of Córdoba and was he not born of a freed slave that belonged to one of your ancestors?'

'He was indeed, Hisham I.'

'He was a great scholar and writer,' she continued, remembering all that she had read. 'His great anthology of literature, "The Unique Necklace", contains many writings from the Eastern Islamic world.'

'That is true. So you have read it?' he asked.

She nodded demurely. She could see he was intrigued. 'It is a book that everyone should read at some time in their lives, because it contains all the culture and knowledge that has been passed down to us,' she said.

'You are right. Twenty-five sections, each named for a jewel, on everything from the art of rulership, war and diplomacy to courtship and food. It is all there. Have you read the complete works?'

'Oh no, my lord, but I have read the section entitled "The Book of the Gem." I love the proverbs that he quotes.'

'Yes, so have I,' he replied. 'It is one of my favourite pieces in the book. I also enjoyed "The Middle Jewel".'

'The thirteenth section?'

'Yes, that's right,' he said, approvingly. 'You know it's hard to believe when you read it, that Rabbihi never travelled to the east. He spent all his life in Córdoba, never leaving the country once.'

'I was surprised that he did not include the work of any Andalusian poets in the book, only those that he had written himself.'

'Maybe he didn't like the competition,' the prince said, with a chuckle. 'Have you read the epic poem "Urjuza"?'

'The one that eulogises the exploits of your father Abd al-Rahman III? Yes, I have; it is at the end of "The Second Adorable Jewel" on khalifas, their histories and battles. It is magnificent and shows how al-Rahman III is a true and worthy khalifa.'

Al-Hakim seemed delighted with her comments and smiled and said, 'Come, Subh, we have talked enough. Sing me something. I would like to hear this sweet voice that Yamut has praised so highly.'

He raised his hand and the musicians, who had been standing in the background, waiting for the moment they were required, picked up their instruments and began to play. Subh's heart was beating so loudly that she feared it would drown out her song. Her plan was working; she had captured his interest, now she just had to retain it.

***

Afra glided silently across the floor and placed the glass of warm anise on the table.

'This will settle your stomach, *Sayyida*. I expect it is because you have been worried about the Khalifa. The nerves in our stomachs always react badly when we are worried.'

'Thank you Afra. Do you remember all those books I used to read to my husband?'

'The ones by the poets? Yes, I remember them.'

'Can you find them and bring them to me. I think reading them again might help my nerves. Poetry is very calming.'

'Very well, *Sayyida*.'

CHAPTER 16

Al-Jundi walked back to the *Dar al-Jund*, where his men were stationed. He had expected to suffer the *Sayyida's* fury over the assassination attempt, but instead she had been relatively calm. Still that did not stop him blaming himself for what had occurred. His son had been shot, could easily have been killed; a hands-width lower and the arrow would have entered his heart. Al-Jundi felt himself turn cold at the thought of losing Ahmad. Not only that, but an attempt had been made on the Khalifa's life, the young man he had sworn to protect. How had it happened? He was certain that this was a planned attack rather than an opportune attempt, but who knew that al-Hisham was leaving the palace that evening? He never went anywhere. How did someone know that he would be going on the hunt? And how did he know the exact spot where the Khalifa would be hunting? Was there a spy in their midst? Had the killer followed them? Or was he already lying in wait for them when they arrived at the foothills? All these questions would have to be answered if he was to discover the name of the assassin and, more importantly, who had employed him, because he was certain it was not the work of one individual.

He entered the *Dar al-Jund,* and went straight to his office, a small room situated close to the office of General Ghálib. The General too was on the campaign, in fact almost all of the army and its commanders were hundreds of miles away. If there was an attack on the city there were few men left to protect it, only his contingent of soldiers and the depleted Palace Guard, but with them he was sure he could at least defend the palace. He brushed the thought away. He was not a commander; he was a simple soldier and his immediate concern was to find this killer.

The young *nazir* on duty jumped to attention as al-Jundi entered his office.

'Soldier, go and round up all my men. I want to talk to them on the parade ground in ten minutes.'

'Yes, *Quaid.*'

Although al-Jundi had been given the title of *quaid* by al-Hakim many years before, he had never led a whole corps of men into battle; he had only a small contingent under his command but they were excellent men. Al-Rashid had been as good as his word and together they had identified a group of some two hundred men whom he felt he could rely on. These made up the Khalifa's new personal guard, and the remainder of the contingent, some eight hundred men, were said to be sound, experienced soldiers. He had been sure he could rely on their loyalty. So who had betrayed them?

He waited until he knew the parade ground was full and then he strode out. Although it was still only midmorning, the late summer sun was beating down on the rows of silent men; he noticed the sweat gathering on the foreheads of those nearest to him. He climbed onto a small dais so that he could see his men clearly, and began to speak.

'You have all heard the grave news about the attack on our young Khalifa. I am ashamed, indeed mortified, that such a thing could have happened under our watch. That an assassin could creep into the presence of the Khalifa without our knowledge is unforgivable. You men were specially selected for your vigilance, your honesty, your loyalty to the throne and, above all, your trustworthiness,' he said, then paused before continuing, 'I admit, I am disappointed in you. We have all failed in our basic duty, which is to protect the Khalifa, and I do not exclude myself from this. It was only the intervention of Allah who saved our ruler from certain death. But we shall find this assassin, and we will deal with him according to our law. *Insha'Allah*.'

He stopped and stared at the rows of soldiers. No-one moved; they stared ahead of them, impassively. Maybe they were expecting some recrimination, penalties, confinement to barracks, a reduction in pay. What good would any of that do? He didn't want to punish them; he wanted them to care as much about the Khalifa's safety as he did.

'But there will be no recriminations, this time. Instead I expect you all to be more vigilant, to be on your guard at all times,' he continued. 'Remember, the Khalifa must never be left alone and unprotected for a moment. The peace and security of this country rests in our hands.'

He turned to the *naqib* in charge of his hand-picked contingent and said, 'Ibn Hassan, I want to speak to you. Dismiss the men and follow me.'

He watched as the soldiers marched out in perfect formation, and then returned to his small office. 'Sit down, soldier. I have much to say.' He pulled off his cloak and unbuckled his sword then turned to Ibn Hassan and said, 'I want you to speak to your men and find out what they know about any strangers in the city. Someone has been skilful enough to find out about the Khalifa's movements and infiltrate the hunting party. He could not do this without help. There is a traitor in our midst. Find him and find out what he knows.'

'Very well, *Quaid*. I have just the man to do that job.'

'Good. And report directly to me. Someone is trying to get rid of the Khalifa and they have a reason for doing so. Find the reason and we will find the real assassin.'

'You think this was planned, *Quaid*?'

'Without a doubt. What, you think someone just happened to be walking in the woods and decided to shoot the Khalifa? With forty soldiers guarding him? No, this has been carefully planned, but, luckily for us, not carefully enough. Be assured we will find the culprit and drag him before the judge.'

'But who would want the Khalifa dead? The only pretender to the throne was the old Khalifa's brother and he's dead.'

'That's what we have to find out. I am relying on you, Hassan. Chose your best men for the job and let's find this killer. Our reputation stands or falls on this.'

'Very well, *Quaid*.' The *naqib* waited for his commanding officer to dismiss him and then left.

Al-Jundi prayed that his soldiers would find out something; it made him uneasy to think that this assassin was out there, waiting for another chance to kill the young Khalifa. Ibn Hassan's words intrigued him. If al-Mughira was dead, then who stood to gain from the Khalifa's death? Not Mughira's sons; they were far too young. Only one name came to mind, al-Mansur.

***

It was well past midday when al-Jundi arrived home. All his sons, with the exception of Rafiq, who was away on the campaign to the north, were seated at the table, waiting for him to arrive so that they could start eating the pigeon casserole that their mother had made.

'*As-salama alaykum*, my children,' he said, sitting down beside them.

'*Wa alaykum e-salam*, father,' they chorused.

'I see you are home, son. How are you feeling?' he asked Ahmad, who was swathed in bandages and sitting with his brothers.

'The doctor said I was very lucky, and in a week I should be well enough to go back to work.'

'Mama has put some of that bitter stuff on it,' little Asim added.

Al-Jundi looked at his wife.

'Myrrh. I applied a paste of myrrh to the wound,' admitted Amina.

'She doesn't trust doctors,' said Qasim, with a smile. 'Not even the Khalifa's own physician.'

'People have been using myrrh for centuries,' she said, putting a plate of food in front of her husband. 'And, by the way, this casserole is made from a pigeon caught by the Khalifa's own falcon.'

'Was there enough to make a meal for all of us? al-Jundi asked. 'The bird seemed to be tearing it apart when I last saw it. I'm surprised there was anything left.'

'Well, I added some other things, too,' she said with a light laugh.

Amina was a good cook, but she did not always share her recipes, many of which originated from her mother, and al-Jundi suspected it was best not to enquire too closely at what went into her tasty stews.

'Have you found the assassin yet?' asked Ahmad.

'Not yet. I'm glad you're here; I want to ask you what you remember about the incident,' al-Jundi said.

'I don't remember anything, Baba. I was handing the knife to the Khalifa and I dropped it. That was when he jumped down from his horse to get it for me. I was looking down all the time.'

'So you saw nothing?'

The boy shook his head.

'What about earlier, did you see anyone you didn't recognise? Anyone that shouldn't have been there?'

'I don't think so, Baba. I knew most of the falconers well. Wait, there was one man I hadn't seen before, but I didn't think it was strange at the time because he was talking to ibn al-Attar, and I've known him for a long time.'

'Who is this ibn al-Attar?'

'He's one of the senior men in the Falcon House. He's worked there for twenty years. I'm sure he would have had nothing to do with the attack on the Khalifa.'

'Tell me about the other man, the one you hadn't seen before. What did he look like?'

'Oh dear, Baba, I'm not sure. He was younger than you. He had a beard, a bit sparse and cut short. Oh yes, there was one thing; he had a scar on his cheek; it was partially hidden by his beard but it was definitely a scar. I remember wondering if a hawk had attacked him at some time.'

'A scar? Didn't you tell me about someone with a scar, who was in the hospital where you work, Qasim?'

'Yes, Baba, but that man didn't have a beard.'

'He was a stranger, right?'

'Yes, no-one knew who he was or where he came from. But there was one thing I didn't tell you, Baba. You remember I said we were keeping him in for a few days to make sure that he was all right? Well, according to my colleague, soon after I left, he went in to check on him and he was gone. He'd taken his weapons and left. Not a word of thanks or anything, just disappeared as mysteriously as he arrived.'

'Do you think it could be the same man?'

'Well, he was thin, aged about thirty, possibly of Berber descent, but he was clean shaven.'

'That could be him,' said Ahmad. 'He wore no cap, just had a pointed hood on his *djellaba*, like a Berber.'

'He could have grown the beard in a couple of days,' suggested Qasim.

'Or it was fake,' cried little Asim, clapping his hands together at his cleverness in having such an original idea.

'Eat your food, Asim, or I will give it to the dog,' his mother said.

'Whichever it is, I think we need to find this scar-faced man. Even if he is not the culprit, he may know something about the attack.'

He picked up his spoon and began to eat slowly, lost in thought, then he asked, 'Did he have a hawk with him?'

His son looked at him in surprise. 'No, he didn't. You're so clever, Baba. He had no birds with him but he had a dog, a skinny dog. Not a hunting dog. At least not one of ours and completely untrained. I think it was probably a stray. That's how I came to notice him; the dog was trying to take a hare from one of the falconers.'

'Did you see anything else? Did he have a bow or any other weapons?'

'I didn't see any, Baba. Just the dog. He'd brought it to flush out the rabbits.'

So that was how he had managed to enter the hunting party unnoticed. But that still left the question, how did he know that the Khalifa would be there on that particular day?

'One more question, Ahmad, and then I will leave you in peace. Think carefully. Did you tell anyone that the Khalifa would be going to fly his hawk that evening?'

His son looked down at his half-eaten plate of food; his face was scarlet. 'Do you think it's my fault?' he asked, barely holding back a sob.

'I didn't say that. I just need to know if you told anyone about the Khalifa's intention to go hunting with you.'

'Well, Baba, it's not like that. The Khalifa has wanted to go out on a hunt for months, but he has had to wait until the bird was ready. So anyone could have worked out that he would be hunting with us, soon.'

'But that specific evening. Who knew beforehand?'

'The Grand Falconer knew because I had to have his permission; you knew and your soldiers.'

'Besides the soldiers. Did anyone else in the Falcon House know about it?'

'Ibn al-Attar might have guessed. I said that I needed to have some caged pigeons that I could loose because we had a falcon that was still on the creance. I didn't tell him it belonged to the Khalifa. Honestly I didn't.' Ahmad was on the point of tears; al-Jundi could see him struggling to hold them back. 'But he could have worked it out. The Khalifa's falcon was the only one that still flew with a creance; all the others could fly free,' he managed to continue, at last.

'And ibn al-Attar would have known that?'

Ahmad nodded.

'Well, it could just be a coincidence, but I must look into it.'

'Will I lose my job?' Ahmad sobbed.

'I don't know, son. We will have to see what your grandfather has to say.'

He was beginning to understand how the attack happened, but what he still didn't know was who was behind it. They had to find this man with the scar on his face but, even if he was still in Madinat al-Zahra, it wouldn't be easy; in a city of that size, it would be like chasing shadows.

He was mopping up the last of the pigeon stew with a hunk of bread when there was a loud knocking on the outside door.

'Who can that be at this hour?' he said, standing up, the bread still in his hand.

'I'll go, Baba. You finish your dinner,' said Qasim.

A moment later, he returned, followed by two of the Palace Guards.

'What is this all about?' al-Jundi said, standing up again. 'What are you doing here at my house?'

'We're sorry *Quaid*, but we have come to arrest your son.'

'My son?'

For a moment he could not understand what they were saying. Which son were they talking about? Did they mean Rafiq?

'Rafiq is away, fighting for his country.'

'Not Rafiq. Your son Ahmad, the falconer. He is wanted for the attempted murder of the Khalifa. We have orders from the Regent, al-Mansur himself.'

'What nonsense is this? My son was injured in the attempt on the Khalifa's life. Everyone knows that.'

Ahmad was standing next to him, his face as white as the snow on the high mountains.

'I can't say anything about that, *Quaid*. We have our orders. We are to arrest Ahmad ibn Makoud for collusion in the attempted murder of Khalifa al-Hisham II.'

'It's a lie,' shouted Ahmad. 'The Khalifa is my friend. I wouldn't do anything to hurt him. It was an accident.'

'Please come with us,' the taller of the Palace Guards said, ignoring the boy's protestations.

'Don't worry, Ahmad. I'll come with you. This is obviously some dreadful mistake. We'll soon get it sorted out.'

Amina was already holding his red cape and held his sword out to him.

'Thank you. Don't worry. We'll have this sorted out in a short while and then we'll be home.' He leaned down and kissed his wife's cheek then followed his son and the Palace Guards out into the street.

His son looked so young and vulnerable as he walked unsteadily between the two guards. He was still weak from his wound and it showed. Well he would make sure that they treated him well until it could all be sorted out.

When he arrived at the prison he went straight to the *nazir* in charge of the prison and explained what had happened.

'*Quaid*, I'm sorry. There is nothing we can do. Our orders were to arrest him and hold him here until the Regent decides to send him for trial.'

'I thought the Regent was away on the campaign?'

'He arrived back in Córdoba, last night.'

'But my son's innocent. How could you think otherwise? He was shot by an arrow. He could have been killed.'

'They say that it was his idea to take the Khalifa hunting that evening,' the *nazir* whispered. He was one of the longer serving members of the Palace Guard and had known al-Jundi for many years.

'But he didn't tell anyone about it.'

'Nevertheless someone knew that the Khalifa would be there. It doesn't look good for your son, even if he is innocent.'

'He is innocent, damn you.'

It seemed that there was nothing he could do except try to find out for himself the name of the would-be assassin.

'Just let me speak to him for a moment, please,' he said.

'It's against orders. You know that.'

It was true. No-one was allowed to speak to the prisoner until he came before the judge.

'I'll only be a minute. He's just a lad. I want to reassure him that everything will be all right. That's all. Come on. You know me. I'm not going to give him my sword or anything stupid.'

'All right, but be quick and leave your weapon here with me. You know I'll be demoted back to the ranks if anyone finds out.'

'Good man. I won't forget this.'

***

Ahmad could not believe that this was happening. He felt sick, and the taste of his mother's pigeon stew rose in his throat as bitter as gall. Why would they think he would hurt the Khalifa? Who had suggested such a thing? Surely not the Khalifa himself.

The soldiers marched him through the streets towards the *alcazaba*. He felt the stares of his neighbours burning into him and wanted to pull the hood of his *djellaba* over his head, but his hands were tied behind his back, so all he could do was bend his head and look fixedly at the ground in front of him. It seemed to be an interminable walk to the prison and when he arrived, the soldiers had pushed him into a small, dark cell and slammed the door behind him. The sound of that door clanging into place was like a blow to his body. He didn't deserve this. He rubbed his shoulder; it was sore from the rough handling by the soldiers and it had started to bleed again, a red stain spreading across his clean bandages. Where was Baba? Why didn't he stop them? He must realise that Ahmad was innocent, but all he said was 'Don't worry.'

How could he not worry? He was accused of trying to kill the Khalifa. That meant the death penalty. Baba wouldn't be able to protect him then.

He looked about him. He was in a cell three paces by three paces, and there was a small barred window which let in a narrow shaft of light. It the corner was a rush mat for his bed and a bowl for washing. Nothing else. A hole in the ground served as a latrine. He sat down on the bed and sobbed. It was just too much. First he had been shot and now he was wrongfully accused of trying to hurt the Khalifa. What was happening to him? It was an awful nightmare. If only he could awake from it.

The sound of someone talking outside his cell, made him sit up. He rubbed his eyes with his sleeve and strained to hear who it was. Was that Baba's voice? Had he come to get him out? Surely he could do something; he was an officer of the Palace Guards. He could tell them to release him, couldn't he? Yes, it was his father and he was talking to one of the guards.

The next minute he heard the key in the lock and the heavy wooden door swung open. It was Baba. At last.

Al-Jundi slipped through the open door and into the cell where Ahmad still sat hunched on the floor. He hugged his son to him and said, 'I haven't got long, so listen carefully. Don't say anything other than what you have already said, that you are innocent.'

'Have you come to take me home, Baba?' he asked.

'No, my son. You may be here for a while but don't worry. I'll make sure you get decent food and treated well.

Your mother will bring you something every day. In the meantime I am going to find the bastard that shot you. I promise you that I will get you out of here as soon as I can. Now, don't cry, Ahmad. You must be strong. Remember to say your prayers every day and ask Allah to protect you.'

Ahmad clung to his father and sobbed. 'Don't leave me in here, Baba. Take me home, please.'

'Be strong, my son,' his father repeated. 'I will find a way of getting you home, I promise.' He hugged his son once more and strode out of the cell, leaving Ahmad alone with his fears.

***

It tore al-Jundi apart to see his young son in prison, unfairly accused. But he would remain focused on what was important and that was finding out who had tried to kill the Khalifa and who was behind it. He would go first to ibn al-Attar and see what he had to say.

The falconer was unable to help al-Jundi. He said he did not know the man, but that his name was Fida and he was a cousin of an old friend of ibn al-Attar, from his home town in Antequera, and that he needed work for a few weeks. He had given him some temporary work in the Falcon House, doing odd jobs, helping with the preparations for the move to Córdoba. He had been working there for more than two weeks when they went hunting with the Khalifa. He couldn't remember anything unusual about him, except the fact that he had not turned up for work on the day after the attack, and he hadn't seen him since.

Al-Jundi was furious. 'You didn't think to tell anyone about this man? A stranger approaches you for casual work and then disappears immediately after there has been an attack on the Khalifa. Didn't you find this strange?'

'No, *Quaid*. I never connected the two things. This man was from my *pueblo*. I have known his cousin for years; we grew up together.'

'But you didn't know this man?'

'No.'

'And you didn't recognise him, even though Antequera is not a large town.'

Ibn al-Attar shook his head; he looked mortified at the thought that it could be his fault that the assassin had gained access to the hunting party.

'Do you know for sure that he is related to your cousin? Or that his name is really Fida?'

'No, *Quaid*.'

'What did you talk about with him?'

'Nothing, *Quaid*. I just told him what he had to do.'

'Did he ask you any questions that seemed a bit unusual?'

'No, *Quaid*. The only thing is, when he knew we were taking the birds out to hunt, he asked if he could come with us and bring his dog.'

'The evening of the attack?'

'Yes. He hadn't been out with us before, but he said he was very keen to learn about hunting with a hawk. He said he wanted to get himself a bird to hunt rabbits and squirrels.'

'So he hadn't been hunting with you before?'

'No, Quaid. As I told you he was just employed to do odd jobs.'

'Did you notice anything unusual about him that evening?'

'Well, only that he turned up with this mangy dog. He said he was training it to flush out the birds but he hadn't done much training as far as I could see. The dog was mad. It chased everything it saw. I almost sent him and his unruly dog packing.'

'So, you didn't tell him about the Khalifa joining you, that evening?'

'No, of course not. I didn't tell anyone. I had guessed the Khalifa would be there to fly his young bird, as soon as Ahmad asked for the pigeons, but I never mentioned it to anyone. The first we knew for certain was when Ahmad arrived with him, to collect his falcon.'

Ibn al-Attar appeared to be speaking the truth. If this Fida was the one who shot Ahmad, he had prepared his plan well. He had got himself a job in the Falcon House and then waited for the Khalifa to join them, as he knew he would eventually.

'One more question, why was this man armed?'

'I didn't think he was, *Quaid*. He had a knife, but we all carry knives, so we can cut up the dead prey. But he had no bow and arrows. I'm sure of that.'

'Could he had hidden them somewhere?'

'It's possible. We often go to that same place to hunt; it's a perfect spot to try out young birds.'

'So he could have hidden his weapons in the woods, knowing that one evening you would all return to hunt and maybe the Khalifa would be with you?'

'Yes. Everyone knew that the Khalifa had taken an interest in falconry and wanted to go out to hunt. But nobody knew when.'

'And it was very likely that you would go to this particular spot to fly a young bird?'

'Yes. As I said, it is a good place for untried hawks. We always go there, particularly when they are still on a creance.'

'And would this man have known that?'

'It's possible, *Quaid*. He used to ask a lot of questions.'

'If this man turns up at the Falcon House again, or if you see or hear of him, I want you to tell me immediately. Is that clear? And keep him there until I get there.'

'Yes, *Quaid*.'

***

A week went by and still there was no sign of the man with the scar on his face, then another week and another; al-Jundi was beginning to think that the man had left the city. If that was the case, the chances of ever finding him were negligible. In the meantime, poor Ahmad languished in jail. Then one morning, when he was checking on matters of security with the *naqib* of the Khalifa's personal bodyguard, a young *nazir* came running up to him.

'Excuse me, *Quaid*. We have found him. We've caught the man with the scar. They're bringing him in now.'

'What? This is good news, soldier. Very good news. Tell them to bring him straight here. I want to look at him before we lock him up.'

'Yes, *Quaid*.'

The man they dragged before him was a wretched creature, thin as a stick, wearing a dirty, torn *djellaba* and smelling as though he'd been sleeping with the goats, which he may well have been. His beard was thick and dark but had not grown over the scar tissue on his cheek, which lay like a rotting worm along the length of his face. He looked like a beggar. Someone had done well to spot him.

'So this is the man we've been looking for,' he said. 'Hardly a king-slayer. What's your name, wretch?'

The man did not speak. He could barely stand and only remained upright because of the soldiers either side of him. His arms and legs were covered in cuts and bruises, and his head uncovered.

'Speak up. What's your name?'

'He refuses to say anything, *Quaid*. Not a word has he spoken since we caught him.'

'How did you find him, soldier?'

'It was the reward, *Quaid*. Two men, one of them a blacksmith, caught him trying to steal a horse from their yard. They remembered about the reward and, instead of just giving him a beating and sending him on his way, they tied him up and brought him to us.'

By the look of the man's condition, they had given him a beating anyway, but that was no concern of his. If they had, it was a light punishment for a horse thief.

'They did right. If this is the man who tried to kill the Khalifa, they will receive their reward,' he said then turned to the prisoner again, 'Where are you from, man? Speak up. If you are innocent, tell us so. Your continued silence condemns you.'

The man remained looking at the ground; he seemed oblivious to those around him.

'Did he have any weapons on him?' al-Jundi asked.

'He had a crossbow, but no arrows, and a large dagger. I have them here.'

He handed the weapons to al-Jundi. The crossbow was identical to those issued to his own men. This was no foreign weapon; it had originated here in Madinat al-Zahra. There were even the same markings on the handle, the insignia of the Khalifa's army. The dagger, however, was unlike any he had seen before; it was more like a short sword, similar to those they used for close combat, with a handle carved from crystal instead of wood, and engraved along the blade were the words, in Arabic: *'Allah is my only judge.'* It was an expensive item, the sort of weapon a prince or a king would own. He read the inscription again. He had seen it before.

'Who gave you this knife?' he asked. 'Where did you get it?'

Still no response from the man, who sagged like a sack of grain between his two captors.

'Lock him up. Later we will take him to Córdoba; maybe the judge can get something out of him,' al-Jundi said in exasperation. He turned to his young *nazir* and said, 'Send a man to the Falcon House to get a falconer called Ibn al-Attar. I want him to see this wretch. Then take him to the prison so that my son can identify him. I need to know if he was the man Ahmad saw in the hunting party on the day he was shot.' He lowered his voice and added, 'Take this knife and find out which family uses this motto. Then come and tell me. No-one else, mind.'

***

Ibn al-Attar confirmed that the prisoner was the same man that had introduced himself to the falconer as Fida, the cousin of his friend, and Ahmad was equally convinced that this was the man he had seen. Nevertheless, even when confronted with their accusations, the prisoner would not speak. He remained sitting on the floor of his small cell, silent and uncommunicative.

'He must be frightened of someone,' Ahmad said. 'Otherwise, why doesn't he confess? Or at least defend himself? He knows I have nothing to do with this. I had never seen him before that evening.'

'It makes no difference. The judge can deal with it now. He leaves for Córdoba this morning,' his father replied.

But it did make a difference. Unless he confessed they could not release Ahmad from the jail. It would be left to the judge to decide which of them was the guilty party or whether they were both guilty of conspiracy. He knew how the system worked; the judge did not waste much time and often people were convicted on the flimsiest evidence. For some reason his mind went back to the execution of Yusuf, his brother's best friend. He had been charged, convicted and executed within the space of a few days and he had been completely innocent. Al-Jundi knew this for a fact because it was his own brother who had committed the crime. Now Ahmad, his son was in the same position. He had to help him and quickly. It all depended on what this wretched man had to say. What reason did he have to kill the young Khalifa? As far as al-Jundi could see, his only motive was money. That was probably why he was still here in Madinat al-Zahra, weeks after the attack; he was waiting to get paid. Maybe he should have a word with the judge and suggest that they let him go, then he could get one of his men to follow him and see who his paymaster was. Al-Jundi decided he would personally go with the prisoner to Córdoba and talk to the judge.

'Get the escort guard ready and send them down to collect the prisoner. We'll leave at once,' he told his next in command. 'Keep a close eye on the Khalifa in my absence. I will be back before nightfall.'

'Yes, *Quaid.*'

'And watch my son.'

'Yes, *Quaid.*'

As soon as the escort was ready, they ushered the prisoner out into the yard. He still seemed weak and unsteady on his feet. Al-Jundi was not sure the man could make it to Córdoba on foot, even though it was barely six Arab miles. They filed out of the *Dar al-Jund,* twelve horsemen leading the way and another twelve, taking up the rear. The prisoner was safely ensconced in the middle of this small entourage, stumbling along, behind al-Jundi's horse, his hands tied in front of him and attached to a rope, which al-Jundi had fixed to his saddle. They left by the North Gate and headed out onto the Nogales Road; it would take them two hours to reach the city at this pace but al-Jundi did not want the prisoner to have the luxury of riding into Córdoba. He would make him walk every step of the way, even though it meant a slow journey for all of them.

In fact, events turned out quite differently from how he expected. The news of the assassin's capture had spread quickly and people were hurrying from their homes and places of work to get a glimpse of the accused, the man for whom there was such a generous reward. By the time the small procession had reached the outer city walls, there were crowds of people, pushing and shoving to see the man who had tried to kill their young Khalifa. Someone shouted out, 'String him up,' another, 'Death to the traitor,' and their cries were taken up and repeated by all around them. 'Why take him all the way to Córdoba?' one man shouted. 'Give him to us. We'll see he gets justice.' 'Yes,' responded the crowd. 'Give him to us.' The growing crowd of spectators was in danger of turning into an unruly mob at any moment. Al-Jundi did not want a confrontation with the citizens of Madinat al-Zahra, but he had his prisoner to protect. He shouted the command for his soldiers to unsheathe their weapons; a show of force might just make the crowd reconsider their actions. The last thing he wanted was the mob to rush them and try to take the prisoner for themselves; if anything happened to him they would never know who was behind the assassination attempt. Sure enough, at the sight of the naked steel flashing in the sunshine, the crowd dropped back a bit, but the chanting continued. He was on the point of stopping, putting the prisoner on the back of his horse and ordering his men to gallop out of there, when he heard a grunt of surprise, followed by a roar from the crowd. He turned in his saddle to see the prisoner on the ground, an arrow in his back. He had been shot.

'Halt,' he ordered the soldiers. 'Keep those people back.'

The soldiers instantly formed a protective circle around al-Jundi and the dead prisoner.

'God almighty. How the hell, did this happen?' he muttered to the soldier closest to him. 'Here, put the prisoner's body on your horse and let's get out of here. We're taking him back to camp. Right away.'

It had all happened so quickly. There was no way to know where the arrow had come from and no sign of who could have fired it. The angry mob, now quiet and subdued, appeared as shocked as he was at this unexpected outcome; one by one, people began to disperse as quickly as they could before any of them were held to blame.

Who had done this? An angry citizen? Someone who believed in instant justice? Or someone who did not want Fida, or whatever his name was, to talk to the judge. Whoever it was, it would be impossible to find him in these crowded streets. And how did that leave Ahmad? How was he going to prove that Ahmad had nothing to do with all this? There was nothing for it, he would have to appeal to the Khalifa.

***

Al-Hisham was stroking Daruj's head and whispering to him, so engrossed in his conversation with the falcon that he did not notice al-Jundi approach through the garden.

'*As-salama alaykum*, Your Majesty.'

'Al-Jundi. I was expecting to see your son. The doctor told me that he would be returning to work today. Daruj is impatient to get back to his training,' he said, with a confidential smile at his falcon.

The bird turned his head ninety degrees and looked at the young Khalifa, his eyes shining with intelligence. He was with his young master almost every hour of the day, either sitting on his fist as he walked about the garden, or resting on his perch in the Khalifa's room; he had become his constant companion.

'I am afraid Ahmad will not be coming to see you today, Your Majesty.'

'But I thought he was recovering. Is his wound worse?'

'His wound is recovering well, Your Majesty and, as you say, he planned to return to work today, but something terrible has happened. Ahmad has been arrested and put in jail.'

'Ahmad is in jail? Why? What has he done?'

'He has done nothing, Your Majesty, except try to do as you requested.'

'I don't understand.'

'They say it was he who told the man who tried to kill you that you would be hunting that evening. As such he is accused of the attempted murder of the Khalifa. If he is found guilty he will be executed.'

Al-Hisham looked at him blankly. It was as if he did not understand the gravity of al-Jundi's words.

'Oh. Thank you for telling me,' he said, turning away from al-Jundi and feeding his falcon with a tiny piece of rabbit.

'But, Your Majesty, can you do nothing to help him?'

'If he is innocent he will go free, will he not? Then he can return to work and we can resume Daruj's training.'

'But he has to prove his innocence and that is not easy. We arrested the man we think tried to murder you and hoped that he would confirm Ahmad's innocence.'

'So, that's it solved then.'

'He has been murdered?'

'Murdered? The man who tried to kill me has been murdered? You mean before he was taken to trial?'

'Yes, Your Majesty. I think someone paid him to murder you and that person did not want him to talk to the judge, in case he betrayed him. So he had him killed.'

'How did it happen? How was this man killed?'

'We were taking him to Córdoba to be tried, when he was shot in the back with an arrow.'

'So how do you know that this was the man who tried to kill me?'

'He was a stranger, Your Majesty, who inveigled his way into the Falcon House. He had been working there for a few weeks, waiting for the opportunity to get to you.'

'And you think someone paid him to kill me?'

'Yes, Your Majesty.'

'But who would do that? Who would want me dead?'

'I have been asking myself that question ever since it happened. All I know for sure is that it wasn't my son.'

'My mother said I had to be protected. She warned me that people might want to kill me,' he said, his face pale and drawn. 'Poor Ahmad, he was shot with the arrow that was meant for me. Did you find any money on this man?'

'No, Your Majesty. We think that was why he was still here in Madinat al-Zahra, waiting to be paid.'

'And nobody saw who killed him?'

Al-Jundi was embarrassed to admit it. 'No, Your Majesty. It all happened so quickly. We were distracted by the crowd.' Thin excuses for his own incompetence. He should have realised that something like that could happen and been prepared. He would never forgive himself if Ahmad was tried and found guilty.

'So the people who want me dead are still free? And you still don't know who they are?'

How could he tell the Khalifa his true suspicions? If al-Mansur got to hear of it he would make sure that al-Jundi was removed from the palace and that would only make things worse for Ahmad, so he said, 'No, Your Majesty. But we will find them, I promise you.

'I hope you do.'

'Will you try to help Ahmad, Your Majesty? He is counting on you.' He was tempted to remind the Khalifa that they wouldn't be in this mess if he hadn't insisted on leaving the palace grounds to fly his damned hawk.

The Khalifa looked at him with tears in his eyes. 'I do not know if I can do anything, al-Jundi, but I will try. This will be in the hands of the Regents and then the judge, but I will speak to my mother. She will advise me. Tell Ahmad that I will do what I can. Now, Daruj and I must get back to work.' He turned and walked further into the garden, leaving al-Jundi with a bitter taste in his mouth.

CHAPTER 17

Al-Mansur was not happy. Things were not going according to plan. True he had returned to Córdoba in triumph, with ten thousand prisoners in chains and with a hundred bullock carts laden with booty, armour, weapons, gold from the Christian churches that they had sacked in Allah's name, all to strengthen the Treasury. People had heard of their victory and come out in their thousands to line the streets into the city, cheering and shouting his name; this time he truly felt he was the Victorious One. But, instead of being hailed as the new Khalifa, and having to cry crocodile tears for the untimely death of al-Hisham, he learned instead of the failure of his plot to get rid of him. It was unthinkable; the child was still alive and well, and now the security around the young Khalifa would have be tighter than ever. At least no-one would be able to link him to it; the only man who knew of his connection was waiting to greet him, his long-time servant, Abbas.

Now al-Mansur would have to reconsider what action to take. Perhaps he had been too precipitous. Perhaps it would have been better to leave the young Khalifa in place; after all, it was a title in nothing but name. He could continue to increase his own power without anyone becoming aware of what was really happening. They would merely see a well-meaning Regent ensuring the safety of the realm. All he would have to do was isolate the Khalifa, cutting him off from anyone who could help him take over the reins of power. If he started now, while al-Hisham was a child, by the time he was grown, the scene would be set for al-Mansur to rule in his place. He would need to be subtle about it otherwise the boy's mother would incite the people to help her son. Yes, he would use this abortive attempt on the young Khalifa's life as an excuse to increase the security around him, effectively making him a prisoner in his own palace.

'Welcome home, my Lord,' said Abbas, stepping forward to greet him. 'Your wife and child are waiting inside.'

'*As-salama alaykum*, Abbas. I'm sure you have much to tell me. Wait until I have spoken to my wife and then come to my room and we will talk.'

'Very well, my Lord.'

He was looking forward to seeing his young bride again. News had already reached him that she had borne a son in his absence. Allah was indeed looking favourably on him.

'*Ahlan*, my husband. I am pleased to see you home, safe and well,' Ismá said, shyly.

'*Ahlan wa sahlan*, wife. You look well. And is this my new son? What a strapping child he is.'

He took the baby from her and held him up so that he could get a good look at him; he had a round chubby face, like most babies, but his dark eyes were keen and, al-Mansur could swear that when the child opened them and looked straight at him, he recognised him as his father. Yes, he would establish a new dynasty for this child. The Omeyyads had ruled for long enough; they were weak now, grown soft with luxury and too much learning, their blood tainted with homosexuality, their fire extinguished, their lust for battle dwindling. Now was his time; he and his descendants would make sure that the world quaked at the name of al-Andalus.

'He looks like you, my Lord,' Ismá said.

'Have you named him?'

'Not yet, my Lord.'

'Good, we will call him Abd al-Malik, servant of the king.'

'A good name, my Lord and maybe, in time, he will become a king, himself.'

Indeed. She was not as dumb as she looked, his pretty little wife; already she had her baby son lined up as a khalifa.

'We will talk more later, dear wife. Now I must change out of my dusty soldier's clothes and put on a clean robe.' He handed the baby back to her and kissed his new son lightly on the forehead.

***

He had just finished bathing when there was a knock on the door to his apartments.

'If that is Abbas, tell him to come in,' he told his manservant and then turned to his masseur and said,

'That will do for now. I will send for you later.' He pulled his robe around him and sat down on a low couch by the open window. The bath had made him sweat and he began to fan himself.

'*Sayyad*. It is good to see you home, safe and well,' Abbas said, bowing as low as his huge bulk would allow him.

'It's good to be home, Abbas. Sit down here with me and tell me what has happened in my absence and why our plans did not go as expected.'

'I am sorry, *sayyad*. I made an error of judgement in choosing that pathetic wretch to carry out your plan. He told me that he had done many jobs like that before, but he was lying. He was no proper assassin - he was a cheap cut-throat who wanted money. When it came down to it, he did not have the nerves for it. I can see that now.'

'Still it was a good plan and it nearly worked. Remember it is important that nothing can be traced back to you, and thus to me. You succeeded with that part of the plan, I suppose?'

'Yes, *sayyad*. They arrested him but before they could take him to the judge, I managed to kill him. There was so much confusion that nobody noticed me. No-one knows that I was involved. And now that the wretch is dead, there is nothing to connect him to me or you.'

'Good.'

'What do we do now?' Abbas asked. 'The guards will be twice as vigilant since the attack. It will be hard to get close to the Khalifa. I could try to poison his food.'

'No. That wouldn't work. There is a taster in the kitchen who tries everything that the Khalifa is served. No. Either we manage to make his death look like an accident or we lock him in his palace and wait for everyone to forget that he exists. The first is quicker but someone might discover who was behind the accident— al-Mansur was thinking of that meddling soldier, who considered himself the Khalifa's bodyguard—or we can take it slowly and wait until time and boredom have done our job for us. If we follow the latter course, no-one can ever accuse me of usurping the rightful ruler of al-Andalus.'

'What do you want me to do, *sayyad*?' Abbas asked.

'Find me some soldiers that can be easily bribed and we will have them installed in the Palace Guard. I want men who can tell me what the Khalifa is doing each day and whom he sees. They must be men who know how to keep their mouths shut. Tell them they will be well paid for their services.'

'Yes, *sayyad*.'

'Knowledge is power, Abbas. And I want to know all about the young Khalifa and his activities. You never know when that information will come in useful. Go now. And tell me when you have located suitable men.'

***

When he saw her, spread out on her couch, the soft light from the oil lamps casting a warm glow on her bare skin, a silken robe scarcely covering her modesty, his heart leapt within him. He had not realised, until that moment, how much he had missed her.

'I hope you are well, my beloved,' he said, emotion causing his voice to waver a little.

Despite her years she was still a beautiful woman, but it was not her beauty that was making his pulse race, it was the memory of their love making, of the thousand and one tricks that she knew to make a man wild with joy, the knowledge that she could satisfy him in ways that no-one else was able to. That was what caused his heart to beat so loudly in his chest and his blood to course through his veins as though he were still a teenager.

'Have you missed me, Abu Amir?' Subh whispered, in her most seductive voice.

'You know I have,' he said, throwing down his cloak and pulling off his tunic.

'Come and sit beside me and tell me all about the campaign,' she said, patting the couch beside her.

'Later. I will tell you everything, later. Now, let me taste your lips. I have been like a man in the desert, dying for want of you.'

It was an exaggeration; he had barely thought of her for months, but now that she lay in his arms, her golden hair spread like a mantle around her, her pale skin, soft and silky beneath his hands, it seemed to him that he spoke the truth. At that moment he wanted her more than anything in the world.

*****

The sound of the cock crowing was enough to wake him instantly. He had not intended to spend the whole night with Subh, but she had been insatiable and, in the end, not long before sunrise, he had fallen into a deep and dreamless sleep.

'You are awake, my love,' she said, leaning over him and stroking his face. 'Did you sleep well?'

'What little time you allowed me to,' he said, with a chuckle. 'And now, sleep or not, I must go; I have many things to do.'

'Of course. But first, tell me, how is your family?'

'You have heard?'

'About your new son? Yes, everyone is talking about what a fine, healthy child he is. Allah be praised.'

'Really,' he said.

'And have you heard about the attack on my son's life?'

'A dreadful occurrence. I don't understand how such a thing could happen. That soldier, the one who calls himself the boy's bodyguard, what's his name?'

'Makoud ibn Qasim, but everyone calls him al-Jundi.'

'The soldier? Well, he's useless; I'm going to get rid of him and strengthen the Palace Guard. The Khalifa's safety is imperative. What kind of message does it give, if anyone can just wander in to the Khalifa's presence and try to kill him.'

'I thought you had only just reduced the number of Palace Guards?'

'Yes, that was before there was an attack on the Khalifa's life. Well now I'm increasing them again.'

'Al-Jundi is a good man and very loyal to the Khalifa. He saved my husband's life, many years ago and since then was constantly by his side until his death. Now he protects my son. I trust him implicitly,' Subh said, taking al-Mansur's hand in hers and caressing it.

'What good is loyalty if he lets an assassin murder your son? Besides which, he is so incompetent that he allowed the prisoner to be killed under his very nose before we could find out why the man did it,' al-Mansur replied, sitting up and reaching for his robe. He must remember that soldier's name. If this man felt duty bound to protect the Khalifa against all odds, through some misguided form of loyalty, then that could be a problem; it was another reason to get rid of him.

'The Khalifa needs men he can trust, men I can trust,' Subh said, a little insistently, he thought.

'Of course he does, but he also needs them to be competent. I will speak to General Ghálib and have him removed. But now, I must get up. I have work to do.'

A scowl passed fleetingly over Subh's face, but was gone as quickly as it had arrived.

'Is everything all right?' he asked. Was it because he was leaving or was there something about this soldier that she was not telling him?

'Yes, everything is fine. Someone tried to kill my son and now you are talking about getting rid of the only man in this place that I can trust. So, yes, everything is fine,' she replied, her voice shriller than normal.

'Come now, Subh, you are exaggerating. Surely you trust me?'

She smiled, touched his face lightly with her hand and said, softening her tone, 'Yes, my dearest, of course I trust you. I was talking of the guards. So many of them are foreigners and some don't even speak our language.'

He laughed and said, 'Do you mean Arabic? There was a time when you didn't speak our language, if you remember.'

'I speak it now,' she snapped.

The *Sayyida* was beginning to get tetchy; it was best not to upset her too much. 'Come, my love, kiss me goodbye because I must leave.'

'You will come and see me again, soon?'

'Of course. Nothing and nobody could keep me away.'

***

As soon as he left the *Sayyida*, he went to the office of General Ghálib. He would tell him that he must dismiss this Makoud ibn Qasim and replace him with someone younger, more reliable.

'*As-salama alaykum*, father-in-law. How are you today?'

'*Wa alaykum e-salam*, my son. I am well and pleased to be home once more with my family. So what do you think of your fine son? He is a sturdy youngster, is he not?'

'I am delighted with him. Already your daughter is proving to be an excellent wife.'

The General smiled with delight. Although he was a hardened soldier and had had a long and successful career in the Khalifa's army, the most important thing in his life, he always said, was his family, and he had a particular soft spot for his daughter Ismá.

'So, to what do I owe the pleasure of your company so early in the day?' he asked, motioning for al-Mansur to sit beside him.

'I have been thinking about the attack on the Khalifa's life. It is unforgivable that such a thing should happen when he was supposed to be being protected by the Palace Guard. I would like you to dismiss that old idiot who is supposed to be his bodyguard. He is obviously past his prime.'

'Whom are you talking about?'

'Makoud ibn Qasim, al-Jundi, whatever he calls himself. He is totally incompetent. He must go.'

'Not so fast, my son. I am in charge of the army until the Khalifa is old enough to take over and I'm afraid I do not agree with your judgement. Makoud is a good man; I have known him many years. The fact that he is old means nothing; he is very experienced. I'm sure things would have been even worse if he had not been there.'

'I can't see how. An attempted murder, a wounding and then, after finding the man responsible - with the help of a substantial reward, I might add - allowing someone to kill him. And what's this I hear about his son being the one who told the assassin where the Khalifa would be that evening? It doesn't sound a very good record for a man of such experience. I insist that you get rid of him and punish his son.'

'The Khalifa won't like it.'

'The Khalifa has no say in the matter. We are his regents. He will do what we say,' al-Mansur said.

'Nevertheless, the soldier is his personal bodyguard. I will speak to him and, if he agrees to get rid of him, he will be dismissed immediately.'

'And if not?'

'If not, then he stays.'

'And his son?'

'That depends on the judge and the evidence against him.'

Al-Mansur leapt to his feet. What was it about this soldier? Why was everyone trying to protect him? The Triumvirate was not working. How could it when one of them was in prison and the other enjoyed stopping al-Mansur from doing what he thought was right? The General was too old; he looked to the past too much and not to the future. He would like to speak openly with him about what he was planning, but he knew he would meet shocked resistance. No, although they were now family and, on the face of it, worked well together, he knew that many of his ideas would be rejected by the General. He was too old; he had served too long with the previous Khalifa and he would certainly never agree to a regime change. Yet the only way to get things moving was to have one leader, not a council of viziers but one vizier, al-Mansur. The General, too, would have to be removed, but not yet. First he had to get rid of al-Jundi.

'Are you leaving so soon?' the General asked.

'Yes, I have matters of state to see to.'

'Of course. *Alla ysalmak*, my son. Come and dine with us this week and bring your wife and the new baby. Already my wife misses him.'

'Thank you, father-in-law. *Ma'a salama.*'

Al-Mansur bowed to the General and left, his mind whirling with plans. He must get Abbas on to it, right away; he was good at discovering secrets and, most assuredly, this al-Jundi would have some secrets. Everyone had something to hide. Find a man's secrets and you could control him. If he couldn't dismiss him then at least he would find a way to destroy him. To leave him in position could prove dangerous in the future; he wanted no weak links in his plan. One way or another he was going to get rid of that soldier.

CHAPTER 18

He had been shocked at the news of Ahmad's arrest. Could it be possible that Ahmad had done this deliberately? He thought that Ahmad was his friend. Why would he want him dead? It didn't make sense. Was it possible that they were all trying to kill him? Wasn't there anybody he could trust? Even Ahmad? He found it hard to believe. But if it wasn't true then why had he been arrested? An intense feeling of loneliness swept over al-Hisham. If Ahmad wasn't there who could he talk to? There was no-one. He had no-one he could turn to. He gently stroked the back of Daruj's neck. No, this was not right. He could not believe that Ahmad wanted him dead. He took hold of the bird's jesses and tied him to his perch. Ahmad had given him these jesses; he had made them himself and given them to him as a present. He thought about how he had brought him the baby falcon and promised to teach him to fly it, how he had come every evening after he had finished work to help him train Daruj, how he had promised that one day he would be the fastest peregrine falcon in the Falcon House and they would fly him free and hunt pigeons and rabbits. No, Ahmad wasn't to blame. It was all his fault. He had forced Ahmad to take him hunting. He had to speak to him. Right away.

'Gassan.'

'Yes, Your Excellency?'

'Go to the prison and tell the officer in charge that I wish to see the prisoner, Ahmad. Tell him to bring him to me, here, right away.'

'Yes, Your Excellency.'

'No, better to bring him to the throne room. I will speak to him there.'

Yes, that was the best thing to do, speak to him himself. He would soon know if Ahmad was lying.

***

He was saddened to see his friend like that. He had heavy iron shackles round his ankles and two soldiers half supported and half dragged him towards al-Hisham. He was bedraggled and dirty, with bruises on his arms. His face was streaked with the marks of his tears and he looked terrified. One of the soldiers pushed Ahmad forward so that he knelt before the Khalifa, then bowed himself.

He could see al-Jundi, standing by the door, watching in astonishment and dismay.

'Get him up,' al-Hisham said. 'Then leave us.'

'But Your Excellency, we cannot leave him unguarded. He might make another attempt on your life,' the soldier said.

'He does not look very dangerous to me. Do as I say, at once,' al-Hisham said, trying to make his voice as authoritative as possible, although he felt more like crying at the sight of his friend.

'Very well, Your Excellency.'

The men withdrew to the far end of the throne room.

'You, too, al-Jundi. I want to speak to your son, alone.'

He waited until al-Jundi had joined the other guards and then he turned to Ahmad and said, 'Is it true, Ahmad? Did you tell that man where to find me?'

The young falconer looked up at him, his eyes full of tears and said, 'No, Your Highness. I would never do anything to harm you. I thought you knew that. I am your loyal subject and, I hope, your friend. I don't know how the man knew that you would be hunting that evening. I told no-one. But ...'

'But what?'

'But it would have been easy to guess that you would be hunting one day soon because everyone knows that the hunting stops while the birds moult. There were only a couple of weeks left until the hunts stopped. The assassin would only have had to wait a a short time to see if you were going on the hunt or not.'

'So you told no-one?'

'No. Please believe me, Your Highness. I said nothing to anyone, not even the Head Falconer. I would never hurt you. Believe me.'

'I believe you, Ahmad.'

He stepped back and called to the soldiers, 'This man is innocent. I want him released at once.'

The soldiers looked at each other, in confusion. They were obviously not used to receiving orders from a boy, even if he was the Khalifa.

'Did you hear me? Unlock those shackles. Now.'

'Yes, Your Highness.'

One of them bent over Ahmad and unlocked the heavy iron padlock. The falconer collapsed on the floor and sat there rubbing his sore ankles. The flesh was raw in places and his bruises the colour of al-Hisham's purple robe. The Khalifa wanted to put his arms around Ahmad and tell him that it was over, that he wouldn't let anyone hurt him again. He felt an intense desire to hug him close to him and kiss his bruised face. For a moment he felt confused, his emotions running riot, but then he remembered his position as Supreme Ruler, took a deep breath and waited while the soldiers returned to their barracks.

'Thank you, Your Highness. Thank you,' Ahmad sobbed. 'Thank you.'

'Go home now, Ahmad, to your family and tomorrow come and see me as usual.'

'I will, Your Highness. Thank you.'

Ahmad could hardly get his words out for the tears that were running down his cheeks, streaking his blackened face even more.

'Go now.'

Al-Hisham felt good. He had acted like a khalifa. He had pardoned an innocent man. It was what his father would have done, he was sure. And now he would be able to see Ahmad again.

***

The next afternoon he could hardly wait for Ahmad to arrive. Daruj sensed his nervousness and kept hopping from one foot to the other. Twice the peregrine bated and each time al-Hisham pulled him back on to his glove and spoke reassuringly to him. At last Gassan came in to say that Ahmad had arrived.

'Good. Send him through to the garden.'

He was impatient to see him again and hurried out to the garden. When he saw the young falconer sitting by the lake, waiting for him, he felt a surge of happiness. He realised just how much he had come to depend on their evenings together, how much he had missed him, how much he loved him.

'Oh, you are here, Ahmad,' he called. '*Wa alaykum e-salam.* Are you fully recovered from your ordeal?'

'Yes, thank you, Your Excellency,' Ahmad replied, standing up and bowing politely. 'My mother is very pleased to have me home. She says she will say extra prayers for you, wishing you a long and happy life.'

'Good. And your wound, is it better?'

'Well enough for us to continue with our lessons, Your Excellency. The Grand Falconer was most insistent that we carry on as before. He was very pleased when I told him how much progress you had made.'

'And the attack on my life? What did he say about that?'

'They caught the man, Your Highness and now he is dead.'

'I heard about that from your father. But are they sure that he was the one?'

'I think so. They were taking him to Córdoba for trial when someone shot him in the back with an arrow. Probably one of your subjects, Your Excellency. It was retribution, they say.'

'Who says?' He is intrigued to think that his people were so upset about the attack on his life that they had killed the man responsible.

'Everyone. It is the main topic of conversation at the moment.'

'Who was he, this man?'

'You remember the man with the unruly dog? The one who kept barking and trying to get the hare?'

'I remember the dog, but not the man. Who was he? Why did he try to kill me?'

'Nobody knows. He was killed before the judge could question him.'

'So we still don't who he was or why he tried to kill me?'

'No, Your Excellency.'

'But he is dead now?'

'Yes, Your Excellency.' Ahmad stroked Daruj's head and said, 'Your bird is looking well. What have you been feeding him?'

'Dead rats, rabbit, partridge, all the things he likes. I just tell the cooks what we want for lunch and they bring it.'

'Dead rats?' Ahmad let out a peal of laughter. 'I can just imagine you ordering a plate of dead rats for your dinner. Your cooks must like that.'

'I don't know why you're laughing. I am the Khalifa; if I want to ask for a dead rat for my falcon, then I can,' he said, trying to sound indignant and failing. It was so good to have Ahmad back.

'But they must have been surprised. It's not a usual dish for a Khalifa.'

'Perhaps they were surprised at first, but now they are used to it. They have plenty of rats in the kitchens; it's an opportunity to get rid of some of them, instead of leaving it to those fat, lazy cats.'

'Well, soon Daruj will be able to catch his own dinner. Come on, let's see what he has remembered.'

'Are we going out?'

'No, not today. The Grand Falconer has forbidden me to take you on any more hunts for the moment.'

'What? What right has the Grand Falconer to say what I can or can't do? I will speak to him at once. I won't stand ffo…or this,' he screamed in rage and stamped his foot hard on the ground.

His anger, red and as hot as fire, had left him speechless with indignation. He was the Khalifa, the most important person in all al-Andalus, yet he was thwarted every way he turned. They wouldn't have treated his father like this. No, no matter what he wanted, Baba only had to say the word and it was done. It should be like that for him, too; he had inherited his father's title. But no, instead they made excuses: it was because he was too young, or it was too dangerous, it was not befitting someone of his status - whatever that meant - and more recently, he had too little experience. He had put up with the Regents ordering his life, he had put up with his mother's interfering but he didn't see why someone like the Grand Falconer should be deciding when and where he could go.

'But, Your Excellency, I am sure it is because they are still worried about your safety. In a few weeks, I expect we will be able to go out again with the others. In the meantime, let's practise teaching Daruj to fly back to your hand,' said Ahmad.

'He did that. Don't you remember, in the woods. He came straight back to me,' he snapped. 'We've been practising getting him to fly to the glove, all summer.' He wanted to go out again and he wanted to do it now.

'Yes, he did. But that was only on one occasion; we want him to do it every time. Then you will be confident that he will always return to you. What you have been practising with him is good, but now we want him to return to you from a much greater distance, when there are many more distractions. You don't want him to fly off and leave you, do you?'

Al-Hisham turned away and ignored him. What was the point of being rich and powerful if he couldn't do what he wanted? But that was just it; it seemed to him that his riches were untouchable and his power illusionary. Then he reminded himself that he had at least secured Ahmad's freedom, even though General Ghálib had visited him that very night to say that he shouldn't have taken the matter into his own hands, that the judge was well able to deal with such things, that in future he must discuss everything with the Regents and not make unilateral discussions about things which he did not understand. He had protested that he understood well enough that his friend had been wrongfully arrested and he was only doing what was right. The General had not argued with him and, better still, they hadn't rearrested Ahmad so that, at least, was a success.

'You're right; I don't want to lose him,' al-Hisham said, his anger beginning to cool as he finally acknowledged the sense in Ahmad's words. 'Very well, let's begin.'

'Do you have some food for him?'

Al-Hisham showed him the pieces of raw rabbit in his bag. 'The cook prepared them for me this morning.'

'Good. Now let's get his perch and put it in the garden.'

Al-Hisham indicated to the waiting slave where he wanted the perch positioned.

'That's good,' said Ahmad. 'Now sit Daruj on his perch and walk away from him.'

Al-Hisham did as he was told, but the bird instantly flew after him and landed on his shoulder.

'See, he comes straight to me,' he said, triumphantly.

'Yes, but he must come on your call. At the moment he is coming to you because he wants to; if something more interesting were to appear, he might ignore you. We need to be sure he will come to you for food and that he will land on the glove. Try again.'

They placed Daruj back on his perch and this time he stayed there.

'Hide a small piece of the rabbit in your glove. Now, call him and when he lands on your fist, give him the rabbit.'

Al-Hisham did as he was told and was rewarded with Daruj responding to his call and landing on the glove.

'Good. I know that we have been doing this exercise all summer but we must be certain that he will come back to the glove before we let him fly free. We want Daruj to come to you when you call even if you are half an Arab mile away.'

'When can he fly free of the creance?' al-Hisham asked impatiently.

'Tomorrow. We will try him tomorrow. We don't need to go out for the first time. You have lots of grounds here in the palace; we can let him fly free in here. But first you must be confident that he will return to your glove whenever you whistle for him.

They worked with the bird for an hour and then Ahmad said, 'I think we all need a rest, especially Daruj. Besides which he has eaten a lot and needs to digest it.'

'Don't go, yet,' al-Hisham said. 'You're the only person I have seen all day except the servants. Stay and play a game of chess with me.'

'I'm not very good at chess,' said Ahmad.

'Well I am. I will teach you some new moves.'

'Very well. I can stay for a while longer.'

'Great.'

He clapped his hands and instantly a young slave was by his side.

'Where is Gassan?' he asked.

'He is in the kitchen, Your Excellency,' said the boy, bowing before the Khalifa.

'Tell him to bring me my chess set. We will play out here in the garden where it is cool and fresh.'

'Very well, Your Excellency. Do you want me to take the bird inside?'

'No, he will stay with us.'

***

True to his word, when Ahmad arrived the next evening, he had a cage with two pigeons in it.

'Today we will let him fly without his creance. I hope you haven't fed him.'

'No, nothing since last night. He's hungry.'

'Good. Let's give him a little titbit now, to remind him that you are the provider of food.'

Al-Hisham went through the usual steps of leaving him on the perch, walking away and then calling him. The bird snatched at the tiny piece of rabbit eagerly. It was so satisfying to have a wild bird come at his command, to feel that rush of excitement when Daruj, now fully grown, flew straight at him, wings outstretched, beak open, pounces ready, and landed with a thump on his glove. It was something he had never experienced before. At first he had flinched each time the bird landed, but not now; now he waited, expectantly, for the thrill it gave him.   And today, at last, he was going to hunt without the creance. His stomach was knotted with apprehension. What if Daruj didn't come back? What if he snatched the pigeon and flew off with it?

'Are you ready?' Ahmad asked.

'Yes,' he said, a little hesitantly.

'Are you sure? We can do it another day, you know. It doesn't have to be today.'

'No, we're ready. Aren't we Daruj?'

The bird swivelled its head and looked at him. Yes, he was ready.

'All right. Now once the pigeon is in the air, release Daruj.'

Al-Hisham could feel his pulse racing. This was the moment he had been waiting for. All at once the cage was open and Ahmad had thrown the pigeon into the air. It fluttered upwards, happy to be free but sensing danger. Al-Hisham waited until the pigeon was high enough and then released Daruj. The peregrine spotted the pigeon immediately and was after it. The pigeon twisted and turned, trying to lose his pursuer but the falcon was too fast for him. He flew straight at him and knocked him from the sky. The unfortunate prey fell like a stone, with Daruj right behind him.

'Where are they? I can't see them,' he cried. He should have waited. Now he would never see Daruj again.

'I have them. Follow me. And call your bird.'

Before Hisham could do anything, there was a whirring of feathers and a thump as Daruj landed on his glove.

'He's back. Look Ahmad. He came back to me. I didn't even call him. What do you think of that?'

He was jubilant. His bird had returned. It was easy.

'Well reward him with some titbits.'

Hisham pulled a dead chick out of his bag and gave it to Daruj. Chicks were his favourite.

'Well done, Daruj. You did really well,' he murmured to the bird.

'Do you want to try again?' Ahmad asked.

'Of course.' This time all he felt was excitement.

***

Flying Daruj without the creance had been exciting but it wasn't enough. Now al-Hisham was restless; something stirred within him, demanding to be free. He could not get rid of this feeling of being caged up. He had not left the palace since the attack on his life. It was stifling him. He had to get out. It wasn't enough for him to fly Daruj in the palace grounds any more; he wanted to take him out across the fields and through the woods and he knew that Daruj felt the same. He wanted to ride his horse, not just in the exercise yard but outside, where he could feel the wind in his face and hear the thudding of his horse's hooves as they galloped across the plain. He wanted to see his falcon soar above him and dive at its quarry; he wanted the companionship of the other hunters; he wanted to go with them hunting for cranes and watch the falcons knock the large ungainly birds from the sky; he wanted to be like any other thirteen-year-old, not a Khalifa trapped in a golden cage. It wasn't fair. He was almost a man and yet they still treated him as a child.

And where was Mama? She had visited him when she heard about the attack but since then he had not seen her. He had sent Gassan to ask her to visit him but the old man returned with a different excuse each time: she was in Córdoba, she was unwell, she would visit him the next day, but she never came. There was always some reason why she was unable to see him. And there were all the extra guards. Al-Mansur, when he returned from his victorious campaign against the Christians, had been angry at the attack on the Khalifa's life. He had threatened to remove al-Jundi and his special guard and replace them with his own men but al-Hisham had stood up to him, and General Ghálib, to his surprise, had supported him. So al-Jundi remained, but now the palace was crawling with extra men, all sent by al-Mansur, to guard him. Sometimes he had the feeling that these soldiers had been instructed to keep him in, rather than keep attackers out; they watched his every move and, he was sure, reported back to the Regents.

'Gassan, ask al-Jundi to come and speak to me. I will wait in the throne room.'

He chose the throne room, not to intimidate al-Jundi, but to have somewhere different to go. His current role as Khalifa did not entail any civic duties at all; no ambassadors came to visit him, no kings or princes, no citizens brought their petitions for him to grant, none of his council members even bothered to tell him when they were meeting. His duties seemed to consist of signing endless bits of paper and giving his army his blessing when they set off to war. When he remembered what the court was like when his father was alive, how bustling with activity, how vibrant, he was saddened and a little confused. In that time, people came from all over the world to greet his father, they brought him exotic gifts, exquisitely engraved pyxis, ceramics from Damascus, glassware from Egypt and books even al-Hakim had never heard of; they brought gifts of slave girls, animals with long necks and enormous trunks that were not seen in al-Andalus, strange herbs and spices, jewels set in the finest gold, weapons, horses, bolts of the finest silk and richly made carpets. Now, most of the court had moved to Córdoba, and that's where the visitors headed. He had heard that when they asked for him, the Khalifa, they were directed instead to his Regent, al-Mansur. Both the magnificent city of Madinat al-Zahra and the Khalifa seemed to be fading from people's memory.

'Your Highness. You wanted to see me?' asked al-Jundi, bowing before him, as a true subject was obliged to do.

'I want to go out into the city. I want to see my subjects. You will accompany me.'

The soldier straightened up and stared at him; he seemed perturbed at his words. Al-Hisham was so used to seeing al-Jundi in the palace, always within earshot of his father and lately, watching over him even more closely, that he had never really looked at him. It surprised him to realise that this faithful soldier was now an old man; the lines that criss-crossed his weather beaten face and the grey hairs in his beard told of many years service, the scars on his arms spoke of battles fought and won, and his ever-watchful eyes suggested he had seen more than he would ever disclose. He was an old warrior but al-Hisham knew he could trust him.

'Well? What do you have to say?'

'If that is your command, Your Highness, then we will do it, but …'

'But what?'

'The Regents have expressly forbidden that you leave the palace. They are worried about your safety.'

'Who is the Khalifa?'

'You are, Your Excellency. May Allah guard and protect you.'

'Exactly. If I have Allah to protect me and you by my side, then what have I to fear? I have not even been allowed to pray in the mosque since the attack on my life.

I have had to pray here, in the palace. Does that seem right to you?'

'Going to the mosque is no problem; as you know, there is a special passageway between your palace and the mosque. I will accompany you this evening.'

'And I want to walk in the city, go to the market, meet the people.'

'I will have to speak to the Regents about that. What you are suggesting puts you in a very vulnerable position. It will be hard to protect you in the crowded city.'

'Well, what if we go riding instead? Up into the mountains? You can bring as many soldiers as you like,' al-Hisham suggested, as though the idea has only just occurred to him. 'I seem to have twice as many guards as before. Bring some of them with us.'

'That sounds a much better idea, Your Excellency.'

'Very well, we'll do that instead. Tomorrow at daybreak.'

'Is that all, Your Excellency?'

'Yes, al-Jundi. I will see you tomorrow.'

***

The next day, at daybreak, al-Hisham was waiting in the stables for al-Jundi and his men to appear, when instead, his mother came towards him.

'As-salama alaykum, my son,' she said and bowed.

'Wa alaykum e-salam, Mama. What are you doing here? Where is al-Jundi?'

'He is not coming. I told him it was a foolish idea. The Regents would get rid of him immediately, if he took you out riding. They would say he was a traitor and leading you into a trap, just like his son. Even if nothing happened, he would be dismissed and maybe even locked up. Would you want that to happen to him?'

'Of course not, Mama. But I would have been perfectly safe with him and his soldiers.'

'Like last time? He was lucky not to have been dismissed last time and his son executed.'

'So he's not coming?'

'No. But al-Mansur is coming to see you later today. He wants to tell you all about their wonderful victory over the Christians. Now you have one less enemy to worry about.'

Al-Hisham felt his eyes sting with unshed tears. It was so unfair. He couldn't care less about al-Mansur and his stupid victory. What did it matter to him when he was locked up in this boring palace, with nobody to talk to.

'Did al-Jundi tell you?' he asked, trying to hold back his tears of disappointment.

'No. There was no need. I have my own ways of finding out what goes on in the palace. You'd have to be up before daybreak to trick me,' she said, rather smugly.

'But I'm bored, Mama, cooped up in the palace all day long. All I ever see are soldiers and servants. I'm not a child any more. I want to meet other people.'

'Why don't you visit the harem? All the women in your father's harem are still there. There seemed no point in getting rid of them until you were old enough to make your own choices. There are some girls there of your own age.'

'I don't want girls to play with, Mama; I want to play with other boys.'

His mother looked at him strangely, but all she said was, 'What about that boy with the falcons? He comes to see you, doesn't he?'

'Yes. He'll be here this afternoon. I was looking forward to telling him that I had been out riding.'

'Well, I'm sorry, al-Hisham, but that's not possible. You will have to wait until you are older and then you can make your own decisions.'

He handed his horse back to the groom and strode back to his private quarters. Even his mother wanted to keep him a prisoner.

***

Ahmad arrived half-way through the afternoon and wanted to begin training Daruj straight away, but al-Hisham had other ideas.

'Come with me. I want to talk to you,' he said.

He placed Daruj on his fist and led the young falconer further into the garden, where they couldn't be seen and, he hoped, overheard. They clambered through hibiscus bushes and hedges of myrtle, until they came to a huge patch of *palmitos*.

'Come here; we can hide in here, behind these dwarf palms' he said. 'No-one will see us here.'

'Why are we hiding?' asked Ahmad. 'What's happening?'

'I want to ask you to do something and I don't want anyone else to know. There are too many spies in this palace; everything I do or say is reported back to the Regents or my mother. I am unable to have any secrets of my own.'

'What do you want me to do?' asked Ahmad, who was crouching behind a line of *palmitos*, with a peregrine falcon and the Khalifa of al-Andalus, as if it were the most natural thing in the world.

Al-Hisham giggled. 'I want to escape from here.'

'What? I can't help you to do that. My father would kill me. And if he didn't then the Regents would have me executed for treason.'

'Not for good. Just for a few hours. Just so we can go and fly Daruj. I'm so bored being in the palace all day and so is Daruj.'

'But how can we do it? The palace is guarded day and night.'

'There must be a way. Maybe we could wear disguises?'

'But what about Daruj?'

'You must be able to think of something. Please, Ahmad. I have to get out of here, if only for a little while.'

The young falconer was silent for a moment then he asked, 'You're allowed to go as far as the old Falcon House, aren't you?'

'Yes, and the stables, in fact, anywhere in the grounds of the *alcazaba*.'

'Well, instead of me coming here tomorrow afternoon, you meet me at the old Falcon House. Bring Daruj with you, and put his hood on him. I'll have a plan arranged by then.'

Al-Hisham felt his heart leap at the prospect of an adventure. He knew he could rely on Ahmad, who was as bored as he was with staying in the palace grounds all the time.

'Good, that's settled then.'

'Can we get out of this bush, now; there's a palm leaf sticking in my bottom,' Ahmad said with a laugh.

'Don't tell anyone, will you? Promise.'

'Of course not. I told you, my father will kill me if he finds out.'

***

The next afternoon, al-Hisham put the bag of titbits they used to train his falcon over his shoulder, called Duraj to his fist and walked out of the garden and through the passageways that led to the old Falcon House. The prospect of riding out of these confines lifted his spirits and he began to hum. The bird cocked his head on one side to listen to him.

As soon as he entered the yard, he was recognised by two of the falconers, who stopped what they were doing in order to bow to him. He waved his hand - regally, he thought - and continued in his search for Ahmad. The Falcon House was no longer the busy, bustling place he had first visited. Half a dozen men were loading the mules with some caged birds, ready to take them to their new home, others were loading camels with sacks of hay and straw. There was no sign of any dogs and the stable was almost empty. He felt a burst of anger when he realised that soon there would be hardly any hawks left for him. These were his birds and they were taking them to Córdoba. It wasn't right. He would have like to have stopped them, told them to put the falcons back in their old cages and leave them alone, but he had to find Ahmad first. At last he found him, waiting inside the bird hospital.

'Come in quickly. No-one works in here now. All the veterinarians have gone to Córdoba, along with all the sick birds. We're safe here,' he said, hurriedly closing the door behind the young Khalifa.

'So, what's your plan?' asked al-Hisham. His stomach was whirring with excitement and he couldn't wait to get started.

'First, put these clothes on and give me yours. They're old ones of mine. My mother was keeping them for my little brother.' He handed him a brown tunic, a dark coloured cloak, some baggy trousers and some soft shoes. 'You'll need to wind this cloth around your head, to hide as much of your face as possible and then put this cap on top.'

Al-Hisham did as he was instructed. This was fun. He loved dressing up. Before he was Khalifa, he had often dressed up in his mother's lovely robes, but she would not allow it now. She said he was too old and besides which, Khalifas did not dress up in ladies' clothes.

'How's that? Do I look all right?' he asked, twirling round so that Ahmad could admire him.

'You look just like a young falconer,' Ahmad said. 'Which is who you are supposed to be. Now, take that expensive hood off Daruj and put on this shabby one. A poor boy could not afford such a beautiful hood for his hawk.'

'You have thought of everything,' al-Hisham said.

'I have tried to think of everything because I do not want us to get caught. I would lose my job and so would my father.'

'I would not allow it,' al-Hisham said, with more bravado than conviction. He had gone against the Regents once but he couldn't guarantee getting his own way a second time.

Ahmad picked up the Khalifa's beautiful, purple robe and wrapped it around all his discarded clothes, then pushed the bundle under a pile of hay.

'Wait here, while I go for the horses. When you hear me come back, just walk out as casually as you can and get on one of them. If anyone speaks to you, just ignore them. I'll do the talking. All right?'

'What if someone recognises me?'

'There are very few falconers here now and they are all working. They will be too busy to look at a poor stable boy. Now are you clear about what to do?'

Al-Hisham nodded. The excitement was tying his insides into knots; he felt he would explode if they didn't leave soon.

They rode out of the palace grounds, past the soldiers on the gate, past the guards on the outer wall, until they were trotting along the Nogales Road, heading for the Sierra Morena. Al-Hisham wanted to cry out with joy; he wanted to scream his freedom to the goats in the fields and the chickens scratching along the verges of the road; he wanted to tell each and every unsuspecting villager that they passed that he was the Khalifa; he wanted to gallop as fast as this rather uninspiring nag could go; he wanted to throw Daruj into the air and watch him soar over the wide plain. But he did none of that. Ahmad had said that they must be inconspicuous; there would be time enough to whoop and holler when they got to the place he had in mind.

They trotted along at a steady pace until they came to a site, very similar to the one he had visited before, but, according to Ahmad, this place was used very rarely by the falconers, so they would be undisturbed.

'We'll stop here,' he said. 'And now let's see if Daruj remembers all we've taught him.'

***

After that first excursion, al-Hisham wanted to go every afternoon but Ahmad advised against it. He said that someone would notice if he no longer came to the palace as usual to see the Khalifa, and they might start asking questions. They would have limit their trips out with Daruj to one a week and they would vary the day that they chose to go. In that way they stood less chance of detection. Al-Hisham had reluctantly agreed because he could see that Ahmad was very worried about being discovered. The risk was far greater for him and his family than it was for al-Hisham. If Ahmad ended up in prison again, he was not sure he would be able to get him released.

Daruj proved to be a very good hunter and was soon pulling birds from the air with ease; he enjoyed the hunt as much as his master, and gave up his prey readily if there was something tasty as a reward. Ahmad had told him that it was not a good idea to leave Daruj with all his kill because then he would have no reason to return to al-Hisham's glove. So the rabbits, partridges, sometimes a stork or a fat pigeon, all ended up in Ahmad's bag to take home to his mother.

He loved being out hunting with Ahmad and Daruj, but it was still not enough. This weekly taste of freedom had only whetted his appetite for more. Each morning when he woke he longed to escape from the *alcazaba*. If only he were like Daruj and could stretch his wings and fly out over the high walls that surrounded him, fly across the plains, soar up into the mountains and see the world from on high, follow the river down to the sea. His father had told him how many of the birds that he saw around him, storks for example, left each winter for North Africa, that they liked to follow the sun and would not return until the following year. How could a bird have more freedom than he had? He was stifled in Madinat al-Zahra. He felt he would die of boredom. Was that how a caged bird felt? What did it think when it looked at the blue sky through the bars of its cage? What did it feel when it saw other birds, singing in the trees? Did it long to be free or did it know no better?

'Gassan. How many song birds do we have in the palace? How many canaries and gold finches?'

'How many, Your Highness? I don't know the precise number but I can find out for you.'

'I want them all released, all the caged birds. Tomorrow morning. Have them all brought to this part of the garden and we will release them together.'

'As you wish, Your Highness. That could take quite a while; there are many of them.'

'Good. I want them to fly free.'

'You do realise, Your Highness, that some of them have come from distant lands; I do not know if they will survive if we release them.'

'At least they will have the opportunity to fly home,' he said.

'Very well, Your Highness. I will see to it right away.'

***

The next morning he rose early, as soon as the sun had started its journey through the sky. Gassan had already organised to have the bird cages set out in the garden. A steady stream of palace servants carried the tiny cages out and placed them in rows. There seemed to be thousands of them already and still the servants came with more. The air was filled with the sound of chattering song as the birds began their morning chorus.

'There are still a few more to come, Your Highness,' Gassan said, putting down a larger cage with a red partridge inside. 'I have instructed them to bring out the partridges as well, although you said song birds. Is that what you want?'

'Yes, Gassan. I want to let them all go free.'

'The cook says, you do realise that there will be no partridge today for lunch if you set them all loose.'

'I will catch one for her, with my hawk,' he said, with a chuckle, 'We will catch all the partridges that she wants.'

He walked along the lines of small cages, looking at the imprisoned birds. Some were drab in colour, like the nightingale, but their song was exquisite, others were bright yellow, others multicoloured, blue, yellow, orange, sometimes with a red cap of feathers on their heads, sometimes green. Like Gassan had said, they were from all parts of the world.

'Here are the parrots and parakeets now,' Gassan said. 'I think that must be all of them. How do you want to release them? Would you like me to instruct the servants to stand by the cages and open the doors on your command?'

'Yes. That sounds good. Let them fly away together.'

Al-Hisham bent down and picked up a cage with a golden canary inside. The bird was clinging to its perch and singing for all its might. 'I will give the signal,' he said.

'Very well, Your Highness.'

Al-Hisham looked around at this unusual scenario before him. Had anyone else ever considered releasing these birds from their prison? No, he was sure they hadn't, not even Baba, but then no-one had felt what he did, the pain of being trapped inside somewhere, able to see the outside world but unable to take part in it. He smiled. This was a good thing he was doing.

'Now,' he said and slid back the bolt of the cage and let the bird free. The servants, all waiting for his signal, followed suit and within moments the air was filled with fluttering birds, chattering, chirping, twittering, warbling, a cacophony of sound that deafened him. He looked up into the sky and watched as first the birds hesitated, alighting in the trees and stretching their wings, then rose and formed a multicoloured cloud of flapping wings which soared and dipped and swirled until it gradually disappeared from view. It was all over in a matter of minutes and the sudden silence was as deafening as the sound of their voices had been moments before. He felt euphoric. They were free. They could fly wherever they wanted to. If only he could do the same.

CHAPTER 19

Subh padded across the cool marble floor, the bells on her anklets tinkling as she walked. It was barely an hour since her lover had left yet already she missed him. As usual he had left her with a churning cauldron of emotions, from the satisfaction of a night spent in his arms to the despair of being parted from him, from the confidence that he was doing everything he could to ensure her son retained his rightful hold on the throne to a growing doubt about his motives. His antagonism towards al-Jundi worried her. On the face of it his anger was understandable but to dismiss the Khalifa's most loyal and trusted servant would leave Hisham vulnerable. Subh did not want anything to happen to her son because, without him, she would return to obscurity, just another slave girl who had risen to the highest position she could only for it all to come to nothing.

'Your bath is ready, *Sayyida*,' Afra said, sprinkling some lavender oil in the hot water. 'Would you like me to massage your shoulders first? You look rather tense.'

'Yes, that would be lovely.'

She took off her robe and lay face down on the table. Afra was a good masseuse; her hands were strong but she was also gentle. She sighed as the slave began to rub her back and shoulders with oil smelling of sandalwood. 'That's a pleasant smell,' she murmured. Already she was feeling sleepy.

'It's a mixture of frankincense, sandalwood and geranium. It's to help release any tension,' her slave said.

'Well, it's working,' she said, a little sleepily as she let her thoughts drift back to before, to her early days in the harem.

***

After that first night, al-Hakim sent for her again, and the night after that, and the next one too. The women in the harem were astonished and badgered her with questions about what had happened.

'What is he like?'

'Is he handsome?'

'Did you dance for him?'

'Did you make love?'

'You are so lucky, nobody has ever been invited to see the prince a second time.'

Some of the comments, such as, 'What does he see in a bean pole like you?' were hardly flattering, but she didn't mind; her plan was working.

'You have bewitched him,' Zahr said. 'It's wonderful. At last someone has managed to get his attention. Now you just have to get him into your bed.'

She looked at her out of the corner of her eye and whispered, 'Or have you managed that already?'

Subh laughed. 'No, not yet. You have to move carefully in these matters,' she said, as though she had been seducing princes all her life.

The general atmosphere in the harem was jubilant. Although some of the women were jealous of her success, they were also happy for her. It reflected well on all of them that the prince was taking an interest in one of the concubines and, more importantly, it had put Yamut and the Royal Wife in good spirits.

'I have never seen Yamut smile so much,' said Zahr. 'He is as proud of you as if you were his own daughter.'

'There is still a long way to go,' Subh said. 'But it is astonishing how kindly the prince treats me. Look, he had this book of poems sent to me this morning. It is from Damascus.'

She showed Zahr a beautifully illustrated book, covered in Arabic script.

'Can you read that?' Zahr asked in surprise.

'Yes, of course. I told you that my mistress taught me to read.'

'I know, but I didn't realise that you were clever enough to read real books.'

It was only now that Subh truly understood what her mistress had been trying to do for her; she had given her a gift, the gift of an education that in her circumstances she would never have had, and by doing so, she had opened many doors for her. Subh doubted that her mistress had intended that she would end up in a royal harem, trying to seduce a homosexual prince, but she would have been well aware that an education could serve her maid in many ways.

'Subh, come here. I want to talk to you, child.'

It was Yamut. He stood at the doorway and beckoned to her to come in from the garden. With him was a woman from the Royal Wife's court; she had seen her before.

'Yes, Yamut. What can I do for you?' she asked, with a slight bow.

'This is Firyal; she is the Royal Wife's hairdresser. She will cut your hair.'

Subh looked at him in astonishment. Cut her lovely long hair? She knew why, but she still protested, 'Does she have to? Why can't I just plait it and put it under my cap?'

'And when she has done that I want you to try on these clothes. I need to see what you will look like tonight when you go to see the Prince,' continued Yamut, as if she had never spoken. 'Make sure that your maid prepares you well for this night.'

Subh called Afra to her and together they followed the hairdresser into the bath house.

'First I will cut your hair and then we will wash it and clean you of any unnecessary body hair. Sit here.'

As the woman began to snip at her golden locks, Subh felt like crying for her to stop but she held back her tears and watched stoically as her hair fell around her like mown corn. If this was what it took to bed a prince then so be it; her hair would grow again, but such an opportunity would come but once.

At last she was finished.

'Afra, bring me a mirror, so that I might look at myself,' she said.

The transformation was incredible; a boyish face with a bob of straight blonde hair stared back at her. Firyal had cut her hair in the latest style for men, short and reaching just below her ears.

'Now your maid can wash your hair and prepare your body for tonight,' the hairdresser said, and turning to Afra, added, 'Make sure that all the hair is removed from her skin and then rub her with this perfume. The Royal Wife has sent it for her.' She placed a phial of perfume on the table and, having gathered up her belongings, left them.

'What is the matter?' asked Zahr, coming into the bathhouse to see what was happening.

'I think I am expected to seduce him tonight,' Subh said. 'The Royal Wife sent her own hairdresser and even some perfume for me to wear.' She handed the bottle to her friend.

'Not very flowery,' Zahr commented as she sniffed it. 'Yes, definitely something a young man would wear. So, you are changing sex tonight?'

'It would seem so. I am to wear those clothes over there,' Subh said, pointing to the white tunic and the voluminous trousers that Yamut had left.

'Well you look just like a young boy with that haircut, so it might work.'

'It feels wrong,' Subh whispered. 'I shouldn't be tricking him like this.'

'Don't be stupid. You're not tricking him; he knows you're a girl. You're just trying to trick his senses. Remember he wants to have an heir as much as his mother does.'

'I feel silly like this,' she said, running her hand through her hair.

'It will look fine when it's washed and then afterwards you can pin it up under a cap until it grows again. Nobody will notice it.'

Zahr was right. If her plan was to succeed she shouldn't be moaning about her lost hair.

'What shall I do with all this?' Afra asked, sweeping the strands into a pile. 'Shall we keep it, to make a wig?'

'Why not.'

***

Just before she was due to leave for the prince's quarters, Yamut came in to inspect her. 'Let me look at you, child,' he said, indicating with his hand that she should walk up and down. 'Yes, I think you'll do. Try not to roll your hips quite so much.' He laughed quietly to himself, a low growling laugh like a hungry bear.

'I've never seen a more handsome youth in my life,' he said. 'If you can't seduce the prince then no woman can.'

Subh touched the woven cap on top of her head and thought wistfully of her lost hair.

'Just one more thing,' Yamut said. 'Your name for tonight is Djafar.'

'Djafar? What's wrong with Subh? I thought you approved of it?'

'Tonight you are a young man; so you must take a man's name. Don't worry, Subh. Just continue as you have been doing and tonight you might succeed in getting into his bed.'

Subh felt herself blush at Yamut's openness. That was her sole purpose, to help the prince begat an heir and she knew she must never forget it. Her own life was worthless but, if she became pregnant all that would change.

'Very well, Yamut,' she said, following him along the now familiar passages to the prince's quarters.

***

The guards at the door stepped aside as soon as they saw her and she was sure she saw a smirk on the face of one of them as he opened the door for her to enter. Well, when she had succeeded in her task, he would be bowing to her, not smirking at her.

'Ah, Subh, it is you. Come here and let me see you. You look different tonight,' al-Hakim said as she entered.

The oil lamps flickered, sending ripples of soft light up the walls

'Yes, my prince. Tonight I am not Subh, tonight I am Djafar, a young man from Baghdad and I am going to tell you a tale from that wonderful book, "Alf Layla", "The Thousand Nights",' she said, her voice low and confident.

'I know it well. But do you think I am going to be like the King of Persia and chop off your head in the morning?'

'I hope not, my prince, because we still have many things to talk about and, so far, I have not recited to you the beautiful poems of my old mistress. You will be amazed at how elegantly she wrote.'

'I only joke, dear Djafar. Your head is far too handsome to be separated from your body. Come and sit beside me and I will listen to your story. These old folk tales should be told to everyone; they teach us much about life and how we should live it.'

So Subh began to tell him the story of 'The Fisherman and the Djinn':

'There once was a poor but honest fisherman who fished every day but only cast his net four times. One day, the first time he pulled in his net there was a dead donkey in it, the second time he pulled in his net there was a pile of stones, and the third time there were shards of pottery and broken glass. So before he cast his net for a fourth time, he prayed to God to send him a good catch and this time he netted a ceramic pot. It was not as good as a netful of fish but at least he could sell it in the market. He took the pot out of the net and opened it to see if it contained anything valuable. As the lid came off the pot, out flew an enormous djinn ...'

As Subh continued with her tale, she felt the prince's hand rest on her leg and begin to stroke it in an absentminded sort of way. He was not an unattractive man, despite his age, and Subh began to feel a stirring in her loins at his proximity. Zahr had insisted she drink a glass of *asafetida* before she left and it was making her feel warm and amorous. She wondered if she should respond to the prince in any way or just wait to see what happened, but before she could decide, the prince had removed his hand from her leg and placed it around her waist. She continued to tell the story and only paused when he leant across and began to kiss her neck.

'Sweet Djafar,' he murmured. 'My sweet boy.'

She heard the musicians creep quietly out of the room; she was alone with the prince, not even a guard was present. She remained quiet while he removed her shoes and pulled down her trousers. Then, still murmuring her new name, he rolled her over and was suddenly on top of her; the tales of 'The Thousand Nights' forgotten by both of them.

***

Before that night, Subh had been a virgin. She only knew what to expect from what she had been told. If anyone had cared about her feelings and questioned her on them, she would have had to admit that, from her point of view, the whole experience had been a great disappointment. However, as far as Yamut and the Royal Wife were concerned, it was a tremendous success and Subh found herself immediately moved into more lavish quarters, with a second maid to look after her and a room of her own.

'You did it,' said Zahr. 'How clever you are.'

'Yes, it was amazing how the prince seemed to look at me for the first time last night. He truly believed I was Djafar. Subh no longer existed for him.'

'See what a lovely room you have now. Just wait until you are pregnant, they will shower you with jewels and fine clothes. You will have rooms like the favourite concubines of the Khalifa.'

'What good will jewels and fine clothes be to me if I have to spend the rest of my life as Djafar?'

'Don't be silly, as soon as you have a child you won't have to see him again. He can go back to the real thing,' she said with a giggle.

'I suppose you're right. Anyway, the Royal Wife seems to be pleased with me, and every time Yamut comes into the harem, he beams at me.'

'Of course. You have bewitched the heir to the throne. Of course they are happy.'

Zahr flung herself down on the silk covered couch and gazed up at her. 'I will miss you,' she said.

'But I'm not going anywhere. We can still see each other all the time. You can brew my *asafetida* whenever you want.'

'I told you it was good,' Zahr said with a giggle.

***

After that the prince called for her every night. He seemed to enjoy her company as much as her young boyish body.

'What will you recite for me tonight, my sweet Djafra?' he asked her one evening.

'I have a poem by al-Ramadi. Do you like his work?'

'You know I do. He understands the workings of a man's heart.' he said, smiling at her.

Subh knew he would like this one and she hoped it would excite him; it was about a man in jail, who fell in love with a young black prisoner. She began, her voice soft and husky:

Your prisoner is one of those whom love deprives of reason;
My bosom is scorched by a fire worse than glowing coal:
He is a crescent, but does not rise in the sky,
He is a gazelle, but does not live in the desert:
I looked into his eyes and became drunken;
No doubt, eyes are like wine in their charm;
I talk to him so that he will answer me, but I
Do so on purpose to hear him scatter pearls:
I am his slave, he is the lord, just like his name:
I have a full share of his company, and he is mine!'

At first the prince said nothing; he just sat there, staring at the ceiling, a wistful smile on his lips. Then he looked at her and said, 'Come here, close to me. You know you are very special to me Djafar; you always seem to know exactly what I need.'

Subh moved closer to him and this time he kissed her on the lips.

She wondered later, when she realised that she was pregnant, if that had been the night she had conceived. She certainly had noticed a difference in his love-making. That night he had been more caring, treating her as though she were someone very precious to him, maybe he had been a little in love with her. She liked to dream that he had.

***

Afra pummelled her back and all the way down her legs before saying, 'Would you like to step in the hot bath now, *Sayyida*?'

Subh gave a contented grunt and sat up.

'Do you know what happened to Zahr? Is she still in the harem?' she asked.

'Zahr? The one who befriended you when you first came to the harem? I don't think so. I'm sure I heard that she had been given her freedom and married off to a local cobbler.'

'I wonder if she is happy.'

Afra gave her a strange look.

'Not as happy as you are, *Sayyida*.'

'When I am dressed I want you to send al-Jundi to me. I must speak to him.'

'Very well, *Sayyida*.'

Thinking about the harem had reminded her of something she had heard back then. The women of the harem, living in luxury with nothing to do except wait for their master to summon them to his bed, had plenty of time to gossip and reminisce. They loved nothing better than to recall old scandals, often embellishing the stories with happenings from their own imagination. But there was one story that she was sure was true. It was to do with a concubine of al Rahman III; her name was Jawhara and she had been captured as a child and brought to Madinat al Zahra and sold into the harem. Yamut would have been a young man, then; it was said to be over thirty years ago.

Apparently a young man from the town had broken into the *alcázar* and tried to kidnap her, but she had raised the alarm and managed to escape from him. In attempting to get away the young man had murdered one of the black eunuchs who was chasing him, then managed to escape over the palace wall. Later a stone mason was arrested and executed for the crime, but his family denied it all. His fiancé had appealed to the Khalifa and said that it was impossible for it to have been him as he had been with her all evening. But nobody believed her. Then the rumours had started that it was true after all, the stonemason was innocent and the murderer had fled the country, thanks to the help of one of the soldiers, his brother.

For some reason she felt that al-Jundi had been involved in it. It was to do with a remark al-Hakim had made to her. He had told her how this young soldier had saved his life in battle and that his father was so grateful he offered al-Jundi large sums of money, precious jewels, a good promotion, anything he wanted. He only had to ask and it would be his. But the soldier didn't want anything in return, except, and this was what struck everyone as strange, he wanted the Khalifa to promise to give his protection to him and all the members of his family, for as long as he lived. Al-Hakim's father had readily agreed to this strange request. Now it seemed to her that the soldier had been hiding something.

***

Al-Jundi bowed before her. It was true what al-Mansur said, he was an old man now, but he was still a handsome man, tall and broad and the muscles in his forearms looked as strong as ever.

'You wished to see me, *Sayyida*?' he asked, straightening up and looking at her with a clear, self-assured air.

She liked men with confidence. It suggested power, and there was something so attractive about a powerful man.

'Yes, soldier. I have been speaking to the Grand Vizier, al-Mansur. He is angry about the attempt on my son's life. He blames you.' She watched him carefully, trying to gauge his reaction but the soldier did not even blink. 'He thinks you're too old for the job and wants to get rid of you,' she continued.

Still he did not speak.

'What do you say to that, soldier?'

'What can I say, *Sayyida*? You know that my loyalty lies with the Khalifa. I would do anything to keep him from harm. I swore an oath to your husband that I would protect his son and that is what I will do, even if the Grand Vizier removes me from my post. But what are your thoughts on this, *Sayyida*? You are the Khalifa's mother. I know you want him to be safe. Is he not safer with me, someone who has sworn allegiance to him, than with a foreign mercenary who would change sides for an extra coin?'

She smiled. 'Indeed, al-Jundi. My son is very important to me and I want whatever is best for him. He is young and vulnerable. He needs good men at his side. When he is old enough to become the ruler of this land, then he can decide for himself whom he choses. In the meantime, the Regents decide for him. But, because he is so precious to me, I will stand by you because I know you have his interests at heart. But I would advise you to take care. Abu Amir is an ambitious man and when he wants something, he usually gets it. Be very careful. If you have any secrets, make sure they are well hidden,' she said, watching again carefully for his reaction to her words.

He bowed and asked, 'Is that all, *Sayyida*?'

'One more thing. Abu Amir believes that someone must have told the would-be assassin that the Khalifa would be out on the hunt that evening? Have you looked into that thoroughly? Do we have another traitor amongst us?'

'I have questioned everyone, *Sayyida* and the only people who knew that the Khalifa would be there were my son Ahmad, the Grand Falconer, myself and my soldiers. I believe I can vouch for all of them.'

'But someone must have told him.'

'It seems possible that it was just a coincidence. Everyone knew that the Khalifa would be going out to hunt one evening. Maybe the assassin was prepared to wait for the right moment.'

'But why there, in that particular place?'

'They always go there with the young birds, it seems. If the assassin knew that the Khalifa was just learning to fly his hawk, then it wouldn't require much effort to find out where they would be going.'

Then it came to her. There was someone else who knew al-Hisham would be going out with the hunt, maybe not that specific evening, but one day soon. Abu Amir knew, because she had told him. They had talked about her son and his new love of falconry, just before Abu Amir left for the campaign. Her mind was racing. Was her lover really capable of murdering her only surviving son? He professed to love her, but was it all an act? She could not accuse him openly; he would only deny it.

'Have you no clues as to who is behind the attack?' she asked. 'Did the man say nothing?'

'The man said nothing. All we have are his weapons: a crossbow and a short sword. The crossbow was standard issue for the Khalifa's army, which tells me that the assassin had some local connection but not much else. There are thousands of identical crossbows. We may have more luck with the short sword. It is an unusual design and it has a family motto engraved on the blade. I have instructed one of my men to find out who the motto belongs to.'

'What does it say?' she asked.

'Something like: "*Allah is my judge.*"'

It was as though a chill wind had entered the room. This was the motto of Abu Amir's family. She had seen it many times.

'I do not recognise it,' she said, looking away.

'Is that all *Sayyida*?' he asked.

'Yes soldier, that is all. But heed my words. There are people who would stop at nothing to get what they want. And Abu Amir is one of them.'

'*Ma'a salama, Sayyida.*'

'*Alla ysalmak.* And be vigilant,' she added.

Everything was pointing to Abu Amir. Could it just be coincidence? Or could he really be plotting to get rid of her son? There was no point in confronting him. He would sweet talk his way out of it as he always did. No, she would watch and wait, and she too would be vigilant.

CHAPTER 20

Al-Jundi was now convinced that the attack on the Khalifa had been planned. It was all too convenient; the only man who could have told them anything was now dead, shot with an arrow through the heart while walking right behind him. He had said as much to *al-Sayyida* when she had called him to her rooms, earlier that day.

That had been a strange meeting. Was she trying to warn him? What did she know about his past? And if she did know about his father or about Omar, who had told her? He couldn't quite work it out. Maybe he was just reading too much into her words. She obviously trusted him and wanted him to remain as her son's bodyguard and, from what he could make out, she didn't altogether trust her lover, al-Mansur.

Al-Jundi had thought that all that was past him once his father died. What did it matter now that his father had been the nephew of Omar ibn Hafsun, the most notorious and the most persistent of the rebels, a thorn in the side of Khalifa Abd al-Rahman III? If the Khalifa had discovered who they were at the time, they would surely have been banished from the city or maybe even suffered a worse fate, but Abd al-Rahman was dead now. Who would care what had happened sixty years ago?

And as for his brother Omar, it wasn't enough that he entered the forbidden area of the harem and tried to abduct one of the concubines, he had killed one of the Khalifa's men, trying to escape. That had nearly been the end for all the family but, luckily, al-Jundi had been at hand and helped him to get away. He had no idea where his brother was now, not even if he were alive or dead and it was better that way. Were these the secrets that *al-Sayyida* was alluding to? Well, he supposed that if someone was trying to get rid of him, that information would certainly furnish them with ammunition. Related to an infamous rebel, who had ended his days by having his bloody head displayed on a stake on the walls of the *alcazar,* and being the brother of a murderer and violator of the Khalifa's harem, were not good references for the bodyguard of al-Hisham. He would have to heed her words and be vigilant, for the sake of all his family.

He hurried through the streets towards his house. He had promised Amina that he would be home in time for the evening celebration. Since the attack on the Khalifa he had hardly spent any time with his family, reluctant to leave al-Hisham's welfare to others, even though he had chosen two of his most trusted men to replace him when he was off duty. But today was *Eid al-Fitra,* the last day of Ramadan and it meant a lot to Amina that he came home earlier than usual. He thought of his lovely wife, the only one he had taken because, from the moment he wed her, she was the one he truly loved. He needed no other. Today she was up before he left, before the sun had even crept over the horizon, before the cock had crowed. The stars still twinkled in an inky sky when she started sweeping and scrubbing the patio. She had roused the children from their beds and they had all gone to early morning prayers together and then visited the graves of their dead. His mother had wept as she had stood by his father's grave and clung to al-Jundi in her sorrow. She still missed Baba after all this time. Then al-Jundi made his way to the *alcázar*, and his family went home. Amina would have spent the whole day cleaning the house and preparing the sweetmeats for this evening: coconut squares, almond pastries, semolina cakes with dates and honey, orange and almond cake, honey and mint syrup cake and cinnamon biscuits. His mother would make her usual, a *tagine* of goat and vegetables. There would be far too much food. There always was.

'You made it then,' Amina said as he entered the patio and started to unbuckle his sword.

'Of course. I said I would be here and here I am.'

'I thought, maybe with all the problems at the palace …'

'No, dearest wife. Tonight I am here with my family,' he said, putting his arms around her and hugging her against him.

'Baba, Baba. Have you seen the cakes?' his youngest son cried, his eyes gleaming with excitement. 'Mama said we couldn't touch them until you came home.' The boy looked up at him expectantly.

'Well, little one, I'm home now. I expect you can have one, if your mother agrees.'

Amina smiled and nodded at her son, who grabbed a piece of honey and mint syrup cake and dashed off.

'Don't drip that honey down your new clothes,' she called after him then added, 'If I make him wait too long, he'll fall asleep and then miss it all.'

'Baba. Someone was asking about you, today,' said Qasim, sitting down beside his father.

'Asking about me? What did they want?'

'Well, I don't know exactly. One of the doctors told me. He said a man was looking for Makoud ibn Qasim and he had heard that his son was a doctor.'

'What did he look like?'

'He'd gone by the time I had finished with my patient but my friend said he was a tall man, very big with thick hair, like straw and a bushy beard. He said he was neither a soldier nor an educated man, but he seemed too confident to be a slave.'

The description seemed to fit al-Mansur's slave, Abbas. He was a brute of a man; the soldiers used to laugh and call him the Grand Vizier's henchman. If it was Abbas, what was he doing hanging around the hospital? And what did he want with al-Jundi? Was this what the Sayyida was trying to warn him about? Had al-Mansur sent his henchman to spy into his past, or maybe to kill him too?

'What else did your friend notice about him?'

'Nothing much. Only that he was enormous. Do you know who he is, Baba?'

'Maybe. It's nothing for you to worry about. Just make sure you're careful and let me know if you find anyone else asking questions about this family. All right?'

His sons were looking concerned now, but they both nodded in agreement.

'Where's Ahmad?' al-Jundi asked his wife.

'He's still getting dressed. You know what he's like when he has new clothes. He's quite a little peacock.'

Al-Jundi laughed. Of all his children, Ahmad was the one who most loved the tradition of getting new clothes at Eid.

'Well he'd better hurry up or we'll have eaten all the food,' he said as his mother placed the covered *tagine* on the table. As she lifted the lid, the aromatic flavours of mint, rosemary and honey drifted out, making his stomach rumble. Ramadan had seemed to last forever this time, the thirty days had seemed more like fifty.

'Help yourselves,' his mother said, and went into the bedroom to look for her preening grandson.

Despite his hunger, al-Jundi could not enjoy the meal as much as he usually did. His mind was racing with questions about al-Mansur. Why had he sent his slave to look for him and why to the hospital? How did he know that his son worked there? Were he and his family in danger? There was not much he could do about it, except to heed *al-Sayyida*'s words.

***

The Khalifa was, as usual sitting in the garden with his hawk, when al-Jundi arrived. A dead canary lay at his feet.

'Look at this, al-Jundi. This is one of the canaries I set free. I thought it would have a wonderful life, maybe flying back to where it came from, but instead, it has stayed here, in the garden and now a cat has killed it.'

'I'm sorry to hear that, Your Highness.'

'And yesterday, Daruj caught another of the song birds, and he had eaten it before I could do anything to help it. I am beginning to feel that my only achievement in releasing the birds was to provide food for predators.'

'Not so, Your Highness. You released many birds. It is only natural that some would not survive. You must remember that they had spent all their lives in cages. They were not used to having their freedom.'

'Like me, al-Jundi. Nobody will let me fly free, either, in case some predator kills me. Since Baba died I have spent all my life, imprisoned here in the *alcázar*. This is my cage,' he said, waving at the palace gardens.

'We are just trying to keep you safe, Your Highness. When you are older, it will be different. Then you will be able to make your own decisions.' He looked at the child, sitting there alone, his only companion, a peregrine falcon. It was not true what he had told him. Even when he was an adult, he would not have the freedom of an ordinary man; the Khalifa could never be truly free.

'When is Ahmad coming to see me?' he asked. 'I miss him.'

'He will be here this afternoon, as usual, won't he?' al-Jundi asked, surprised. He thought his son saw the Khalifa every afternoon.

'Yes, I know. But I want him here all the time. Tell the Grand Falconer that he must be here with me, every day.'

'Yes, Your Highness, but don't you have other things to occupy you, preparations for the day you take over the rule of this beautiful country?'

'Other things to occupy me? No. I have nothing else to do. When I told my mother I was bored, all she said was that I should visit my harem.'

He rubbed his eyes, brushing away a few tears and continued, 'I don't think I am ever going to be a proper Khalifa, al-Jundi. They are not going to let me rule. Not until I am old and grey. Maybe then, if I'm lucky.'

'That is not the case, Your Highness. You are the Khalifa and when you come of age, you will have to rule your kingdom. That is the law.'

'If I am still alive.' The tears were running down his cheeks now.

'Of course you will be alive. That is my job, to ensure that you live a long life. I am here to protect you,' al-Jundi said, with more emotion than conviction. The child was not stupid. He knew that he wasn't being protected; he was being imprisoned. The Regent had no intention of handing over the reins of power to him, not now nor later. Al-Hisham was beginning to understand his situation. Like the songbirds, he was a prisoner in everything but name.

'Well I don't care. I will find other things to do with my life. Tell the Grand Falconer that he must send me some more birds. The Falcon House is almost empty. I am the Khalifa and I deserve to have the best birds at my disposal. What use are they to me if they are in Córdoba?' al-Hisham said, standing up and stamping his foot to emphasise his words.

'Yes, Your Highness. I will tell the Grand Falconer what you have instructed.'

'And Ahmad. Don't forget to tell him about Ahmad.'

'Very well, Your Highness.'

'Do you play chess, al-Jundi?' the boy asked.

'Chess, Your Highness? No, I'm sorry, I don't play.'

'Pity.'

'Is there anything else you would like me to do?' he asked, feeling sorry for the boy, who was the richest person in the Western world and had no friends and nothing to do each day.

CHAPTER 21

Al-Mansur was furious. The Khalifa was meddling again. He had released that boy from prison, without a word to either of the Regents. It was too bad. With Ahmad in prison he had the perfect scapegoat. There was no way the falconer could have proved his innocence, especially if al-Mansur had instructed Abbas to say that he had seen him with the assassin the day before the murder attempt. Now he must make sure that nobody dug too deeply into Fida's background and connected that incompetent lout to him. With luck, Abbas had left no trace of the man and his past, so no-one would find out that al-Mansur had once - years before when he was working as a lawyer - done the man a service. Fida should have been dead long ago, and he would have been if al-Mansur had not persuaded the judge that it was a case of mistaken identity and that his client was an innocent man caught up in a family feud. The bodies of the dead woman and her child, whom Fida had thrown in the Guadalquivir, were never found, so it had been easy to convince everyone that just because they were missing did not necessarily mean that they were dead. He had suggested that it was much more likely that they had run away or, if they were dead, then the culprit was probably a relative, the husband or the brother, rather than a stranger who had nothing to gain by their deaths. The judge had not been wholly convinced, but al-Mansur had sown enough seeds of doubt to have the case dismissed and Fida walked free. There were a number of men, like Fida, who owed him their lives and from time to time he called in a favour. It was so much more useful than having to use his own men to do his dirty work. Unless he was very unlucky, their actions could never be traced back to him. And his luck took the form of a muscle-bound slave called Abbas, who was more than happy to remove any unwanted connections to his master. He smiled to himself. Yes, Abbas was a trustworthy servant and one well worth rewarding generously. He understood that the richer al-Mansur became, the richer he became.

'Dirar, find Abbas and send him to me. I will be in the garden.'

'Yes, *sayyad*.'

***

Al-Mansur strolled leisurely through the gardens of the half-finished palace. They promised to be spectacular when they were finished. The flower beds had been newly planted with roses and lavender and already two lakes had been dug and filled with crystal clear water piped up from the Guadalquivir. He planned to fill the lakes with golden carp. Marble fountains were being built in sheltered corners of the garden and the water from them would flow through narrow channels into tiny pools filled with water lilies. Myrtle bushes would line the pathways.

These gardens were going to be far better even than those in Madinat al-Zahra; he would make sure of that.

'You wanted to see me, *sayyad*?' a deep voice asked.

It was Abbas, his growling tone more like that of a bear than a man.

'Yes, I have much to talk to you about. Come and sit here beside me. I do not wish us to be overheard,' al-Mansur said, sitting down by the side of the lake.

'Yes, my Lord.' The slave squatted on the path beside him.

'Now, first of all, have you discovered anything further about the soldier, al-Jundi?'

'Not much, my Lord. Nobody has anything to say about him. He is a soldier and always has been. Some years ago, he was fortunate enough to save the life of al-Hakim in battle and was rewarded by the Khalifa. His family are unremarkable. His father was a potter and they came to Madinat al-Zahra to work. Nobody seems to know where they lived before that, but that's not unusual because many people flocked to the city at that time to help with the construction. Al-Jundi's father is dead now, and his mother lives with him and his family. I have to admit that nobody has a bad word to say about him, but there were some rumours about his brother.'

'What kind of rumours?'

'It was said that he broke into the Khalifa's harem and killed one of the eunuchs. But this was many years ago, when al-Rahman III was ruler.'

'So why wasn't he charged at the time?'

'They charged another man, a local workman. He protested his innocence but was executed nevertheless. It was only afterwards, when al-Jundi's brother had disappeared, that the rumours started. Al-Jundi worked at the *alcazaba* at the time. They say that he helped his brother to escape.'

'That is a treasonable offence.'

'But nothing was proved. And by the time the rumours started, al-Jundi had the protection of the Khalifa and his son.'

'Well, it's something to hold on to, just in case. You never know when such information could be useful. Good work, Abbas.'

'If you think he is a problem, just say the word and I will get rid of him for you.'

'I don't think that will be necessary. He is an old man now. Maybe we will just let nature take its course.'

'He's nearly sixty. I doubt if he can be much of a threat to you, my Lord.'

If only he could be sure about that. Nevertheless he said, 'You're right. I will leave him where he is for now. I have my spies inside the palace so I will soon hear if he is brewing trouble.'

'Was that all, my Lord?'

'Yes, that's all for now, Abbas.'

'*Ma'a salama*, my Lord.'

'Here, take this for your excellent work with Fida,' al-Mansur said, handing his slave a small sack of gold *dirhams*. 'The poor man never had a chance to collect it, so you might as well have it.'

He felt no remorse over the death of the assassin. He knew the wretch had been guilty of murdering the woman and child, but thanks to al-Mansur, he had been acquitted and lived ten more years of freedom. So what did it matter that now he was dead? Justice was served in the end.

PART 3
983 AD

CHAPTER 22

A column of black smoke rose into a bright blue sky, momentarily blotting the sun from his gaze. It gave him great satisfaction to see the flames licking around the bonfire, red, yellow, orange, blue, quite a kaleidoscope of colour. One of his men threw a few more books into the fire and the flames leapt up hungrily and pulled them down with the rest. The crowd roared their appreciation.

'What about these, my Lord?' asked one of the Palace Guards, holding up two beautifully illustrated books for his inspection.

'Are they copies of the Quran?' al-Mansur asked.

'I don't think so,' replied the guard.

'Burn them with the rest. All those blasphemous books, filthy scientific tracts. Burn them all.'

It had been an inspired idea to burn all the science books. It marked him out as a zealot, someone who cared for the spiritual wellbeing of his people, an uncompromising man when it came to religion. He would not let them be corrupted by books of astronomy, physics, astrology, chemistry, logic and all the rest of the mumbo-jumbo. No. Science was wicked, heterodox propaganda. These books had been unknown to their ancestors. It was only al-Hakam who had introduced such heresy to their city. Such books were written by foolhardy men who claimed to know the actions of Allah. In their hearts everyone knew that only Allah knew why the sun moved through the sky and why the stars were where they were. It was foolish pride to think that because you were learned that you could understand the workings of the universe. Only Allah understood that. To state otherwise went against Islamic law.

The fire was hungry now. The soldiers obediently flung baskets and baskets of books into the flames, which crackled greedily, sending showers of glowing sparks into the air, fountains of tiny stars rising higher than the walls of the *alcázar*. They fed its insatiable appetite until the air was thick with the smell of burning parchment and paper, and the smoke hung in a huge black pall over the square.

'Excuse me, my Lord. What about these books on medicine? Do they burn as well? And the ones on botany and herbs? There are many of them.'

'No. For now we will keep them. And the ones on mathematics. They may stay in the libraries for the moment. But make sure that your men bring all the other science books, every last one of them. I do not want people to be tempted into heresy by reading the lies they contain.'

'Very well, my Lord.'

Al-Mansur coughed, the smoke was choking him. He smiled to himself, the people were enjoying the spectacle. The fumes from the fire did not deter them. Each time new fuel was fed to the blaze, a roar of appreciation accompanied it. Yes, it had been a clever idea to burn the books. Now they would recognise him as a man of strict religious principles and see the Omayyads as the degenerate dynasty it had become. With this move he had taken another step in his journey towards becoming supreme ruler.

He turned to the officer by his side and said, '*Quaid*. Make sure this fire burns until they have all been destroyed. Leave not a single one behind.'

'Yes, my Lord.'

He pulled his cloak over his mouth and nose so that he could breathe more easily and walked back to his horse. He would ride along the river bank to his new palace. It was almost finished. Ismá and his children were already living there, as was his mother-in-law. It had been his wife's idea to take her mother to live with them after her father died. Al-Mansur would have been happy to leave her to rot.

General Ghálib's death had been most fortunate. His father-in-law had become a nuisance of late, rarely agreeing with him about anything. He certainly would not have agreed with today's actions. He had been a staunch supporter of al-Hakim and would have fought hard to stop the destruction of tens of thousands of his books. But his opinions were of little consequence to al-Mansur because the General was no longer here to make them heard.

In the end it had been his antagonism to al-Mansur that had led to his death. Foolish man to think he could take on the Grand Vizier of Córdoba and win. In a moment of rashness, he had allied himself with the Christian King Ramiro and declared war on the Regent. Al-Mansur could hardly believe it when he heard the news. His own father-in-law, his old mentor and protector, had challenged him to a battle because he did not agree with his policy of *jihad*. He did not want the Regents to pursue a religious war, he wanted al-Andalus to return to the strategy of the previous khalifas, to respect the borders of their Christian enemies and live in peace. Why couldn't he see that it was impossible to do that? How could they live in peace with the infidel? The Christians had to be defeated. There was no other solution. Only then would they have peace. He and Ghálib had argued about it for two years, and in the end the silly old fool had joined forces with Ramiro and declared war on him.

But Allah had been on their side that day. At first the General had acquitted himself well in battle, scattering the Berbers on al-Mansur's right flank and then breaking through his left flank, but before he could attack the centre, something spooked his horse and it reared up, unseating him. Ghálib's age had slowed his reactions and he was thrown forward and hit his head on the pommel of his saddle. When they picked up his body later from the bottom of a ravine, he was dead. It was clearly a sign from Allah. It had been easy work then to dispatch the Christian forces and al-Mansur had ridden home in triumph once more. As a lesson to anyone else who was considering disputing his policy of *jihad*, he had his father-in-law's head chopped off and displayed on the gateway to his new palace, al-Zahira.

That was where he was headed now. He felt very pleased with himself. The new *alcázar* was almost complete and it was more beautiful even than Madinat al Zahra; there was nothing to rival it anywhere. This was his bequest to the city of Córdoba, his legacy, one of the things for which he would be remembered. He had picked the site with care, on the eastern side of Córdoba, as far away as possible from the Khalifa and his palace, and north of the river. It was protected by the Sierra Morena to the north and by the Guadalquivir to the south. The land was flat and well watered, and it lay on the main road into Córdoba. When men rode towards the city from the east they would see his beautiful palace from miles away. Yes, he was pleased with what he had achieved. Everything was going to plan. He had completed the relocation of all the government departments back to Córdoba, his army was substantial - thanks to his many victories - and he had even persuaded Subh that she should spend all her time at al-Zahira, near him. He had been true to his word and built special rooms in the palace for her, spending a fortune furnishing them to her liking. Yes, his plans were taking shape nicely. The only cloud on the horizon was that al-Mushafi was being released from prison today, he had served his time, and although he would not be allowed to return to his duties, technically he was still one of the Khalifa's regents. Al-Mansur was going to have to do something about that, and soon.

***

When al-Mansur rode through the gates to his palace, the head of his household came out to meet him. He looked worried.

'What is the matter Dirar? Has something happened to the children?'

'No my Lord, your family is fine. There are some men waiting for you in the Great Hall. They are from the university and they are very angry.'

'Oh, is that all. It will be about the books. Send for the *imam*. Tell him I want him in the Great Hall, immediately.'

'Yes, my Lord.'

Al-Mansur handed the reins of his horse to the waiting groom. 'Rub him down well; he is covered in ash from the fires.'

'Yes, my Lord.'

'Now. Where are these blasphemous professors?'

He threw his cloak to one of the slaves and strode through the portico and into the Great Hall. He had modelled it on the one in Madinat al-Zahra and, apart from the lack of a throne at the head of the room, it was just as sumptuous. One day. One day he would have a throne built. But enough of that. First he must deal with these troublemakers.

'*As-salama alaykum*, gentlemen,' he said, bowing slightly. 'What can I do for you?'

'*Wa alaykum e-salam,*' the professors chorused.

Some of them he recognised. They were mostly mathematicians and scientists, as he had expected but there were also others whom he knew were writers and philosophers. What were they doing here?

'Well?' he repeated.

'You know very well why we are here. What you are doing is barbarous,' a grey bearded man said, his voice shaking so much with emotion that he could hardly get his words out.

'Our books are priceless. You cannot destroy them like that,' said another.

'Do you not realise that learned men journey thousands of miles to visit our libraries and study our books? We have the most important collection of scientific books in the world,' said a younger man, whom al-Mansur recognised as one of the philosophers.

'Had.'

The man looked puzzled.

'Had. You *had* one of the most important collections of scientific books in the world. They are no more. Sent through the flames back to the devil who begat them. These books that you revere so much, are blasphemous. They fly in the face of our religion. They are an insult to

Allah. And I will not stand for that. The people will not stand for it.'

'Those books were collected by the Khalifa al-Hakim himself, a deeply religious man,' the man with the grey beard said, still struggling to control himself. 'You had no right to destroy them. It will take years to replace them.'

Al-Mansur stared at him. 'Replace them?' he said. 'There will be no thoughts of replacing them. There will be no more science taught in Córdoba. I have already instructed the head of the university and he will be speaking to all of you. There are going to be significant changes.'

'But you can't do that.'

'You can't destroy all we have worked for.'

'It is scandalous.'

They all began talking at once, their voices rising in their agitation, their faces contorted with anger, their fear and frustration increasing with every word. He turned away from them. It was futile of them to protest and they knew it. It was rhetoric, nothing more. Isolated words caught his attention: 'barbaric', 'disastrous', 'irreplaceable', 'tragic', 'devastating', 'appalling'. It was just as he had expected.

'You sent for me, my Lord?' a quiet voice asked.

It was the *imam*, dressed in a plain white *djellaba* and carrying a copy of the Quran.

'Yes. I want you to explain to these so called men of learning why I was forced to cleanse our libraries and universities of these corrupt books.'

The *imam* bowed and turned to the group of professors, who looked at him in silence. Their rage had subsided and now they waited in despair.

'I know you all. You are God-fearing men. I see you at the mosque every week. You all know our laws. You know that Allah is not a vindictive God. Indeed, we are not a vindictive religion. We are happy to let the people of the Book worship their religion in their own way. You, yourselves, know many Christians and Jews who lead contented lives here in our great city; they hold important posts in the government, they even teach in our university. We are a tolerant people. But what our law does not tolerate is that anyone should try to turn a devout Muslim from the correct path,' the *imam* began.

Some of the professors nodded in silent agreement.

'These books of supposed scientific fact are filled with lies. Lies that suggest that we, lowly creatures that we are, know more about the universe and its laws than its creator. Only Allah knows how the universe was created. Only Allah knows why the stars are in the firmament. Only Allah knows why the wind blows one day from the east and another from the west. All these questions with which you fill your trusting students' heads are questions for Allah. They can be answered by reading one book, and one book only.'

He held up his copy of the Quran to emphasise his point.

'When you encouraged your students to read one of those books you were unwittingly turning him from the true path of his religion. That is why the books have been destroyed. Go back to your students and explain to them that this action was for them, to maintain their purity, to keep them from straying from the path of a true believer. And *insha'Allah,* let us pray that such an act will never be necessary again.' The *imam* bowed to the professors and said, 'May Allah go with you, my sons.' Then the *imam* left the room as quietly as he had arrived, leaving the men staring at the floor, their faces filled with anguish and hopelessness.

'Well, gentlemen, I must leave you. I have business to attend to. I hope you marked well the words of our holy man, and that I will hear no more of this,' said al-Mansur.

He knew that the mutterings would continue, but the professors would not go against the words of the *imam*. In time they would accept the situation or they would leave the city. It was all the same to him. What was important was that the people of Córdoba recognised him as a strict upholder of their religious beliefs.

'Dirar, is *al-Sayyida* in her quarters?' he asked.

'Yes, my Lord. She is waiting for you.'

***

The Khalifa's mother was lying on a low couch, strewn with silk cushions of various hues of blue; she looked as though she were floating on water, her golden hair, already streaked with silver, spread out below her.

'Subh, my love, are you well?' he asked, bending and kissing her on the mouth. She tasted of honey.

'I am well, my dearest but my mind is troubled,' she said, sitting up and pulling her long robe down over her feet. 'The people of the city are saying that the Khalifa is dead. It has been such a long time since anyone has seen him that they are saying you have murdered him.'

'You know that is not true, my love. You know that I would never harm your son. He is alive and well. You must have seen him yourself when you last visited him. When was that?'

Subh looked away. 'I have not seen him in many months. I have been far too busy here, settling in to my new home,' she said.

'Well, I can assure you he is unharmed. You mustn't listen to such rumours. You know how people love to gossip, and they don't care if it is the truth or a lie that they repeat.'

'I believe you when you tell me that Hisham is alive but rumours like this have a way of becoming fact in the minds of simple people. It would not go well for you if they thought you had murdered the rightful ruler of al-Andalus, the Khalifa, a boy you are supposed to be protecting.'

There was the hint of an accusation in her voice but he could see the sense in her words.

'So what do you want me to do?' he asked.

'Bring him here. Let the people see for themselves that he is alive. He can stay here in the palace.'

So once again she was trying to persuade him to allow the Khalifa to live in Córdoba. Well his answer would be the same as before. He would never bring the boy here. No, the Khalifa had to stay in Madinat al Zahra. If he brought him to the palace now, it would undo all that al-Mansur had achieved. Al-Hisham was eighteen now. If he were to live in Córdoba, in plain sight of his subjects, then it would not take long for people to question why he still needed a regent and why he could not rule himself. No, al-Mansur couldn't risk that. But Subh was right in one aspect. He could not allow rumours that he had murdered the Khalifa to circulate. The people needed to see for themselves that he was alive.

He sat down on the couch beside his mistress and stroked her arm. 'I will arrange for al-Hisham to attend the mosque in Córdoba this Friday. We will pray together. Then people will see that he is indeed alive and that the rumours are no more than that. Will that satisfy you, my love?'

'If you think that is sufficient, then yes,' she replied.

He knew she would prefer to have her son in Córdoba but she would not oppose him.

'So that's what we will do then.'

He kissed her neck and whispered, 'I will come and see you later, dearest. Now I have business to attend to.'

As he left Subh's rooms, ibn Dirar was waiting for him.

'Al-Mushafi would like to speak to you. I have sent him to the Great Hall.'

'Very well. And the professors?'

'They have left, my Lord.'

'Good. Well let's see what this jailbird wants with me.'

It was proving to be a day fraught with irritations. How much simpler life was when he was on a *jihad*. Then you had but one enemy and you knew who it was. There was no need for diplomacy nor negotiation nor intrigue. You had an enemy to fight and that was all you needed to concentrate on.

'*As-salama alaykum*, al-Mushafi, my dear friend, how good it is to see you again. Are you well?' al-Mansur asked, stepping forward and hugging his former friend.

'*Wa alaykum e-salam*, Abu Amir. It is good to be home with my family,' al-Mushafi said, returning the embrace.

'Your children must be happy to see you again. It has been a long time.'

'Yes, five years. They have grown into young men since I last saw them.'

'So what can I do for you?' al-Mansur asked. He did not want to waste time speaking of trivialities.

'I have not come to ask you for anything, my friend. I have come to tell you that I am back and I am at your disposal. I realise that I cannot hold any post of importance any more but I would like to work. I was deeply saddened to hear of the death of our good friend General Ghálib, but then I realised that you would need my help more than ever now.'

'Indeed.'

'And what of the boy? He will soon be able to take over his role as ruler, will he not?' al-Mushafi asked.

'He is remaining in Madinat al-Zahra for now. I fear he is rather immature, still.'

'How sad. Well I will be happy to spend time with him, acquainting him with what he needs to know until we deem him to be ready.'

We? We deem? Did this man, so recently released from prison, think that he would be helping al-Mansur to make such decisions? The impertinence of him. It was all he could do not to strike him down, there and then.

'I was pleased to see that the court has moved back to Córdoba. It is a short distance from my home. I would be able to start work right away, if you would like me to,' al-Mushafi continued, seemingly unaware of the affect of his words on al-Mansur.

'That is wonderful news but you should at least give yourself a day or two to spend with your family. I have urgent business this afternoon, but why don't you come here again tomorrow and we will talk about the future,' al-Mansur said, forcing himself to remain calm.

'Of course. Thank you Abu Amir. I won't take up any more of your time. *Ma'a salama.*'

'*Alla ysalmak*, dear friend. Until tomorrow, then.'

There was no ignoring it now. He had to do something about al-Mushafi, and quickly. He knew that the wily politician was not deceived by his smiles and warm embrace. True, the ex-Grand Vizier could not know for sure that it was al-Mansur who had instigated the investigation into his finances which had led ultimately to his imprisonment, but he would certainly have his suspicions. In which case he was dangerous and he would be looking for revenge. It did not do to ignore vengeful men.

***

His bodyguard was in his private office, squatting on the floor, awaiting his return. His huge form was hunched, his legs pulled beneath him. Light, coming through the slatted windows, fell on his gleaming muscles, Abbas, the Lion, fierce and unswerving in his loyalty to al-Mansur. Thank goodness he had someone like him to rely on.

'Ah, Abbas. I want to speak to you.'

'Yes, my Lord.'

'I am unhappy about the Khalifa's behaviour. You remember how he took it upon himself to release the prisoner Ahmad?'

'Yes, *sayyad*.'

'That was a pity. I don't want him thinking that he can do anything he wants, especially now that he is eighteen. I can't have that. I can't have him believing that he can go against the Regents and get his own way. We need to do something to discredit the Khalifa, to make him more unpopular with the people.'

'What do you have in mind?'

'His father was homosexual. Everyone knows that. But somehow he managed to father two children. Now, it could be that they were not his children after all. Maybe someone else was the father. Maybe it's time that people started questioning the legitimacy of our young Khalifa.'

'But he has a strong resemblance to his father. The red hair and the blue eyes. Those are not the characteristics of an Arab.'

'Indeed they are not but his mother, the queen, is of fair complexion. Who is not to say that her own father did not have red hair? Who is not to say that she did not sleep with someone of al-Hakim's colouring, so that the child could be passed off as his own?'

'But she was in the harem. She would never have been allowed to go anywhere without a guard.'

'The Royal Wife was desperate for her son to have an heir; the *Sayyida* has admitted as much to me, herself. She said that the prince's mother would have gone to any lengths to get one, maybe even allowing a concubine to leave and find another lover. Anyway I have heard from the *Sayyida's* own lips, that al-Hakim allowed her to leave the harem from time to time as long as she was dressed as a boy. She even went to the mosque with him once to pray, and nobody recognised her.'

'So you want me to spread some rumours that the Khalifa is a bastard?'

'Exactly. But be discreet.'

'I will be arrested if I am caught. It is a serious crime to spread sedition.'

'And even more serious to speak ill of the Khalifa, but you will do it and do it well. Just drop the odd comment here and there. Nothing too overt. I have great confidence in you, Abbas.'

'Very well, *sayyad*. Was there anything else?'

'Yes. I have an important job for you to do but nobody must trace it back to me. Is that understood?'

'Naturally, my Lord.'

'The old Grand Vizier, al-Mushafi has been released from prison. I would like it if he were to disappear.'

'Very well.'

'However it must look like an accident. I do not want his sons clamouring at my door, accusing me of getting rid of their father.'

'I understand, my Lord.'

'And it must be done soon. This is a task of great urgency.'

'I will see to it straight away. Do not fear, my Lord, no-one will ever know.'

'And I do not want to know the details.'

The eunuch nodded his great shaggy head.

'Is that all, my Lord?'

'Yes, for now. Report back to me when it is done.'

Abbas, bowed and left the room. It was done. He knew that his slave would not let him down. What a pity they had not kept al-Mushafi in jail longer and then this would not have been necessary.

CHAPTER 23

Subh wandered around her new rooms, examining the quality of the tapestries that hung on the wall, feeling the silk sheets, inspecting her private bathroom. Bit by bit, Afra had transferred all her clothes and jewellery from the *alcázar* in Madinat al-Zahra and installed it in this new palace in Córdoba. It was all as it should be, expensive and of a quality suitable for the mother of the Khalifa, but somehow it lacked the sumptuousness of her old rooms.

Al-Hisham had not been happy when she told him she would be spending more time in Córdoba. He had clung to her and begged her to stay in the old palace, and for a moment she almost weakened. He looked so lonely, standing there with his falcon on his wrist, surrounded by guards and household slaves, but no family and no friends. He was eighteen now, but he looked much younger; there was hardly any beard on his face and his voice was still very feminine. He was legally a man, but he seemed to her to be still a vulnerable young boy. How could she leave him there alone? But then she reminded herself that she was doing this for him. If she stayed in Madinat al-Zahra with her son, they would both soon be forgotten and who knew what might happen to them?

There were already rumours circulating that al-Hisham was dead. It would be so easy to dispose of the Khalifa now the court had gone. True there were hundreds of Palace Guards to protect him but they were under the command of al-Mansur. Her lover's power was growing all the time. She needed to be in Córdoba to keep an eye on him, for her son's sake as well as her own.

'Here is your water, *Sayyida*,' Afra said, placing a jug of cool water and a glass on the table beside her.

'Thank you, Afra. Have you been into the city this morning?'

'Yes, *Sayyida*. I went to buy you some new ribbons.'

'Well? What news?' Afra always came back from her shopping trips with the latest gossip. It was an excellent way to gauge the true feelings of the people of Córdoba. 'Sit down beside me and tell me what they are saying in the market about al-Mansur,' Subh instructed her.

'His wife has just given birth to another son,' Afra said.

'Indeed.'

Al-Mansur had not mentioned that Ismá was pregnant again. So now he had three sons.

'They have called him al-Rahman.'

'Servant of the beneficent. The name of a khalifa? How pretentious.' What was al-Mansur thinking, calling his new son Rahman? Did he intend to set his sons up as rulers ? What else did he have in mind for his family?

'Is that all you heard today?' she asked, pretending that the news was of little interest to her. 'What do people say about him? Is he popular?'

'Oh yes, *Sayyida*. He is very popular, especially since he reconquered the fort at Gomaz.'

Yes, that had been a great success for him. The loss of that fort to the Christians had been devastating; it was in a strategically strong position, close to the Duero and said to be vital to the security of the realm. Some years earlier al-Mansur had made an attempt to recover it when he had sacked the city of Ledesma but had failed. She knew how much it had hurt his pride to ride back to Córdoba and admit defeat. He had spoken to her many times of his determination to recover that fort for al-Andalus. So, when two years ago, he had taken his army and made a successful raid on Gomaz, he had returned to Córdoba with his head held high and his popularity secured.

'That man who was in prison, you know, the one who was the Grand Vizier years ago, he's dead,' Afra continued. 'Some people say he was poisoned, others say he committed suicide but most people think it was his wife's cooking. She is so mean she always buys fish that is at least two days old. They say that he died of food poisoning from a fish stew she had made the day before, and some say that if he hadn't been in prison all those years, she would have accidentally poisoned him long ago.'

'You mean al-Mushafi? He's dead?'

'Yes, that's him. Died last night, in agony, they say. They got a doctor to visit him but it was too late; he could do nothing for him.'

'How dreadful. The poor man.'

She couldn't believe it. He had come to see her only the day before, and they had spoken at some length. At first she had been reluctant to see him, but he had been so contrite, saying that he had made a terrible mistake and he had paid for it, so full of remorse, that she could not deny him an audience. He said how all he wanted now, was to offer his services to the Khalifa. He promised to do everything he could to protect him and help him become the ruler he was destined to be. He had said that the time for a Regency was over, that al-Hisham should be ruling his kingdom, not the Regent. And she had believed him. Now he was dead.

Al-Mushafi was dead. General Ghálib was dead. Al-Mughira was dead and his sons exiled. The only one who remained, who stood between al-Mansur and total power, was her son, al-Hisham. She felt herself shiver, as though a cold breeze had entered the room.

'I got your ribbons, *Sayyida*. I hope you like them. They are a new range, just arrived from the East.'

Her maid laid a collection of silk ribbons in front of her to inspect, but Subh's mind was not on ribbons, it was frozen with fear. If anything happened to al-Hisham she would be thrown out of the palace to fend for herself. Al-Mansur said he loved her, but she was not so naive as to think that any love he had for her would be enough to overcome his ambition. A man who could have his own son beaten to death for a minor infringement of the law, would not hesitate to get rid of an old lover. It occurred to her that it had been a long time since her lover had wanted anything from her other than sex. He no longer discussed matters of state with her or confided what was troubling him. Maybe he shared this information with his wife, but she doubted it; he was too imperious for that. He was drawing away from her bit by bit. It bothered her. If she was to hang on to her comfortable life then she had to exert a stronger influence over him.

'Oh, there is something else,' Afra said. She seemed hesitant. 'It may only be a rumour, of course.'

'What is it, girl?' Subh snapped. 'What have you heard?'

'Al-Mansur is going to take another wife.'

'So soon? Who is she?' she could barely keep her voice steady.

'It may only be a rumour, *Sayyida.*'

'Who is she?' she asked, with an icy calm.

'They say she is the daughter of Sancho Garcés, the King of Navarra. Her name is Abda. They say she is very beautiful.'

'A political alliance, nothing more.'

'And only eighteen.'

Eighteen. The same age as her son. She turned away from her slave so that Afra could not see her tears.

'Leave me now. I have listened enough to your silly tittle-tattle.'

'Yes, *Sayyida*.'

There were no bounds to her lover's ambitions; she knew that now. She must be careful and look out for her own interests and those of her son. She would convince him that her son should be left in Madinat al Zahra, that he would be no threat to him, that he could continue to rule as Regent and that al-Hisham was more use to al-Mansur alive than dead. He would surely recognise that even his popularity was not that strong that the people would allow him to depose the rightful Khalifa, the lawful successor to the Prophet. If anything happened to al-Hisham, the suspicion would surely fall on al-Mansur. He must see that.

She wiped away her tears. She would not waste them on al-Mansur. It was the birth of her sons which had given her her current position and it would be their deaths that would take it away.

A pigeon came to rest by the pond. She watched the bird bend its purple neck and drink from the clear water, its beak setting up a series of ripples that spread across the surface of the pond, growing and growing until, finally they could grow no more and dispersed. Was her life like these circles on the water? She had come to Córdoba as a young slave girl with nothing, then she became the Prince's concubine, becoming richer and more powerful with each year, until she became the most powerful woman in the kingdom, the Khalifa's mother, *al-Sayyida al-Malika,* but now her power was diminishing and it would soon disappear into nothingness, just like the ripples on the water. The pigeon's mate, a drabber version, joined him and together the birds drank their fill then flew off with a noisy flap of their wings.

'Afra. Afra,' Subh called.

'Yes, *Sayyida*?'

'I am going to visit my son. Pack some clothes for me and arrange transport for us. Let everyone know we will be gone for a few days.'

'Very well, *Sayyida*. When do you want to leave?'

'Right away.'

She had to see Hisham as soon as possible. She needed to be sure that he was all right.

CHAPTER 24

Al-Jundi was about to go home when he was stopped by one of the palace guards.

'Excuse me, *Quaid*, there is a soldier outside, wanting to speak to you. He says it's urgent.'

'Send him in.'

A young *nazir*, whom al-Jundi recognised from the barracks, hurried up to him, bowed abruptly and said, 'Excuse me, *Quaid*, but we have arrested a man who has been spreading vile rumours about the Khalifa. You need to see him, right away.'

'Why the hurry, soldier? Can't he just rot in the cells until I have time to see him?'

'No, *Quaid*. With respect, you must deal with this right away.'

'And why is that? Who is this treasonous rumour monger?'

'His name is Abbas. He is one of al-Mansur's slaves.'

Now he understood. How astute of the young *nazir*. He knew that once al-Mansur heard about the arrest of his man, he would have him released at once.

'I thought you would want to know as soon as possible,' he added, bowing politely.

'You thought correctly. You have done well, *nazir*. Take me to this villain, right away.'

He followed the young soldier out of the Khalifa's private quarters and into the *Dar al-Jund*, where the man was being held. He had been locked in a small cell and a number of al-Jundi's hand-picked men were gathered around, discussing what they should do with the prisoner. They all stood to attention when al-Jundi entered the jail.

'At ease men. Now, will someone please tell me why this man, a trusted servant of the Grand Vizier, has been arrested and thrown in the dungeons?'

'He was overheard making treasonous statements about the Khalifa. We have five witnesses to prove it.'

'Indeed and what did he say that was so treasonous?'

'He made a number of statements to the effect that al-Hakim was not really the Khalifa's father and that therefore he was an imposter.'

'A bastard, is what was said,' added another soldier, rather more outspoken than the first. 'He has been telling everyone that al-Hakim was not capable of siring a child and that the concubine Subh was allowed to couple with another man in order to become pregnant. He says al-Hisham is not the rightful heir to the throne because he has no Omayyad blood in his veins.'

'And can he prove this?' asked al-Jundi.

'I think not, *Quaid*. I think he is just trying to stir up trouble. It has been said that he has been spreading this rumour in Córdoba, as well.'

'We thought you should know before the Khalifa gets to hear of it,' said the young *nazir*.

'You did well to alert me. You have witnesses, you say. Bring them here and get their written statements. We will take them and this treacherous wretch to the judge.'

'Shall we transport him to Córdoba, *Quaid*?'

'No, that's not necessary. We still have one judge left here in Madinat al-Zahra. We will take him to Abu Adil. I have no intention of losing another prisoner on the journey to Córdoba,' he added, ruefully. 'While you are doing that I will speak to the Khalifa's mother. I hear she is here in Madinat al-Zahra at the moment. And while I am away, guard the prisoner with your life. I want no-one to go near him, no-one except you men. Is that understood?'

***

Al-Sayyida was in her old quarters in the *zenana*. He sent her a message to say that he wanted to speak to her and, reluctantly he thought, she agreed to meet him in the palace gardens.

'Well, al-Jundi, what is it now?' she asked, tetchily.

'I have come to tell you that we have arrested a man for spreading vile rumours about your son's blood line,' he said, a little unsure how she was going to react.

'His bloodline? His bloodline is that of the Omeyyads.'

'I know, *Sayyida*. But this man has been spreading lies about him and you.'

'What exactly has he been saying? Speak up, man.'

'He says that al-Hakim wasn't his father. That he is a bastard.' Better not to elaborate on how she was supposed to have left the harem to meet the man who fathered him.

'What?' she screamed at him. 'Who is this man that's telling such lies? Where is he now?'

'We have him in the dungeons, *Sayyida*. He will go before the judge this evening. I will personally take him there. We have witnesses to prove his treason,' he added.

'So what is his name? Where is he from, this liar, this traitor? I want him executed.'

'His name is Abbas, *Sayyida*. He is a slave in the household of Abu Amir.'

He watched the colour drain from her face.

'Abu Amir? Are you sure?' she asked, her voice changed. She looked like a woman who had seen a ghost.

'Yes, we are certain. He is one of his most trusted servants.'

So she knew nothing about this, he could tell from her demeanour. The servant of her lover was spreading lies about her and her son. What could that mean?

'Go back to the prison and make sure that this servant receives the full punishment of the law. Treason cannot be tolerated. My son must be protected at all cost. And let me know when it is done.'

'Yes, *Sayyida*. Do you want to tell the Khalifa or should I? he asked.

'I will tell him, but not yet. I need to find out why this man has been spreading these lies. I will tell my son when the danger has passed.'

'Very well, *Sayyida*.'

He was tempted to tell her than she should move back to Madinat al-Zahra, that her son needed her, but he knew it was not his place to offer advice unless asked for it. Al-Jundi had seen a change in his charge over the last few months. He was no longer the same shy, vulnerable boy eager for friendship who had been thrust into the role of Khalifa, he was instead sullen and introverted. With puberty had come an interest in his harem and he spent many hours there. Like his father before him, he had a preference for young men, and most of the women in his harem had been dismissed, either married off or found jobs as servants in other parts of the palace.

Al-Hisham still loved his falcons and continued to see Ahmad every day, but al-Jundi was beginning to worry about the amount of time his son spent at the palace. He was twenty-two now and he needed to start thinking more about his career and maybe even marriage. Al-Jundi's eldest son, Qasim—named after his grandfather as all first-born sons were—had married the previous year and now had a house near the hospital. It was time Ahmad gave some thought to his own future. He and Amina had discussed a suitable bride for Ahmad and even approached the girl's father. The girl in question was the daughter of one of his men, a man he liked and trusted. She was comely and seemed to both him and Amina to be a perfect wife for Ahmad.

He sighed. If he was truthful with himself, he wanted to get Ahmad away from the Khalifa's influence. He could see that al-Hisham was becoming very attached to Ahmad, and not just as a friend. So far, his son seemed unaware that the Khalifa's interest had taken a more sexual turn. He did not have the same opportunities as al-Hisham to explore his own sexuality. He would remain a virgin until he took his first wife, like most commoners. He had no harem waiting for him each night. No, it would be better if Ahmad married as soon as possible. Tonight they would speak to him about it. But now, he must see to the prisoner.

***

Abbas was taken to the law courts that evening and the judge's decision was swift and final. The condemned man was to be returned to his cell and executed the following morning at first light. His head was to be displayed on the parapets, along with common thieves and murderers. No clemency was offered. The judge spoke briefly and with gravity of the severity of his crime, and explained to all present that treason against the Khalifa was not a crime that would ever be tolerated.

Abbas had stood, silent and with his head bowed until the sentence was passed then he said, 'Please tell my master that I am sorry to have betrayed his trust.' They were the only words he spoke.

Was he trying to suggest that al-Mansur had known nothing of this? Al-Jundi found it hard to believe. Abbas was too astute to go around making such dangerous statements about the Khalifa unless he thought al-Mansur would protect him. This time he was wrong. By the time his master received the news, Abbas's head had already parted company from his body.

As soon as the execution had taken place and Abbas's headless body was thrown into the lime pit outside the city walls, al-Jundi went to check on the Khalifa.

***

That evening, when al-Jundi and his family were about to sit down to dinner, they had an unexpected visitor. It was al-Jundi's brother Ibrahim.

'Ibrahim. What a surprise. Is something the matter?'

He hadn't seen his brother in almost two years, despite the fact that he lived in Córdoba, not that distant. Whenever they met they promised to see more of each other, but Ibrahim had made his life in Córdoba and between his pottery business and his growing family he was kept very busy, and al-Jundi never liked to stray far from the Khalifa's side.

'Can't one brother visit another without something being wrong?' he asked, kissing al-Jundi on both cheeks.

'Not when he arrives at dinner-time, unannounced. I suppose we'll have to lay another place for you.'

But his wife had already got out an extra plate and moved the children along so that Ibrahim could sit down.

'True, brother, but can we speak in private first?'

They went outside onto the patio and sat by the fountain. It was a clear, cold night, with the moon hanging large in the sky, like an enormous lantern.

'So what is it?' al-Jundi asked, feeling apprehensive.

'You will never believe it,' Ibrahim said excitedly. 'I have had a message from Omar. He is on his way home. He should arrive in Córdoba in a couple of months time.'

'No. He can't come back. He knows that.'

'But the Khalifa is dead now, and his son. Baba is dead too and Omar is an old man now. There is nobody left that could identify him.'

'He cannot return.'

'But he is homesick, al-Jundi. He wants to be with his family again. He wants to spend his last days here in Madinat al-Zahra.'

'You must send him a message and say that he cannot return just yet. It is still too dangerous.'

'But why do you say that? So many years have passed. What does it matter now?'

'Believe me Ibrahim. There are people to whom this matters. Powerful people, who are trying to find out if I have any skeletons in my cupboard so that they can discredit me and remove me from my post. If Omar returns and anyone should recognise him, or if he inadvertently tells anyone who he is, it could bring disaster to my family, and probably to all of us.'

'So he is destined to spend the rest of his life in exile? How cruel.'

'I know. He has been paying all his life for the foolishness of a young man. But you must contact him and warn him. It is still not safe, not here, nor in Córdoba.'

If Omar could be persuaded to stay away, it was very unlikely that anyone would find out about al-Jundi's involvement in the whole sorry business. In time, al-Mansur would give up; other things would become more important than looking into al-Jundi's past. He no longer had his henchman by his side, so he would have to find someone else that he could trust. And that was not so easy, not in this city of intrigue and conspiracy.

'The food is getting cold,' Amina called from inside the house.

'We're coming, wife,' al-Jundi said, then added, 'Do as I say, Ibrahim. It's for the best.'

CHAPTER 25

Subh was beside herself with rage. Al-Mansur was behind this, she was sure. No-one else would even dream of starting such a rumour. To suggest that the Khalifa, her son, was illegitimate was too much. Everyone could see that he was al-Hakim's son. He was so like him, the same blue eyes, the reddish-gold hair, his same way of talking. He was his father's son. There was no doubt about that. What was al-Mansur trying to achieve by spreading such lies? She remembered clearly how pleased al-Hakim had been when she told him that he was to become a father

***

She was pregnant. There was no doubt about it; her breasts were tender and she had not bled for two months. She went straight to the Royal Wife to tell her the news.

'My dear child. I am so pleased. You have done very well. Very well indeed. I knew that if anyone could seduce my son, it would be you and you have proved me right,' the Royal Wife said, her face alight with pleasure. 'His father, the Khalifa will be delighted when I tell him.'

'Thank you, Your Highness,' Subh said, bowing politely.

'Have you told my son the good news yet?'

'No, Your Highness. I will tell him tonight when he sends for me.'

'Good. That will scotch these rumours that my son is impotent. Now, child, you must take good care of yourself. This baby that you carry is very precious. One day he will be the ruler of all al-Andalus.'

From that moment her life changed. If she had thought she lived in luxury before, it was nothing compared to the riches that her father-in-law, the Khalifa showered on her now: jewels, gold, land and houses. She wanted for nothing. But better than that she was now the official favourite wife of Prince Hakim and he treated her with love and respect.

The months passed quickly as her body changed shape and the child grew inside her.

'There is a doctor here to see you, my lady,' Afra said.

'A doctor? But I'm not ill.'

'The Royal Wife wants her to examine you to make sure everything is all right.'

'Very well, send her in.'

A young Jewish woman, in black robes and with her hair plaited around her head, came into the bedroom. '*As-salama alaykum*, my dear. My name is Rebecca. Your mother-in-law is concerned about your pregnancy.'

'*Wa alaykum e-salam*, Doctor Rebecca. There is no need. I am very well.'

'I understand that this is the baby that the Royal family have been hoping for, for many years. You will understand if the Royal Wife is rather anxious.'

'Of course, but really, I am fine.'

'If you wouldn't mind, I will just examine you. Could you please remove your outer garments; you can leave your undershirt on, if you chose.'

The doctor asked her questions about her appetite and whether she still suffered from the early morning sickness. She examined her breasts and listened to her stomach.

'You can hear the baby's heart beating,' she said. 'It sounds a strong child. Now, let me see your ankles. They are a little swollen but I can give you an infusion that will help with that. What about sleeping? Do you get plenty of sleep?'

Subh looked around her and smiled, 'Yes, I lead a life of rest and repose.'

'Good. Tranquility is very good for the baby. A tranquil mother will have a contented baby. Now, I will come and see you each week to make sure that everything is going well.'

She wrote out a prescription for Subh's swollen ankles and handed it to Afra. 'The pharmacist will make that up for you. It's a mixture of lavender, cypress and juniper berries, very good for tired limbs. Mix a spoonful with warm water and leave it to infuse for five minutes and then strain it and give a cup to your mistress,' she said, picking up her bag and leaving.

Subh lay down on the couch with her feet on a cushion. She would see the Prince this evening as usual. She had already planned to recite some of her old mistress's poems for him tonight. There was one she particularly liked, about the miracle of birth; that would be very appropriate. The Prince no longer made love to her, but he still sent for her every evening to ask how she was feeling and to listen to her stories.

Once the little prince, Abd al-Rahman was born, a chubby, fair-skinned baby boy with blue eyes and a wisp of reddish hair, the Khalifa gave her the name *umm al-walad*, mother of a son. She had fulfilled her purpose. Nobody would ask any more of her. But that was not the end of it because, to everyone's surprise, a true friendship had grown between her and al-Hakim and he continued to send for her, not every night as before, but often. They would talk about poetry or she would entertain him with tales from 'The Thousand Nights'. He taught her how to play chess and they would sit in the cool of the garden during the hot summer months, playing far into the night. He still visited the other parts of his harem where the young men lived, but he did not neglect his wife. Unlike the other women in his harem, Subh was allowed to leave occasionally to visit the markets or wander around the city, but only dressed as a young boy and with Afra to accompany her. Sometimes al-Hakim would make her hide her hair in a cap, wind a scarf around her head and face, put on men's clothing and accompany him to the mosque to pray. The deception excited them both and when they returned to his rooms, he would make love to her. In this way, her second son was conceived and, when al-Hisham was born, Subh's place in the Omayyad royal family was secured forever.

***

She pulled her woollen cloak around her and set off to see al-Mansur. She knew he would be in the Treasury at this hour. He was very preoccupied with money at the moment; according to the gossip, his new palace was costing much more than he had intended and there was less tax revenue to pay for it because he had cut the tax on olive oil the year before - another move to gain popularity with the citizens of Córdoba. And it had worked. He was now more popular than ever and he was about to leave again to fight another *jihad*. That would swell the coffers of the Treasury, no doubt. Some even said that the *jihads* were really just about looting and sacking Christian churches and monasteries - always a rich source of treasure - and nothing to do with religious fervour. But no-one said it to his face. Her lover was becoming too powerful for dissent. The army had increased greatly in size since the days of al-Hakim, and al-Mansur had incorporated whole tribal units from North Africa into it, some over a thousand men strong. It was said that he was creating his own private army, rather than an army loyal to the Khalifa. She knew she could do nothing to curb his power or his ambition, but she had to do something to protect her son. This business with Abbas had worried her. She was sure the slave would never have dared to spread such lies unless he had been asked to do it.

She arrived at the studded wooden doors of the Treasury and said to the guard, 'Tell Abu-Amir that the Khalifa's mother has come to see him.'

'Yes, *Sayyida*,' the guard said, unlocking the heavy door and letting it swing open. 'Please wait inside, out of the cold wind.'

'Thank you.'

She thought he would keep her waiting, just to emphasise his power over her, but he appeared at once.

'My queen, what can I do for you?' He was obviously surprised that she had come to his place of work. 'I thought you were in Madinat al-Zahra, visiting your son.'

'I was, but now I must speak to you about him,' she said. 'It is important.'

'Very well, dearest one. I hope he is well. Come with me.'

He led her through stone passage ways into the interior of the building and eventually they came to a small, but beautifully furnished room, with low couches and intricately woven carpets on the floor.

'This is where I like to sit and plan my day's work,' he said. 'In peace and solitude.'

'It is very pleasant,' she said, removing her heavy cloak and sitting down on a couch.

'So, what is so urgent?' he asked, bending down and kissing her neck.

'Have you heard the disgusting rumours about my son? And about me?' she asked, her eyes blazing with anger in the knowledge that he knew all about them.

'No, dearest, I have heard nothing of that nature. But you know I do not pay any attention to gossip. I leave that to those who have nothing better to do.'

'They are saying that al-Hisham is illegitimate. That he is not the son of al-Hakim. That he should not be using the title of Khalifa.'

'But how can they say that when you are his mother?' al-Mansur asked with an ingratiating smile.

'Because they say that I tricked Prince Hakim and slept with another man. Can you imagine such treason?'

'Disgusting indeed. Who is saying such things? They should be flogged.'

'People.' She watched him carefully to see if he was lying.

'But we have to know who exactly, if we are to do anything about it,' he said. 'I will see what I can find out for you, my dear, and we will punish these people. We will punish them severely.'

'Well, fortunately they have caught the man,' she said, her eyes never leaving his face.

'Indeed. Well that is good news, is it not. Who is the wretch?'

'Someone you know, my love. An old servant of yours, Abbas.'

She was sure his face went white as she said the name, but it was hard to tell because of his thick beard.

He sat down beside her and put his arm around her. 'I can't believe that Abbas would spread such lies. Are you sure that is what he said? He has always been such a loyal servant.'

'There are witnesses.'

'Well, everyone knew that al-Hakim was homosexual. It was like a miracle when you conceived. Everyone said as much. Maybe that's all he meant,' he said, rather lamely she thought.

Subh pulled away from his embrace and turned to face him. 'Do *you* think it was a miracle? Don't you think I was capable of seducing him? Don't *you* find me seductive?' she asked.

'Dearest, of course I do, but I am a normal man. I was only saying that it was a miracle that you were able to seduce him because he truly preferred men to women.'

'Al-Hakim knew how important it was to have an heir. He took his responsibilities as the Khalifa's son very seriously.'

'I'm sure he did. All I'm saying is that maybe Abbas was referring to that. Maybe it wasn't as serious as you think. I will arrange to speak to him and we will get to the bottom of this.'

'It's too late. He was executed this morning. The judge had no doubts about his guilt.'

Now Abu Amir did turn pale. 'What judge? If he was tried by a judge I would have known about it,' he blustered. 'Are you telling me someone has murdered my servant?'

'No. He was tried in Madinat al-Zahra, last night, and sentenced to death by the judge, Abu Adil.'

'That old fool. And you are sure it was Abbas? I find that very hard to believe. Maybe there is some mistake.'

'There is no mistake. You can see for yourself if you ride to Madinat al-Zahra. His head is on the city ramparts,' she said, relishing his discomfort.

'I just cannot believe that Abbas would do such a thing,' al-Mansur said, trying his best to look contrite. 'That a servant of mine would betray me in this way, I find hard to understand.'

'That is not all, my dear. I have been considering my position, and now that you are married and have a growing family, I feel I should return to Madinat al-Zahra and be with my son. He will be old enough soon to become our ruler. I want to be there to help him and to make sure there are no more poisonous rumours about him and his family.'

'What's that? I thought we'd agreed that you would live in Córdoba. I have had a special suite of rooms built for you here in my new palace, far better than anything you had before.'

'My son needs me.'

He pulled her towards him and whispered, 'I need you. I need you with me, Subh.'

'You have your wife. And I hear you are about to take another one.'

'It's you I love. They mean nothing to me. Please, Subh, you must stay in Córdoba with me.'

'But you won't allow Hisham to come here to live with me,' she said. 'If he has to stay in Madinat al-Zahra, then so will I. What if someone tries to kill him and I am not there to help?'

'If that happened, I doubt if there would be much that you could do. If someone really wants to get rid of the Khalifa then they will do it.'

She stared at him. His face was serious and she knew it was a veiled threat to her and her son. She remembered how helpless she had felt when they told her that someone had tried to kill al-Hisham when he was out with the hunt, how powerless she had been and how the realisation that her own future depended on her son staying alive had become very clear to her. Despite all their precautions, despite bodyguards and soldiers, on that occasion someone had still managed to get close enough to her son to try to murder him. There was the slightest flicker in his black, piercing eyes, enough to tell her that they understood each other. She would have to tread carefully with this man. He was a lot more dangerous than she had first thought.

'I'm sorry, my love, my place is with my son. I will leave tomorrow,' she said, biting back her tears.

She would give up the life at court and stay with Hisham. He would be pleased. He was always asking her when she was coming back to live with him. It would make him happy to have his mother by his side.

CHAPTER 26

Al-Hisham was excited at the prospect of visiting the city of Córdoba. He hadn't been there since his father had died. In fact he hadn't been anywhere. For his own safety, or so they said, he had been kept in Madinat al Zahra. Now at last it looked as though things were going to change. This was excellent news. When he saw al-Mansur, he would talk to him about moving the court back to Madinat al-Zahra, so that he could get more involved in governing his country. He knew it had been necessary before, but now that he was eighteen - legally allowed to rule - there was no need for all the administration to be in Córdoba while he continued to live elsewhere.

Madinat al-Zahra was deserted now. All the big houses were empty; their owners had flocked to Córdoba to protect their jobs and their positions. Those who had stayed behind - a few old families, loyal to al-Hakim - had lost all their influence and most of their money. Córdoba was where the decisions were made now. He would change that. He would encourage people to return to Madinat al-Zahra. It would be scary, taking control of the government, but he was the Khalifa, and eventually he had to start to rule.

For this, his very first trip as Khalifa, he had an enormous entourage. Four hundred soldiers were ordered to accompany him and he insisted on Gassan and al-Jundi riding beside him. Everyone was to wear their best uniforms and he wanted the full splendour of arriving in the city, riding on horseback, surrounded by his closest servants. He himself wore his finest white robes and a purple cloak, trimmed with gold. On his right hand was a gold ring set with an enormous ruby, given to him by an ambassador from India, and around his neck hung chains of fine gold and pearls from the Black Sea. He was pleased with his appearance. If only he didn't look so young, but that was mostly down to the fact that his chin was barely covered by a handful of red wispy hairs. Gassan had said that it was just a matter of time and then his beard would grow long and thick. He had to be patient. It seemed to him that people had been telling him that all his life. Well, beard or no beard, his moment had come at last.

As they rode through the *Bab al-Sura*, the ceremonial gate to the city and out onto Almunias Way, the road once used by visiting ambassadors, he was delighted to see that people were lining the roadside to see him, and the closer they got to Córdoba, the more people there were, cheering and waving, obviously delighted to see their reclusive Khalifa at last.

'They are very happy to see you, Your Excellency,' Gassan said. 'Listen to their cheers.'

Al-Hisham beamed and from time to time lifted his hand in greeting, trying to maintain a dignified and royal bearing. At long last he was meeting his subjects. This had been an excellent idea of al-Mansur's. Surely now he would have to give up the Regency and allow al-Hisham to reign.

He could see Córdoba ahead, high walls and turrets, with the splendid outline of the mosque at its heart, all bathed in the warm amber light of the evening sun. As they trotted across the Roman bridge towards the mosque, swallows swooped and dived around them, skimming across the sluggish water in their search for insects. Thousands of people had turned out to see him and a cordon of soldiers lined the road, holding them back. From astride his horse he could make out the crowds stretching back as far as he could see, filling all the roads around the mosque, cramming into the squares, climbing on walls to get a better view of their ruler. There were so many people, men, women and even children, all stretching for a glimpse of their Khalifa, craning their necks, jostling and pushing, desperate to see him. Suddenly he felt panic grip his heart. The mosque would be filled to capacity. There would be no room to move, no room to breathe.

He had never seen so many people before. What if they stopped cheering? What if they turned on him? He would never be able to escape from them. He would be trapped. Nobody would be able to help him, not Gassan, not al-Jundi. There were too many people. Their faces, which a moment ago had seemed so warm and welcoming, so pleased to see their Khalifa, now seemed threatening. Were they smiles of welcome or sneers of derision? Was one of them an assassin? Anyone could slip through the crowd and plunge a knife in his back; it would be so easy. Doubts began to crowd his mind. Why *had* al-Mansur invited him here after all this time? Why now? Was it because he was now eighteen and legally old enough to rule the country? Had he become a threat to the Regent? Was this a trap? Was something bad going to happen to him? Suddenly he could go no further. He had to go back to Madinat al-Zahra. He would be safe there. They must leave right away. No delays. Soon it would be dark. The feeling of panic increased and he thought he would faint. His breath started to come in short bursts and he felt as though there was an iron band around his chest, crushing him.

'What is wrong, Your Excellency? Are you feeling all right?' Gassan asked him. 'You are very pale.'

'Home. We must go home,' he gasped, clutching at his chest. 'Take me home. Now.'

Gassan spurred his horse forward so that he could speak to al-Jundi, 'The Khalifa is not well. He wants to go back to Madinat al Zahra. Now.'

Instantly al-Jundi called the procession to a halt and rode back to be at the Khalifa's side. 'What is it, Your Majesty? What is wrong?'

'I can't do it. I can't go among all those people. Take me home. Please al-Jundi. Take me home,' he gasped, shaking uncontrollably.

***

He was already in the garden, with his falcon, Daruj, on his gloved fist, when Ahmad arrived. His dear friend was wearing a new *djellaba* and had already removed his cap, leaving his head bare and his dark, glossy hair gleaming in the sunshine; he looked more handsome than ever. Al-Hisham felt his heart leap with excitement.

'*As-salama alaykum*, Your Highness. Are you well?' Ahmad asked, sitting down beside him and reaching across to stroke the peregrine.

'*Wa alaykum e-salam*, Ahmad. Yes, I am very well. Very well indeed. So, are we going to fly the new bird today?'

'We can try. Have you selected a name for him yet?'

'Yes, I am going to call him Ahmad.'

'Ahmad? But that's my name.'

'Yes, I want to call him after my dearest friend,' al-Hisham said.

'Well if you want to, but it will seem a bit strange when you call him. I'll think you are calling me,' he said with a chuckle. 'Let's have a look at him.'

Al-Hisham put Daruj back on his perch and took up the new bird, holding the jesses tightly in his hand.

'He comes back to me, already. I think he will be an excellent hunter,' he said. 'Not like Daruj, of course, but fast nevertheless.'

He loved Daruj. The bird was rarely far from his side. Even at night he slept on a perch by the side of his bed.

'I have some news for you, Your Highness,' Ahmad said. He seemed nervous and stood there twisting the spare set of jesses around in his fingers.

'Has something happened? What's the matter, Ahmad? Tell me. I would do anything for you, my friend,' al-Hisham said.

'I am leaving. I have a new job in the Falcon House in Córdoba.'

At Ahmad's words, al-Hisham felt as though his world had stopped. He could not believe what he was hearing. His beloved Ahmad, his dear friend was leaving.

'But you can't,' al-Hisham said, his voice wavering like a petulant child. 'I need you here. Who is going to help me with my birds?'

'A new man is going to replace me. He is very experienced and will look after you well.'

'I don't want someone to look after me. I want you. You are my friend.'

' I am to be married next month,' Ahmad said, quietly. 'We will live in Córdoba, with her parents.'

'What? Married? You have never mentioned anything about wanting a wife before? Who is your bride? What is her name?'

Why had Ahmad never said anything before? He had never even hinted that he was interested in marrying. He never talked about women in the way some of the other men did.

'Her name is Aisha. She is the daughter of one of your Palace Guards.'

A cold chill crept over him as he stood there, refusing to believe what Ahmad was saying. At last he found the strength to speak. 'But you can't marry her, Ahmad. I love you. Your place is here with me. You can't go to Córdoba.'

'I am truly sorry, Your Highness, but it now time for me to marry.'

'But how can I live here without you? I will die here alone. Please. Doesn't our friendship mean anything to you?' he pleaded. 'Don't leave me, Ahmad.' He leaned forward and took Ahmad's hand.

'Of course, Your Highness. I am very honoured to be your friend,' Ahmad said, disentangling his hand from al-Hisham's. 'I hope we can remain friends and I will come and see you whenever I can. But one day you too will want to get married. It is the way of the world. Men must marry and have families.'

This serious young man did not sound like his fun-loving Ahmad, who had helped him slip out of the palace, who had ridden across the plains with him and taught him all he knew about flying a hawk.

'You are lying to me. You are just trying to tease me,' he said and leaning across, kissed Ahmad full on the lips. Now Ahmad would understand why he couldn't leave him. He had wanted to do that for so long, dreamed about it. But straight away he knew something was wrong. Ahmad's lips did not open in response to his own. He did not speak. He did not move. He sat there frozen.

'What? Didn't you like me kissing you, my dearest friend?'

'Friends don't usually kiss like that,' Ahmad said, not moving.

'So, how do they kiss then?' al-Hisham asked, growing bolder and, putting his arms around Ahmad, pulled him towards him and kissed him more passionately.

That was when Ahmad leapt to his feet and said, 'I'm sorry, Your Highness, I have to go now.'

'Go? Why? You have only just got here. We haven't flown the birds yet.'

'I must leave now. I am sorry.'

'You cannot go. I command you to stay. We will fly the birds and then we will sit and talk. You can tell me more about this nonsense about marriage. It's your father isn't it? He is forcing you to marry. Well I'm telling you that you don't have to. I can stop this.'

'I am sorry, Your Highness. I know we have been friends for many years, but I can never be the sort of friend you want me to be. I can never love you. I love Aisha.'

The Khalifa couldn't hold back his tears any longer and even then Ahmad was unmoved. He just stood there and watched him. That made al-Hisham angry and he spat at him, 'Go then, you ungrateful creature. Wasn't it I who had you released from prison? I who saved you from execution? Is this how you repay me? Marrying some slut and leaving me here alone? Go. I don't care. I hate you. Go.'

He was in a rage by then and almost summoned the guards to take Ahmad and lock him up, but even in his anger he knew he could do nothing to hurt his friend.

'Your Highness, I am so sorry. If I were made differently, I would be honoured to stay with you, but I'm not. I'm in love with Aisha and I want to marry her. I want to be a husband and have many sons. But I will always be your true loyal subject and your friend.'

'Just go. And don't come back,' al-Hisham shouted.

This last comment was unnecessary because he already knew that Ahmad was never going to return. Their friendship was over. There was no turning back now. The Khalifa had declared his love for him and he had been rejected.

***

Al-Hisham woke to the sound of the *muezzin* calling the faithful to prayer. It was still dark and the lamps in his room cast eerie shadows in the half-light. The boy from the night before still lay at the foot of his bed, his naked body half covered with a silk sheet and his arm stretched across al-Hisham's leg. Al-Hisham kicked the arm away and said, 'It's time to go.'

The boy blinked sleepily and rolled over.

'Get up. You must go now,' al-Hisham repeated, more loudly.

He was a young one this time, no more than thirteen, he guessed. Not really to his taste but he had asked for someone who was as different from Ahmad as possible and this young Yoruba slave was just that. Ahmad. He had promised himself that he wouldn't think about him any more. It was too painful. They had been such friends and then he had spurned him. Him, the Khalifa. He was lucky that he hadn't had him thrown into prison again.

'Get out,' he shouted in exasperation at the slave. 'Gassan, get this boy out of here.'

'Yes, Your Highness.'

He lay there watching as Gassan directed the servants to remove the sleepy child and take him back to the harem. The old Chief Black Eunuch was dead now and a new one, Aswad, was in charge of the harem. He understood al-Hisham's needs better than anyone, better even than he himself. As soon as Aswad had seen how little interest the Khalifa had in the women of his harem he had brought him a young man. That was when everything changed for al-Hisham, when he realised what his body had been trying to tell him for some years now. And that was when he began to look at Ahmad through different eyes, when he began to realise that he was more than just a friend to him. He was no longer satisfied with Ahmad's friendship, he wanted his love.

Ahmad was to be married today. He knew because al-Jundi had told him. He had sent one of his most trusted men to be al-Hisham's bodyguard while he went to attend his son's wedding. There was nothing he could do to stop it now.

The young slave had finally woken up and was hurriedly pulling on his robe. He was a nice child, soft and pliable in bed but it had been a distraction, nothing more. It hadn't eased the pain in his heart.

Having ejected the sleepy slave, Gassan returned and said, 'Your Excellency, *al-Sayyida* is here to see you.'

'My mother? Here in the palace? What does she want?'

'She did not say, Your Excellency, just that she wanted to see you.'

'But I am expecting Barakah to come and play chess with me.'

'Yes, Your Excellency. So what should I say?'

'Well, I suppose I will have to see her. Here take this wine back to the kitchen before she sees it. She will only moan at me. And lay this chess set out on a low table, ready.' It was one that had been given to his father by a visiting ambassador from the Byzantine Empire. The pieces had been exquisitely carved from ivory and onyx and the board was made of two different coloured marbles. He had thought of giving it to Ahmad as a token of his love, but that was before the young falconer had rejected him.

'Very well, Your Excellency,' Gassan said, picking up the two wine glasses and the half-empty jug of wine. 'Maybe you'd like to chew this?' He handed him a small stick of arak to sweeten his breath.

'You think of everything, Gassan.'

He picked up the King from the chessboard and twirled it between his fingers; it was the piece that everyone wanted to capture or kill. He lined them up, the Rhuks, the Archers, the Knights, the infantry; they were all represented on the chessboard, all except the Queen. He smiled, here was a game his mother could not participate in.

'Hisham, my son. How are you?' his mother asked, coming through the archway, her dress floating behind her like gossamer shimmering in the sunshine, a satin cap holding her hair in place.

'*As-salama alaykum*, Mama. You look well and happy. What has brought you here, unannounced?'

'*Wa alaykum e-salam*. I wanted to see you, my son. It's been too long since I have spent time with you.'

'It has indeed, Mama. How many months has it been? Or is it years? It certainly seems like it,' he replied bitterly. 'I thought you were far too engrossed with your lover, Abu Amir, to come and visit your son, the Khalifa. Maybe I should have sent my soldiers to bring you to me.'

'I know you're angry, Hisham, but I have tried to explain that I was only trying to help you. I thought if I stayed close to Abu Amir I would be able to keep an eye on him and his plans.'

'And what plans are they?' he asked, with a yawn. It was the same old story. She was doing it all to protect him. He was tired of hearing it.

'He has got rid of all opposition to his power. He is the sole regent now. There is no longer a Council of Viziers;

he is the only vizier, the Grand Vizier. There is only one person who can oppose him and that is you, my son, the rightful Khalifa of al-Andalus.'

'So? What do you want me to do, command my soldiers to arrest him? On what charges? He will say the same as you, everything he has done has been to protect me. Anyway, I don't care. He can govern the country, if that is what he wants to do. He can wage a *jihad* against the Christians. He can fill the Treasury with booty from his campaigns. But he will never be Khalifa. I am the Khalifa, like my father before me and his father before him, part of the Omayyad dynasty, a dynasty of strong rulers and just men, of men who built magnificent palaces and mosques, who united the country in which we live, men of culture and learning who were respected throughout the world, men of tolerance, the political and religious successors to the Prophet Mohammed. Who is this Abu Amir anyway? He claims his ancestors arrived in this country with Tarik, in the first invasion, and who can prove otherwise? He says he is of true Arab blood but how do we know? What I do know is that he is an ambitious man and a dangerous one. I do not intend to cross him. Why should I? I have everything I need right here, my palace, servants, riches and my title. I will never give that up.'

'And your harem?'

'Yes, my harem.'

'I did not expect you to oppose him, my son. I have come here to tell you that you must be careful. I do not know what plans Abu Amir has for you, but I know they do not include returning to the court in Córdoba.'

'I have no intention of returning to Córdoba,' he said, thinking of his abortive attempt to go to the Great Mosque and how terrified he had been that evening.

'That is a wise decision, my son. I have decided that, from now on, I will live here in Madinat al-Zahra, with you. I will have my belongings brought here next week. I assume my old rooms are empty?'

'They are indeed, Mama, waiting for your return. But you must realise that I am no longer your little son; I am a man now and I am the Khalifa. I will do as I wish. I am happy for you to live here - it is after all, your home - but you must not interfere with my life.'

He replaced the chess pieces on the board and smiled at her. It was true; he was pleased that she had returned.

CHAPTER 27

Al-Jundi was tired. He would have liked to have been at home, sitting in his shady patio, surrounded by the pots of sweet smelling flowers that Amina liked to grow, listening to his wife talk about Ahmad's wedding. Things were different now. Madinat al Zahra was like a ghost town, or perhaps more accurately, as his sister had remarked when she had come to visit them just before his mother died, like a military barracks, because everywhere you looked there were only soldiers. Soldiers and Palace Guards. The place was a fortress and he knew that the reason for such a heavily armed presence was because of the Khalifa - not to keep him safe but to keep him a prisoner. Nobody said as much openly but everyone knew it was so.

His thoughts went back to the day, some years before, when the young Khalifa had released the birds. Al-Jundi had stood with the rest, watching the cloud of chirping, chattering birds being given their freedom: canaries, chaffinches, gold finches, linnets and larks. They wheeled and turned as one, a multicoloured cloud that gradually dispersed as each bird made its own destiny. Was that what al-Hisham wanted? To be free of his golden cage? But who was brave enough to release him? Who was kind enough to let him fly free? And if he was given his freedom after all these years, how would he fare? The boy had panicked when they had gone to Córdoba to visit the Great Mosque. It had been such a shame. He had been so excited to be leaving the confines of the *alcazaba*, and then he was not able to go through with it. He had run back to the only place he felt safe, the opulent palace that had always been his home.

Al-Hisham was a man now, but still the remaining regent, al-Mansur, had not relinquished his power. Al-Jundi doubted that he personally, would live long enough to ever see it happen. Power was a potent drug. Once you had a taste of it, it was not easy to give up and there seemed to be no sign of al-Mansur slackening his hold on the reins. Al-Jundi worried for al-Hisham. He had done what he could, placing his own men at strategic places within the royal household, spending as many hours as he could possibly manage by the Khalifa's side, double-checking the new arrivals in his all-male harem, but he feared it was not enough. If al-Mansur decided to get rid of the Khalifa, there was probably nothing he could do about it. It depressed him and it made him angry.

The young Khalifa still took an interest in his falcons but the Falcon House stood almost empty - the Grand Falconer had not returned all the birds as the Khalifa had ordered - and only a handful of men had stayed behind to care for them.

Even Ahmad had asked to be transferred to Córdoba. He and his new bride would live in that city from next month. Al-Jundi had been both happy and sad when

Ahmad had given him the news, delighted that he had agreed to marry the young girl that he and Amina had chosen for him, but sorry that it meant he wanted to move to Córdoba. Ahmad said he could not remain in Madinat al-Zahra; there was nothing here for him. Al-Jundi was sure something had happened between his son and al-Hisham, but Ahmad would not say what it was. He rarely came to visit the Khalifa anymore. It was strange. They had been friends for such a long time. He had tried asking his son why this was but he would not tell him.

'I must think about my new wife now, Baba. I cannot be at the beck and call of the Khalifa all the time,' he said.

Al-Jundi could understand his concern. For the last few years, Ahmad had spent every day at the palace, more as a companion to the Khalifa than as a falconer. They had continued with the falconry - it had become an obsession with al-Hisham - but Ahmad was also expected to play chess and dominoes, to read to him, to play quoits with horseshoes from the stables and even a new game with playing cards. It had been fun for him at first but Ahmad had a living to make and was soon grumbling about having to 'baby-sit'. On many occasions al-Jundi had been tempted to say something to the Grand Falconer about it, but it was so good to see the Khalifa happy that he had refrained from mentioning it.

'*Quaid*, the *Sayyida* wants to see you. She is waiting in the reception hall,' one of his men said. 'Can you come right away?'

'Very well. Stay here and wait for the Khalifa, he is in his harem. I will be back directly.'

What did *al-Sayyida* want with him? Was she checking up on her son?

'*As-salama alaykum*, *Sayyida*. You wanted to see me?'

'*Wa alaykum e-salam*, al-Jundi. Yes. I need to speak to you. Will you walk with me in the garden?'

He followed her through the narrow passage way that led into the south gardens. The sun had risen but it was still early and the dew lay like a sparkling carpet of tiny lights on the ground. They walked as far as the first of the lakes and then *al-Sayyida* stopped and sat on a low bench by the water's edge.

'Sit beside me for a moment, al Jundi.'

Obediently he sat next to her. This was most unusual. Normally the Khalifa's mother was very formal. They sat in silence for a few moments and then Subh asked, 'How is my son?'

'The Khalifa is in good health, *Sayyida*.'

'But how is he? Is he happy?'

'That is not for me to say, *Sayyida*. I can only tell you that he is well.'

'But what does he do all day?'

What should he say? Should he tell her that since Ahmad had left, the Khalifa spent most of his time with various young men of the harem? That he had a new lover brought to him every day. That his Chief Black Eunuch was charged with scouring the city for suitable boys and if he could not buy them he was to bring them to him anyway. Should he tell her that her son spent much time drinking wine, although it was forbidden, and no longer enquired after his subjects or had any interest in the government of his kingdom? Should he say that al-Hisham had turned into a rude arrogant master, insulting his servants and throwing his food on the floor if it did not please him? Should he admit to her that he often heard the Khalifa ranting and raving to himself as he paced up and down in the garden?

'He has never had very much to do, *Sayyida*. So he plays games and he frequents his harem. I cannot tell you any more,' he said at last.

'He goes to the harem now, does he? He's a man at last. So we might have an heir one day?' she asked with a smile. 'I would like to be a grandmother.'

When al-Jundi did not answer, her smile faded and she said, 'Oh, so he is like his father then?'

'In some ways, *Sayyida*, but he does not have al-Hakim's strength.'

'No, I realise that. He has always been a weak child.' She paused, pushing her greying hair back from her face. 'I am worried about him, al-Jundi. I think there may be men who would like to get rid of him. I can mention no names but you can probably guess whom I mean.'

'Yes, *Sayyida*.'

'You may not believe it, but I love my son and I do not want anything to happen to him. He is all I have.'

'I will do my best, *Sayyida*. You know it has always been my sworn duty to protect him.'

'I know that, but I have made a decision. I am returning to Madinat al-Zahra. There is nothing for me to do in Córdoba now. I will live here with my son and maybe together we can protect him.'

'I am sure your son will be pleased with the news, *Sayyida*.'

'Yes, I hope so. I will go and tell him right away. Please let the rest of the household know that the Khalifa's mother will now be in residence.'

'Very well, *Sayyida*.'

He stood and bowed to her, then made his way back to his post. Well, he hadn't expected that news, but he had to admit he was pleased. *Al-Sayyida* was old now but she was still a strong-willed woman, and she would protect her son to the death. At last he felt he had an ally.

CHAPTER 28

His servant, ibn Dirar approached him. 'I have a letter for you, *sayyad*, from the Khalifa's mother. A messenger brought it and is waiting outside for your reply.'

Why was Subh writing to him? Oh, of course, she regretted her hasty decision and now wanted to return to him. Well, he would agree, but not right away. He'd let her stew for a bit, make her wait for a week or two and then he'd take her back. Yes, then she would be so grateful, she would do anything to please him. He felt his loins stir at the thought of his beautiful mistress.

'Give it to me and tell the messenger that I will send a reply when I feel like it.'

'Yes, *sayyad*.'

Al-Mansur broke the seal and unfolded the letter. So what was her excuse for wanting to come back? He started to read:

'Dear esteemed Abu Amir' she began. 'As you are now aware, I have moved back to Madinat al-Zahra with my maid servants and all my belongings. I tried to explain to you that my son's safety was now more important to me than our love. He needs me and I must be by his side. That has never been clearer to me.

'I realise now that you will never give up your powerful position as Regent and my son will never get to fulfil his destiny as Khalifa. Once I thought I would fight you tooth and nail for al-Hisham's right to rule but now I know that I can never win. You have too many people on your side. So I am prepared to make a deal with you. I know many things about you, Abu Amir, some good and some bad, some you have told me yourself and some I have learned from others. I know that you were behind the attempt on my son's life, when he was still but a child, and I know that you murdered al-Mughira, and probably al-Mushafi, as well. Don't ask how I know these things - I too have sources within the palace.

'I'm sure the people of our country would be very interested to know that the pious warrior, al-Mansur, was really a murder and a traitor. So, if my son were to die suddenly, from a bout of food poisoning, a strange illness, a stray arrow, a mysterious fall, anything at all that led to his sudden death, I would make sure that everyone knew that you, Abu Amir were behind it. You might get away with many things, but the people of al-Andalus would never forgive you for murdering the Khalifa, the rightful ruler to the throne. You have set yourself up before them as a man who stood by their laws and upheld their religion. How could such a man kill the anointed ruler of their country? They would never stand for it. All your popularity, all your power would disappear in a single moment, melting away like the winter snows in the springtime.

'For my part of the bargain, I will keep my son in Madinat al-Zahra, out of harm's way. He will be Khalifa in name only and you will be left to rule unchallenged. al-Sayyida al Malika'

Al-Mansur was furious. He tore the letter up and threw it on the floor. Still she treated him like a servant. Did she not realise whom he had become? He was the most powerful man in Córdoba, no, in all al-Andalus. And what was she? An ageing concubine, living off her past glory. Because her son was the Khalifa, she thought that made her better than him, well it didn't. Who was she to warn him in this way? Not even the courtesy to speak to him face to face. He was well rid of her. She had become too jealous and possessive lately, especially since his latest marriage. He did not need her any more. He had stronger allies than her, now. Good riddance to her.

'Is everything all right, my Lord?' asked Dirar.

'Yes,' he snapped. 'Everything is fine. Pick up those pieces and burn them.'

But the letter rankled him. How did she have the gall to write to him in that way? To take it upon herself to write and warn him that if anything happened to her son, she would publicly accuse him. She wouldn't be able to prove anything; he was certain of that, but she knew it would ruin his reputation. Then this she-wolf had had the temerity to offer him a deal. What made him angrier than ever was the fact that she was right. It was too risky to murder al-Hisham. Since Abbas's death he had no-one he could trust in the same way.

He strode out into the garden. Two of his sons were playing with one of the kitchen cats. They stopped when they saw him and bowed, saying, '*As-salama alaykum,* Baba.'

'*Wa alaykum e-salam,* my sons,' he replied.

Maybe he should accept her deal. The boy was useless, inept, he would never make a ruler. Look how he had panicked when all he had to do was enter a crowded mosque, running back to Madinat al Zahra as if the hounds of Hell were after him. Spineless, that's what he was. No, he would never be a real threat to al-Mansur. She was right. Let them both live their lives as recluses. He could arrange that without a problem. She would soon regret her decision when she was stuck in that decaying city.

In the meantime it wouldn't harm to spread some more gossip about their young Khalifa. For the second time the people had a ruler who was homosexual. That in itself would not bother anyone, they were used to such behaviour from the elite classes, but the fact that there might be no descendants would. With no heirs, the Omayyad dynasty was in grave danger of coming to an end. He would encourage people to look at the possibility of a new ruling family, his own of course. He knew he had the support of the people, they were all firmly behind him in his *jihad* against the Christians. They liked having a strong ruler. Yes, although he hated to admit it, Subh's advice was sound, as always, self-seeking maybe, but sound nevertheless. He would move slowly.

With both the Khalifa and his mother incarcerated in the *alcazaba* in Madinat al-Zahra, people would soon forget about them. All eyes would be on Córdoba and al-Mansur and his family of healthy sons.

But for now he needed to do something that would impress the populace even further, and reinforce his position as a religious leader. He would go ahead with his plans to double the size of the Great Mosque. It had been built two hundred years before, by the emir al-Rahman I, but it had soon proved to be too small and despite being extended by two successive rulers, it was still not large enough to house the huge numbers of the faithful who came to worship there each day. It would not be an easy task to increase the size. He had already spoken to the architects and builders, who said that the Great Mosque's closeness to the river posed a problem. The only logical area to expand was eastwards into the city, away from the river, and this would mean tearing down existing buildings. It would be costly. The owners would want indemnification. He had to talk to the accountants in the Treasury and see what they advised. His head filled with new plans, he strode out of his palace and headed for the Mint.

CHAPTER 29

Subh was surprised at the change in her son. She studied him carefully as he set out the chess pieces on the board. He was taller and his chest had broadened since she had last seen him. The deep auburn of his hair was very evident now and he bore a strong likeness to his father, al-Hakim. How could anyone doubt his ancestry? It was written all over him that he was an Omayyad. He even had his grandfather's hooked nose. Not as handsome a man as his father, she would admit, but not unattractive. What a pity he preferred the young men that Aswad brought him, to the beautiful women that used to inhabit his harem. She would never be a grandmother, she could see that. Where was the young Subh capable of seducing *her* son? How unlikely that she would find any woman that could worm her way into his bed.

He had changed in other ways too. He was cold and cynical for such a young man. Had they done that to him? The Regents had wanted him to keep out of the way, and encouraged him to amuse himself with games and pastimes; they had done nothing to help him prepare for his role as ruler. Now she could see that she had been blind. Abu Amir had never intended that her son should rule and he had succeeded. There was no fight in al-

Hisham, no interest in government, no sense of duty and responsibility. All the things that al-Hakim had ruled by were absent in her son and she knew she was not blameless in this. Children were not born with a sense of duty, even if they were the heirs to the Khalifa. When it had mattered, when al-Hisham had needed her help and guidance, she had failed him. Not for the first time, she wished that her husband had lived long enough to help her son become a good ruler. She could have stood up to Abu Amir in the beginning, right after al-Hakim's death, but she was spell-bound by her lover and had truly believed him when he said his actions were for the best. Al-Hisham had been such a sweet child, unworldly, ill-prepared to be Khalifa. He was her only child. She had feared for his life then and continued to do so. It was too late now to wrest the reins of power back from Abu Amir, but she could still try to protect al-Hisham and his dynasty. After all, Abu Amir had nothing to fear from her pleasure-loving son now.

'Hisham, I would like to make some changes to my old rooms. I take it you have no objections?' she said.

'No. They are your rooms. Do as you wish, Mama.'

'I thought it was about time that we spent some of your money on this palace, instead of pouring it all into buildings in Córdoba. The Khalifa lives here, after all.'

'How true. They tell me it makes no difference where I actually live; I am the Khalifa and it is important that my government is well housed and my court is lavish, even though I am not allowed to go there to see it. It would reflect badly on me, they say. Visitors would think that the Khalifa was no longer a wealthy man, that he was no longer the most powerful ruler in the Western world.' Her son burst out laughing at his own words. 'Can you believe that, Mama? Abu Amir said that. Powerful? The Khalifa is too scared to go into Córdoba. The Khalifa is frightened of crowds. The Khalifa is not allowed to leave the *alcazaba* without the Regent's permission. The Khalifa is anything but powerful.'

The bitterness in his voice tore at her heart. What had they done to him, her lovely child?

'Ah, there you are Barakah. You can be black today, all right? I will play the white.'

A tall thin, young man, wearing a saffron robe, sat down opposite al-Hisham.

'This is my mother. You will address her as *Sayyida*. You will see a lot of her. She is going to be living here from now on,' al-Hisham said, with a smile.

Maybe he was pleased to see her after all.

'*As-salama alaykum, Sayyida*,' Barakah said, standing and bowing politely to Subh.

'*Wa alaykum e-salam*,' she replied.

'Come, Barakah, let us begin,' her son said.

She bowed and went in search of Gassan. He would help her to organise her new rooms, and tomorrow Afra would arrive with the first of her luggage.

***

Within a couple of months Subh had the household running better than it had in a long time. She employed artisans from Córdoba, and further afield, from Damascus and Bagdad and soon the palace was bustling with activity. Stonemasons, plasterers, painters and carpenters set to work, and the servants were instructed to polish the marble floors and buy new rugs and tapestries. Her son had little interest in the interior of the palace and from what she could see, he spent most of his life outside with the falcons or in the harem with a string of new male concubines. He took no interest in what she was doing, made no comments but neither did he make any objections. Until she mentioned the falcons.

'Gassan, why are the falcons always here, inside the palace? Why aren't they in the Falcon House? We do still have a Falcon House, don't we?'

'Yes. *Sayidda*. But the Khalifa likes to have his birds close to him.'

'Well I think it's rather unhygienic. Have the servants clean up that mess, at once and send for the falconer.'

'Yes, *Sayyida*. The Khalifa won't be parted from his favourite falcon. He takes him everywhere with him, even into the harem at night.'

'One falcon, yes, but fifty? The place stinks.'

'Do you want me to speak to him, *Sayyida*?'

'No. I will do it.' She walked into his private quarters, stopping first at the door to ask the guard to inform the Khalifa that his mother was outside.

'Mama, what do you want at this hour?' al-Hisham asked, pulling a silk sheet over his naked body. 'Is there a fire? Has someone died? Why wake me for anything less?'

'*As-salama alaykum*, my son,' she said, bowing before him. She knew that he liked her to follow protocol, although he rarely did so himself these days. 'I have come to talk to you about your birds.' She sat down on his bed and smiled at him.

'What about my birds?' he asked.

'They need somewhere to live. An aviary, perhaps.'

'They have the Falcon House,' he said.

'I know, but wouldn't it be nice if you could keep some of them closer to you, if we built an aviary for them here in the garden?'

Her son sat up, excitedly. 'What a great idea, Mama. I will see to it, straight away. Now, if there is nothing else, please leave me. I must bathe and get dressed.'

He snapped his fingers and the falcon flew from his perch and landed on his hand. Subh jumped back, nervously. What an enormous bird he was and his talons looked incredibly sharp. The falcon stared at her, his head tilted slightly. He seemed to be asking himself who she was and what she was doing sitting on his master's bed. His eyes, black as night gleamed in the fluttering light of the oil lamps.

She walked back to her rooms, feeling a little sad. She could see that al-Hisham no longer needed her, not in the way he had when he was younger - she had left it too late. Still she was here now, by his side, and this would be her home until the day she died.

EPILOGUE

Al-Hisham II was the third caliph of al-Andalus and the last one in the Omeyyad dynasty. He was born in 966 AD and died in 1013 AD.

He inherited the title of Khalifa in 976 AD, at the age of eleven, on the death of his father, al-Hakim II. Too young to rule, his mother and her lover Abu Amir agreed that a Regency should be formed to rule in his place until he came of age.

Unfortunately, by the time al-Hisham was old enough to rule, Abu Amir, an ambitious and ruthless man, had other plans for him. Abu Amir moved the Court and all the departments of government back to Córdoba and left the young Khalifa alone in Madinat al-Zahra, where he lived in isolation, a prisoner in his own palace until his death in 1013 AD.

There were a number of attempts to wrest the title from him. In 976 AD two powerful eunuchs plotted to put al-Hakim's half-brother, al-Mughira, on the throne, but before they could do so, he was killed.

Then in 1009 AD Muhammad II, the great-grandson of al-Rahman III, lead a revolt against al-Hisham and imprisoned him. Al-Hisham was re-installed as Khalifa the following year, but in 1013 AD a second revolt took place and al-Hisham was killed. The next Khalifa was Sulayman al-Mustain.

***

Abu Amir, also known as al-Mansur because of his victories against the Christians, became the absolute ruler of al-Andalus in the year 997 AD and moved all the caliph's treasure to his own palace. He continued to wage *jihad* against the Christians and died in 1002 AD returning from laying waste to the region of Rioja. He was succeeded by his son Abd al-Malik. The institute of the caliphate had been fatally damaged by al-Mansur's actions and he brought an end to the Omayyad dynasty, opening the way for the country to break up once more into small quarreling princedoms.

GLOSSARY

Al-Andalus the Islamic name given to Moorish Spain

Alcázar palace, fort or castle

Alcazaba walled fortification

Alla ysalmak response to goodbye

ammu uncle

As-salama alaykum Hello

Arab mile is between 1.8 and 2 kilometres

Baba father

Dar al-Jund soldiers quarters in the palace

dirhams units of currency

Djellaba a hooded cloak

Djinn a mythical being from the spirit world

Ghifara a crocheted cap

Hadith reports of the deeds and sayings of Mohammed

Hamman baths

Imam holy man

insha'Allah God willing

jihad holy war

Jinete horseman

Ma'a salama goodbye

Mihrab niche in the wall of the mosque

Quaid officer in charge of a corps of 10,000 men

Quran the central religious holy book of Islam

Sayyad master or sir

Sayyida queen, queen mother

Tagine North African stew of spiced meat and vegetables

Teta nickname for grandmother

Wa alaykum e-salam Peace be upon you

Zenana the innermost apartments where the women live

The Eye of the Falcon

www.ingramcontent.com/pod-product-compliance
Lightning Source LLC
Chambersburg PA
CBHW051212120726
47905CB00004B/1082